A Haunt for Jackals

Seven Cows, Ugly and Gaunt: Book Three

Mark Goodwin

Technical information in the book is included to convey realism. The author shall not have liability or responsibility to any person or entity with respect to any loss or damage caused, or allegedly caused, directly or indirectly by the information contained in this book.

All of the characters, places, and incidents are products of the author's imagination or are used fictitiously. Any resemblance to actual people, places, or events is entirely coincidental.

Cover design by Deranged Doctor Design
www.derangeddoctordesign.com

Copyright © 2016 Goodwin America Corp.

All rights reserved. No part of this publication may be reproduced, stored in a retrieval system, or transmitted in any form or by any means without the prior written permission of the author, except by a reviewer who may quote short passages in a review.

ISBN: 1535502738
ISBN-13: 978-1535502733

DEDICATION

Blessed is the nation whose God is the LORD; and the people whom he hath chosen for his own inheritance. The LORD looketh from heaven; he beholdeth all the sons of men. From the place of his habitation he looketh upon all the inhabitants of the earth. He fashioneth their hearts alike; he considereth all their works. There is no king saved by the multitude of an host: a mighty man is not delivered by much strength.

Psalm 33:12-16

This book is dedicated to the soldiers who have given their lives for the freedom of America and to the wives, mothers, fathers, sisters and brothers who have shared in their sacrifice. It is also dedicated to the stalwart men and women of God, who have fought the spiritual battle in an attempt to keep our nation on a straight course that we might retain the blessings of our Creator and avoid the calamities portrayed in this series of books.

ACKNOWLEDGMENTS

Thanks to Mom and Dad, for the investment you made in my young imagination in the form of Legos, Hot Wheels, and Star Wars action figures. It's proving to have a rather favorable return.

Thanks to my beautiful bride, best friend, and editor-in-chief, Catherine Goodwin. I would also like to thank the rest of my fantastic editing team, Ken and Jen Elswick, Jeff Markland, Frank Shackleford, and Claudine Allison.

CHAPTER 1

"Arise, go up to the wealthy nation that dwells securely," says the LORD, "Which has neither gates nor bars, Dwelling alone. Their camels shall be for booty, And the multitude of their cattle for plunder. I will scatter to all winds those in the farthest corners, And I will bring their calamity from all its sides," says the LORD. "Hazor shall be a dwelling for jackals, a desolation forever . . ."

Jeremiah 49:31-33 NKJV

Danny rolled over in the bed Friday morning and picked up his watch. It was time to get up, but his back and muscles were racked with pain and he was shivering beneath the covers. While the beginning of April could still have a few cooler days in South Carolina, this particular morning was in the high sixties, which didn't warrant the cold trembling sensation coursing through Danny's body.

"Are you getting up?" Alisa pulled her sweater over her head as she finished dressing.

Danny stuck his head out from beneath the quilt. "I think I'm sick."

She bent down to place the back of her hand on his forehead. "You're burning up!" She ran her hand down into the covers. "You're soaking wet, too!"

Danny's eyes burned with fever. "Sweating is good. Maybe I'll sweat it out."

Alisa looked at him with compassionate eyes. "You better put on a dry tee-shirt. And I'll go get you some water. You have to stay hydrated."

"Tell Nana that I won't be down for breakfast."

"I will. You just rest. I'll be right back with some water." Alisa closed the door softly behind her.

Danny felt miserable. He didn't bother to change his shirt. Instead, he pulled the quilt back over his head, leaving just a small opening to breathe through.

Minutes later, Alisa returned with a big glass of water and two aspirin. "Come on, sit up and take a drink. You have to keep fluids in you. Cami said she'll make you a jug of Gatorade."

Danny sat up and took the aspirin and the glass. He sipped slowly to wash down the aspirin then put the glass on the bucket which served as a make-shift nightstand. "Cami has Gatorade?"

"Well, she's going to make something up. She has Kool-Aid packets. She said it's just Kool-Aid, sugar and a little salt; I guess you can call it *homemade-orade*."

Danny forced a smile. He knew Alisa was trying to make him feel better, but he felt absolutely miserable. "If I can choose, tell her orange would be best. If not, any flavor will be fine. It's just that I don't have much of a taste for anything."

"I'll tell her. What's your second choice if there's no orange?"

"Punch, I guess. Thank you." He put his hand on hers.

"No problem. Anything to make my baby feel better. Do you think you could eat some grits?"

"No way, but thanks." Danny finished the glass of water and lay back down.

She kissed him on the head. "Alright. You rest and feel better. We'll all be praying for you."

As Alisa closed the door, Danny shut his eyes and drifted back to sleep.

Danny awoke to Alisa putting her hand on his forehead.

"What time is it?" he asked groggily.

"Nine-thirty. You've been out for about two and a half hours. The aspirin should have helped by now, but you feel just as hot as before. I brought your Gatorade, it's orange. Can you drink a glass for me?"

"Okay." It took all of Danny's energy just to sit up.

Alisa handed him the glass. "Cami is coming up in a minute."

Danny nodded and sipped his drink.

A gentle knock on the door preceded Cami's voice. "Hey. Can I come in?"

Alisa stood to open the door.

Cami walked in the room and took a seat on the side of the bed. She felt Danny's forehead. "Wow. You are hot. I think you picked up typhus or typhoid fever from the dead bodies of one of Schlusser's goons. You looked like you were kind of dragging yesterday. When did you start feeling bad?"

"Probably last night. But you're right, I didn't have much energy yesterday. JC, Jack, Chris, and Clay all handled the dead bodies when we burned them. None of them are sick."

"They're not sick yet. The incubation period could be anywhere from a week up to four weeks, depending on whether it's typhus or typhoid." Cami set a small plastic pill bottle on the bucket next to Danny's drink. The bottle had a picture of fish swimming past coral.

"What's that?" Danny nodded toward the bottle.

"Ciprofloxin. Typhus and typhoid are both bacterial. This should kick either one."

"It's for fish?" Danny's mind was a bit clouded by the fever, but he was even more confused by the bottle of fish drugs.

Cami opened the bottle and took out two pills. "It's the apocalypse, Danny. The pills are for whoever needs them."

"Are you sure they're safe for humans?" Alisa

sounded somewhat concerned as well.

"They're manufactured in the same plant as human antibiotics and they come in the same dosage. The pills have the same colors and the same numerical markings as pills dispensed in a pharmacy." Cami handed the two pills to Danny.

"Fish Flox." Alisa read the label as she examined the bottle. "These are expired."

Cami nodded. "We bought them a while back, but they're good for five to ten years past expiration. Even then, they don't go toxic. They simply loose potency, so you have to double up the dosage."

Danny looked at Alisa to see if she thought it was a good idea.

She shrugged.

Danny washed the two pills down with his orange drink.

"Trust me, Danny. These fish pills might save your life." Cami crossed her arms. "Worst case scenario, you'll be able to breath under water."

"You're joking, right?" Danny asked.

She patted him on the leg as she stood. "Yeah, just kidding. Take two every eight hours. And just so you know, Nana is downstairs boiling some herbs she picked in the woods. She's making you some kind of voodoo tea. It smells awful. I'd be more worried about that than the fish antibiotics." She winked as she walked out of the room.

Danny finished his orange drink and resumed his position on the bed.

Alisa stroked his head. "I'm going to go finish my chores. Do you need anything?"

"Just keep Nana away. I don't want any part of her voodoo tea."

"Sorry, you're on your own with that one." Alisa kissed his head and stood to leave.

Nana walked in with a kettle and a tea cup before Alisa had a chance to exit the room. "Sit up Daniel. This here will put you right."

"What is it?" Danny curled his nose.

"Never you mind what it is. You just drink it."

"Nana, I'm not drinking it if I don't know what it is."

"It's tea. A little willow bark and sumac leaf. Now you sit up and drink."

"I appreciate it, but Cami gave me some medicine. I think it's going to help. I'm sure I'll be much better tomorrow."

"Listen here. You sit up and drink this tea."

Danny knew he wasn't going to win this argument and he had no strength to dedicate to such a doomed endeavor, so he sat up and sipped the concoction Nana handed him. It didn't taste as bad as he expected and the warmth seemed to dissipate his chills to some degree.

"The willow bark will help your aches and pains, and the sumac will help you get shed of that fever." Nana sat on the side of the bed and refilled Danny's cup when he finished it.

He drank the second serving and handed the empty cup to Nana. "I can't drink anymore."

She took the cup and stood. "Come on Lisa, let's leave him alone so he can get some rest."

"I'll check on you in a few hours." Alisa blew him a kiss as she left.

Danny forced a smile and covered his head, and soon drifted back to sleep.

Danny looked at the trunks of the trees which lined the bank of the creek. They seemed to swell and shrink, swell and shrink. He felt dizzy and tired, yet he continued walking toward the creek. He made his way toward the section of the creek where the banks were cleared with gentle slopes so the tractor could drive across. He'd always loved that place as a child. He loved to stand on the bank and watch the minnows swim against the gentle current. When he reached the bank, he tossed a stick in the water to watch it float downstream, just as he had done as a youth. The stick was soon caught up on an obstruction protruding from the water. Danny bent down to retrieve a rock to throw at the stick in hopes of freeing it, to continue its journey down the creek. Perhaps if he could dislodge it, the stick would reach a river somewhere, and then on to the Atlantic Ocean, where it might catch the Gulf Stream and travel the world. Danny knew he'd never travel the world now. He was blessed to be alive. But he wondered, what if the stick were a boat and what if he could ride the stick down the creek, to the river, into the ocean and catch the Gulf Stream. What would he see? Nick said the lights had been turned off all over the world. Were the inhabitants of other lands getting along as poorly as Danny's compound? Or were they treating each other in a more civilized fashion?

The stick was still lodged. Danny tossed another stone, landing inches away but creating enough of a ripple to move the stick. "Almost, but not enough." He picked up one more pebble, but before he could cast it at the trapped stick, the obstruction just below the surface of the water began to move. Danny stood still, wondering what it could be.

It rose slowly from the water. It resembled a horn. "It is! It is a horn!" And then he saw a second horn rising from the water only inches away. Danny saw what looked like the head of a cow coming up from beneath the water. "How can that be? The creek is a foot, maybe two feet deep at most."

Nevertheless, the head of a cow seemed to float to the surface then protruded upwards. The bovine's neck stuck up from the troubled creek as it gasped for air.

"That tea. She must have put some hallucinogenic in that tea." Danny knew that Nana would never intentionally give him something to make him trip out, but what if she had accidentally picked the wrong plant for her potion.

The cow continued to rise up from the water. It stared into Danny's eyes and walked towards him. Its flesh was torn in places, as if it had been dead and was in the process of decomposing. As the reanimated creature approached him, he tried to turn and run, but he was frozen, unable to move, unable to scream.

The rancid beast stood inches away from him and opened its mouth. The lower jaw seemed to melt like wax and dislocate like a snake as the top of its mouth covered Danny's head to swallow him. Unable to move or resist the assault of the filthy creature, Danny was soon in the stomach of the rotting animal.

Danny's body was paralyzed, but his mind was acutely aware of the horror as it occurred. He felt unsteady as his ability to move returned to him. He leaned against a rib that towered over him in the cavernous pit to keep from slipping into the pool of foul smelling digestive juices puddled about his feet. "This is no hallucination. This is a dream, another terrible nightmare."

Soon the sides of the animal's stomach melted away and he was in a vast open field. It was still dark, but a faint glint of moonlight filtered through the dark clouds all around. He could make out what looked like thorn bushes all around. He was standing in the middle of a desert.

Something moved from behind one of the bushes and ran to take cover behind another of the plots of dried brambles. Danny peered into the night, but couldn't tell what it had been. Then another one; out of the corner of his eye he saw a four-legged creature dash to the thicket behind him.

The silence was interrupted by a high pitched howl, like a ghost or specter calling out to harass a realm where it was not wanted. The sound, much too high to be that of a wolf or coyote, chilled him to the bone. It was answered by yet another distant howl. Soon, the wretched beasts hiding in the briar patches all around him began to sing out in unison with their hideous yelps. Danny squinted to make out the shape of the four legged beings. They had long ears and a pointed snout like a fox, yet their bodies were much more akin to a small wild dog with a bushy tail. Soon, they were all around him, howling and snarling with their jagged teeth showing. "Jackals," he said, as he recognized the species of his tormentors.

Dream or no dream, Danny was terror-stricken. He looked down, the sand was now up to his knees and he was sinking. As soon as he realized his predicament, he began calling out to Alisa to wake him. "Alisa! Wake me up! Wake me up! Alisa!" It was no use; she was off doing chores. She couldn't hear him, but he continued to call out. "Help! Alisa!"

Suddenly, Danny crashed to the floor. He'd fallen out of bed. Danny bumped his elbow pretty hard, but he didn't care. He was simply happy to be done with the macabre vision. He sat on the floor for a while, rubbing his head and trying to process what he had just seen. He whispered softly to himself, "I've had some weird dreams in the past few months, but that one takes the cake. I wonder if it was prophetic or just a product of my fever induced delirium. Of course, it could have been Nana's voodoo tea."

Danny's shirt was wet with sweat, so he took a dry one from the dresser. As he changed, he noticed that he didn't feel quite as bad as he did earlier. "Something must have helped; either the voodoo tea or the fish pills."

He made his way down the stairs to get another glass of Gatorade and perhaps see if he could eat.

"Hey man, how you feeling?" Steven stood in the living room, a crutch under each arm.

"Better than I was. How's the leg?"

"It still throbs. The consensus is that it's fractured, which means I'll probably be out of commission for at least another four weeks. I hate being a burden to the rest of the group."

Danny shook his head and smiled. "You took one in the leg, defending the rest of the group. Everyone here appreciates your sacrifice and no one thinks you're a burden. Besides, you're on watch like twelve hours a day. That's a job that would have to be done by somebody. Where's your sidekick?"

"You mean Jason?"

"Yeah, he's been hanging around you almost all the time since his dad was killed."

Steven lowered his head. "Yeah, I don't mind it. I like having him around. He keeps me company. Nana has him and his sisters in the back field working the garden. It helps them to keep their minds busy. There's a fine line between grieving and depression."

Danny nodded. "Plus, between Korey and Rocky being killed, and you and Nick being injured, we actually need their help."

Steven hobbled toward the kitchen. "Yeah, and if we get hit again, they might be on their own, so they better learn whatever skills they can. It's a tough world."

Danny grimaced as he followed Steven into the kitchen. He was just starting to feel better. He did not want to think about another assault on the compound.

Alisa and Dana came in the back door. Alisa took off her shoes before coming in. "Look who's feeling better!"

Dana removed her shoes also and followed Alisa. "How are you doing?"

"Weak, but much better. My fever is way down."

Alisa put her hand on his forehead. "Wow! Something worked. I don't see any scales, so no adverse side effects from the fish pills. What about the voodoo tea?"

Danny pursed his lips. "I don't know. Something gave me some pretty crazy dreams."

JC walked in the back door. "Hey kid. How you doin'?"

Alisa answered for him. "Better, but he had another dream."

"Ay-ay-ay. I don't think we can handle another one of your dreams. At least let us recuperate from the last attack. How 'bout I give you my coffee rations and you just stay awake for the next few weeks," JC quipped.

"So let's hear it. What happened in the dream?" Dana sounded anxious.

"Get him something to eat first. He's weak." Steven made his way to the table and took a seat.

"Nana has some soup for you. Sit down with Steven and I'll warm it up for you." Alisa retrieved a bowl from the cupboard.

Danny complied. "Can you bring me a glass of that Gatorade? I'm super thirsty."

"I'll get it," Dana said.

"Where are you guys getting Gatorade?" JC took a chair next to Danny.

Steven motioned toward the back woods. "Minimart just opened up back by the fence."

"Get outta here." JC fought back a grin.

"Cami made it. But it really tastes like Gatorade," Danny explained while he waited for his soup.

Alisa and Dana brought Danny's soup and drink to the table, and then took a seat.

"Okay, let's hear it!" Alisa crossed her arms and looked intently at Danny as she awaited his reply.

"Before everyone gets all excited, let me preface this by saying that I had a very high fever, had drunk some concoction that Nana made, and was taking fish antibiotics. The dream was very trippy and surreal; not like the others. All my other dreams seemed like reality when I was having them. This one seemed like a bad drug experience."

Dana made a circular motion with her hand, indicating that she wanted Danny to proceed. "Okay, okay, get on with it."

Danny gave his account of the dream and everyone at the table listened quietly. When he was finished, they all looked to Alisa.

She shrugged. "What are you guys looking at me for? I don't have any idea what that is supposed to mean."

Dana kept looking to Alisa. "So maybe it was just the fever?"

"I guess. I never claimed to be an interpreter," Alisa replied.

Steven leaned in. "But you've had an understanding of every dream so far."

"Until now," she said.

"Hopefully, it was just a bad dream then." Danny continued eating his soup.

JC stood up suddenly. "I've got to get those

clean rags and get them back over to Cami. She's in the process of changing Nick's bandages and I told her I'd be right back."

Danny waved. "See you later."

JC patted him on the back as he walked away. "Feel better."

Danny ate his soup and drank his drink, while the conversation among the remaining people at the table soon progressed beyond the topic of his nightmare.

After lunch, Danny felt a bit more energetic. He stripped the damp sheets from his bed and took them outside to wash. Without the conveniences of an electric washing machine, washing sheets would consume what little strength he had built up. He removed his pistol belt and hung it from a nail on the small out building near the pump. He drew a tub of water from the hand pump and mixed in a small bit of detergent. He pushed the sheets down into the water, pulling them back up, and then down again to get the soapy water mixed in.

Alisa walked up. "What do you think you're doing? You should be in bed."

"There's no sheets on the bed. Anyway, I feel much better."

"You need to rest. Go lie down on the couch. I'll finish this." Alisa took over the sheets.

Danny didn't have the energy to argue, so he thanked her, put his pistol belt back on and walked off. Danny had been in bed all day and needed to move around a little more before returning to his vegetative state on the couch. He walked around to the pinnacle to see who was on watch.

JC was sitting in a chair, near the entrance of the fox hole. His rifle was leaned up against the sandbags and the radio was in his hand. "You got cleared by medical?"

"Not really." Danny smirked. "I've been instructed to return to the infirmary, but I'm taking the scenic route."

JC snickered then his expression became more solemn. "So nobody had anything else to say about your dream, huh?"

"No. We pretty much wrote it off to delirium from the fever."

JC pursed his lips. "I wouldn't be too quick to do that."

"Why? Do you have any ideas?"

"This is just between you and me. I wouldn't be showing you this if it hadn't been for that dream." JC handed Danny a folded piece of paper.

Danny took the note. "What is it?"

"I was going to leave that for Melissa last night. I was planning to head out this morning, but I could tell you were getting sick last night, so I wanted to wait and make sure it wasn't going around. Night watch is too lean as it is."

"And go where?" Danny was confused.

"Try to infiltrate Schlusser's organization."

Danny furrowed his brow. "What? JC, you can't do that. You'll get yourself killed."

"Maybe not."

Danny shook his head. "You were going to take off and not tell anybody?"

"I was going to leave the note, but otherwise, no;

I wasn't going to say anything. Melissa wouldn't want me to go, Jack and Chris would want to come along. There's no point arguing with Melissa about it, and the compound needs Jack and Chris here. We're spread way too thin on shooters even with both of them."

"We'll be spread even thinner if we lose our tactical coordinator."

"Nick can handle that. He knows what he's doing. It don't matter, though. This is the only way we have a chance. I've got to get information on what their plans are, where and when they're moving. If we sit around here and wait to get hit again, we'll all be dead."

"So, what's your plan?"

"Drive up to Charlotte, see if he's hiring."

"And?"

"That's it. If I can get inside, I'll get information and try to get it back to you down here. If an opportunity for sabotage presents itself, I'll take it."

"How will you get information back to us?"

JC snickered. "That's a good question."

Danny got a curious inclination. He tilted his head to the side as he asked, "And why are you telling me all of this? You're not telling your wife or your sons, why am I being included in the scheme?"

"Your dream."

"What about it?"

JC lowered his glasses on his nose and peered over the tops. "Where were you in the dream?"

Danny tried to make a connection to something, but had no idea what JC was hinting at. "The cow's stomach."

"Right, and where am I going?"

Danny shook his head, "Charlotte?"

JC sighed. "The belly of the beast."

A chill shot down Danny's spine. He instantly understood where JC was going with all of this. "Oh no. I'm not going to Charlotte."

"And I would never ask you to. But, what if your dream was a message from God? In your dream, you were in the belly of the beast. I'm going to infiltrate the belly of the beast.

"And jackals, eastern European cultures think they are companions of Satan. The Egyptians have Anubis, a man with a jackal's head, as their god of death. Those filthy animals will dig up a buried body and eat the entrails out of it. They feed on death and slip around in the night, just like Schlusser and his goons."

Danny crossed his arms. "In the dream, I was swallowed up by quick sand. I don't really want to put myself in that position."

"What if the mission depends on you coming with me? Danny, this thing is a long shot and if it has any chance of success, we need all the help we can get from God."

"Then why even risk it?"

JC stared out toward the road. "It's the only chance we have at survival. Schlusser got our coordinates from the radio in the Hummer. Sooner or later, he's comin' here with every ounce of strength he has. We don't stand a chance. He'll kill every one of us. Maybe take the kids as slaves. The only other possible alternative is to run, and I don't have any idea where we would run to. You heard Nick and Cami's account of what it's like out there. And I guarantee it's worse now than it was two weeks ago when they were hiking home."

"It's been almost a week since the attack. Maybe he's forgotten about us."

"Oh no. He's getting organized. We hurt him. We took out every soldier he had in Greenville. He's probably been focused on getting enough people moved down to Greenville to hold his position. If it were me, I'd split the people from Spartanburg to hold the base in Greenville then send reinforcements to both from Charlotte as soon as I could get new recruits trained."

"So that's why you think it'll be easy for us to get a job? Because Schlusser needs to replace the men we killed off?"

"Yep."

"What makes you so sure he'll hire us?"

"I'm pretty sure he'll give me a job because of my experience."

"Yeah, as a beat cop, right!"

JC tilted his head to one side. "My resume might be a little more extensive than that."

"So you've eluded. You can tell me. I won't say anything."

"I was a captain for NYPD ESU. Before that, I worked a while in narcotics."

"What's ESU?"

"Emergency Service Unit. SWAT, basically."

"Oh!" Danny's eyes lit up. "What makes you so sure he'll give me a job?"

"Your dream. Where God guides, God provides."

"And what's our cover story going to be?"

"We'll figure something out on the way. So you're on board?"

"Do I have a choice?"

"You always have a choice, but I don't see any other way to protect the group."

Danny sighed heavily. "Yeah. I guess I'll come along. When will we leave?"

"As soon as you feel better. I'll give you a list of stuff to start putting together for the trip tomorrow. Once we get actionable intel, I'll send you back home with a plan. As long as you have a non-combatant job, you probably won't be missed if you desert."

"But if I am, and I'm caught, what happens?"

"Schlusser will probably kill you. He can't have people changing their minds about being in his organization. Warlords don't last long if they run an easy camp."

"And if they find out we're spies?"

JC shook his head. "Don't even talk like that. You don't want to know. Never admit you're a spy. Deny, deny, deny; no matter what."

Of all the visions Danny had dreamt before, this one was quickly becoming his least favorite. "I'm not sure I can leave without telling Alisa."

"Do what you want, but if you tell her, she has to understand two things. Number one, she ain't going. It ain't no kind of environment for a girl. And number two, she can't say anything to anyone. If you decide to tell her, I'd wait until right before we leave.

"You still look a little pale. You should go get

some rest. I don't want to take a chance on you getting real sick on the trip, so we won't leave until you're back to 100 percent."

"Yeah, okay. I'll talk to you later." Danny waved as he walked away. He had plenty to ponder on his way back to the house.

CHAPTER 2

And in those times there was no peace to him that went out, nor to him that came in, but great vexations were upon all the inhabitants of the countries. And nation was destroyed of nation, and city of city: for God did vex them with all adversity.

2 Chronicles 15:5-6

Danny woke up on Saturday with a slight fever. It wasn't nearly as bad as the previous day, but it still left him with little energy. Nana brewed him another batch of the tea which seemed to taste worse the second time around. Alisa double checked that he was continuing the antibiotics which Cami had given him. Cami had said to take them for at least seven days to keep from encouraging a drug resistant strain of the bacteria. He ate very little and drank a lot; soup, water, homemade Gatorade, and Nana's potion was the entirety of his diet for the day.

Danny spent as much time as possible in bed, but boredom got the better of him from time to time, so he had to get up and stretch his legs. Besides sleeping, he read his Bible for several hours, and then looked over some of Nana's old *Reader's Digest* magazines, memoirs of a world that no longer existed. Puddin', Dana's cat, would wander in from time to time, like a nurse making her rounds in a hospital. She'd jump up on the bed, as if to check his vitals, stay for a brief scratch, get bored, and move on to inspect some other part of the house.

Alisa came up to check on him just after sundown. "How are you feeling?"

"Pretty good actually, but I'm going to take it easy. It seems I feel the worst when I first wake up."

"That sounds like a good plan. Do you think you could eat some more soup?"

Danny nodded. "Yeah, I could eat. What did you guys have for lunch?"

"Rabbit and cornbread."

"Are there any leftovers?"

"Maybe some cornbread. No rabbit."

"I think I could eat some cornbread with my soup."

"Do you want me to make you a tray and bring it upstairs?"

"That's sweet of you to offer, but I need to stretch my legs. I'll come down to the kitchen, if no one is worried about me being contagious, that is."

"Cami said she has a pretty good stockpile of antibiotics, so I don't think it's that big of a deal; not that anyone wants to get sick in the first place. I'm just saying it won't kill anybody."

"How are Tracey and Pauline holding up?"

"Tracey is doing okay. I think she is forcing herself to keep it together for the kids. Pauline, on the other hand, is a mess. She slept in her house alone last night, and I haven't seen her all day."

"Is she okay?"

"Nana went up there at lunch and took her some food, but said she wouldn't eat. She left it there."

Danny shook his head. "They'd just moved all of their stuff to the trailer."

"Yeah, to be safer. I feel sorry for her, but I don't know what to do to help. We're all so busy trying to keep up with the chores, there's not a lot of time to hold her hand while she grieves."

"At least Nana is looking in on her."

Sunday morning came and Danny had recovered enough to attend church in the barn. Steven read from 1 Corinthians 15, teaching on the glory of the resurrection body. Tracey Reese bawled like a baby during the sermon. Cami put her arm around her to comfort her.

Danny wished that Pauline was present to hear the message, and that perhaps she could have gained a glimmer of consolation through the knowledge that she would see Rocky again someday.

After church, Danny's appetite returned and he ate a hearty lunch of biscuits, fried chicken, sweet potato greens, and rice.

JC sat next to Danny at the communal picnic tables in the courtyard. "Looks like you're feeling better."

Danny made sure Alisa wasn't listening in. She wasn't. She was deeply engaged in conversation with Dana. Danny turned his attention back to JC. "Yeah, much better. I'm still taking my antibiotics. You think tomorrow?"

JC shook his head. "Tuesday at the earliest. I want to see you back up to 100 percent, rested and ready."

"Okay." Danny would have the anxiety of the mission hanging over him for the rest of the day, but he still made every effort to make the most of the time with his wife, family, and friends.

On Monday, Danny continued to take it easy, conserving his strength for the next morning. That night, as he and Alisa got ready for bed, he took out his large backpack.

"What'cha doin'?" Alisa looked at him curiously.

He tried to hold back the tears. The thought of leaving her, perhaps for the last time, hit him all at once. Before he could speak, he began to cry.

"Hey, come here." She held him in her arms while he dried his eyes.

He looked up. "Sorry about that." He slowly began to recount the dream, and his conversation with JC.

Now it was Alisa whose face had lost every trace of joy and happiness. She shook her head in opposition and began to weep. "No, Danny. You can't leave me. I can't do this without you. I can't lose you. I can't be here all alone like Tracey and Pauline."

"There's no other way. If we don't figure out a way to stop Schlusser, we'll all be dead."

She gripped his hand tightly as she continued crying. "Then take me with you."

He shook his head as he looked her in the eyes tenderly. "Not this time, baby. Pretty girls only have one function in a den of jackals like Schlusser's camp."

"I'll stay outside of town, camp out in the woods. I'll listen in on the radio. If you get in trouble and you can get to a radio, you can call me and I'll come home and get help."

"Alisa, you have to trust God. If he has given me a mission, you have to believe that he is going to get me through it."

"He didn't get Rocky or Korey through it." She crossed her arms in anger.

Danny didn't know how to respond. He sat quietly for a moment. "But he delivered the compound, against impossible odds. And they're in heaven, waiting for their families."

She took his hand again. Her voice softened. "I know. But I don't want to live if you die."

Danny pulled her close and the two of them held each other silently for the next hour.

Danny's alarm went off at 4:00 AM Tuesday morning. He turned it off, got dressed and kissed Alisa goodbye.

"You come home, Danny Walker." Alisa gripped his arm tightly, as if she did not intend to let him leave.

"I will. I promise." Danny knew it wasn't up to him, but he would make every effort to keep that promise.

"You better." She bit her lower lip and let him go.

He slung his pack over his shoulder and blew her a kiss. "I love you."

Her voice cracked. "I love you, too."

Danny closed the door behind him and walked softly down the stairs.

JC was waiting outside in the courtyard.

Nick had been on night watch and was sitting at the picnic table next to JC. "We'll be praying for you guys. I'll tell everyone you said *goodbye*."

Danny sighed. "Thanks."

JC handed Danny a brown paper bag. "Here's your breakfast. Did you get everything on the list I gave you?"

"Yeah, everything except the bikes." Danny looked inside the bag and took out a biscuit. "Since we're going to be stashing the rifles in the woods anyway, wouldn't it be better to take a couple that we took from the soldiers we killed?" Danny bit into the biscuit and stuck it back in the bag.

JC shook his head. "We can't take a chance on getting picked up with anything that will identify us as having been involved in killing Schlusser's men.

We don't know how good he is at record keeping. For all we know, he has a ledger with the serial numbers of every gun in his arsenal.

"Do you want to drive?"

Danny finished chewing. "Sure, what are we driving?"

"The Fish's truck." JC tossed him the keys.

Danny caught them. "Catfish lent you his truck?"

"Sorta."

"Sorta?" Danny looked at Nick who simply shrugged.

"Come on, I'll tell you on the way. I want to drive by the Greenville outpost on the way. We need to get there well before sunrise." JC led the way to Catfish's old truck and tossed his backpack in the bed.

"Godspeed!" Nick waved.

"Thanks. I think I'm going to need all the help I can get." Danny threw a hand in the air as he hustled to keep up with JC.

Once in the truck, they drove around to the barn, stuck two bikes, and an eight-inch PVC pipe with an end cap and a clean-out plug in the bed. Next, they were headed toward Greenville.

Danny kept his eyes on the road, scanning for stalled vehicles so he'd have plenty of time to avoid them, while still maintaining a steady pace. The headlights on the old truck weren't very bright, so he had to concentrate on the road. "I got the feeling that you didn't tell Catfish we were taking his truck."

"I told him I needed it. I just didn't specify how long I'd be gone. He won't mind." JC retrieved two magazines for his AR-15 from the inside of his jacket pocket and stuck them under his leg. He adjusted the collapsible stock on his rifle to the shortest length possible. "Stay on US-29 all the way to the interstate. Hopefully, we won't see any trouble for the short stretch we have to travel on I-85."

"We'll take I-85 all the way to Charlotte?"

"No we'll get back off and take 29 when it diverges from I-85."

"Then on to Spartanburg?"

"We ain't goin' through Spartanburg. After Greenville, they'll be on their toes and possibly looking for us."

Danny glanced over at JC. "What do you mean?"

"We're going to take a little detour by the Greenville Airport. It backs right up to the convention center where Schlusser has his outpost. We're gonna find a good sniping position on one of the out buildings at the airport and cause a little chaos."

Danny's heart started beating harder. He hadn't planned on getting into a fight so early. "But then they'll be after us. Won't that compromise the broader mission?"

"Nope. It'll buy us some time. If we kill a couple of their guys at the Greenville outpost, they'll have to spend time and resources figuring out how they're going to stop a similar attack from happening. They can't start planning an attack on our compound until they get that place secured.

"While we're there, I can assess their general state of military readiness. If they look like they're about ready to launch an attack, we'll have to hustle back home, load up as many supplies as we can into ever how many trailers we can pull and get out of dodge. We'll take 'em to a campground or state park. Of course, that presents a whole new list of potential threats."

"Would we still attack them if they look like they're ready to launch an assault?"

"Yep, it'd still buy us some time."

"What if they catch us?"

JC shook his head. "It won't happen. We're coming in from the back side of the airport. Even if they had someone waitin' in a vehicle ready to roll as soon as we start shootin', we'd be through the neighborhood and long gone by the time they got around the fence to the airport."

Danny wasn't convinced. Maybe it was because JC had sprung it on him out of nowhere, but it felt like something he'd thrown together at the last minute. "Are you sure? If the airport is close enough for us to shoot them, then we're close enough to get shot."

"They'll be dead before they know where the attack is comin' from. Trust me."

Danny grunted. He wished he could be as confident as JC, but it sounded risky. The airport was just under an hour away, which would leave them a little more than an hour before sunrise.

When they arrived in Greenville, JC guided Danny down the street behind the convention center. "Take it slow. I want to see how many vehicles they have back by the loading docks."

Danny continued at a snail's pace, driving with

his lights out.

JC held a small pocket spotting scope to his eye. "Not much of nothin' back here."

Danny followed JC's directions around to the back entrance of the airport. JC jumped out to cut the lock at the flight school gate. From there, they drove across the runway to the building adjacent to the convention center.

"Pull up to the corner of that building."

Danny looked at the structure. It was a two-story building which contained offices for various aircraft-related companies. It was constructed with corrugated metal which was painted white. The building had an awning extending out from the entrance, which was the only thing that kept it from looking like a hanger or a warehouse. "How are we going to get on top of it?"

"We'll drive right up to the awning. We can climb from the bed of the truck to the top of the cab and that will give us enough height to get up on the awning."

"You think that awning will hold us?"

"Oh yeah. That thing is heavy duty corrugated sheet metal. From there, we can climb that drain pipe to the upper roof."

Danny absolutely did not like this plan. Even without shooting into a hornets' nest, the climbing alone was frightening. He dug down deep for courage and prayed a silent prayer. *God give me strength.*

Danny parked the car and the two of them quietly got out, leaving his door open for a hasty retreat. JC led the way up on the cab of the truck, and then to the overhanging awning. He helped Danny up next. Each of them had their rifles slung across their backs and two extra magazines in their back pockets.

JC worked his way up the metal drain pipe to the second level then lowered his hand, once again, to give Danny a lift. They walked softly to the apex of the roof and knelt down.

JC took the small spotting scope from his pocket and looked all around. "I don't see much in the way of heavy machinery. Just a few pickups and a couple of Humvees. There's two old Deuce and a half at the end of the parking lot, but those are just for troop transport."

JC pointed to the two men sitting in chairs at the entrance of the convention center, 30 yards from their position. The two men had AR-15s, but nothing else about them was the same. One wore a black long-sleeve shirt and ACU camouflage pants, while the other had woodland camo pants and OD green jacket. It was obvious that Schlusser was still operating beyond his means.

JC whispered. "You take the one on the left, I'll take the one on the right. As soon as the men inside hear gunfire, they'll come running. Once the reinforcements arrive, empty the rest of your magazine, and then scale back down to the truck. I'll change my mag and dump another 30 rounds to let them know we're serious. As soon as you hear me drop back into the bed of the truck, take off like a bat out of hell. Get back on 29 west for about two miles then take 292 north til it ends at Boiling Springs. We should have enough distance then. You can pull over and I'll jump back in the cab. Got it?"

Danny understood, but he wasn't ready for all of this. "I guess so."

"You'll be fine. I'll shoot first. You shoot as soon as you hear my first round. Let me know when you have your target and you're ready."

Danny took a prone position on the metal roof and steadied the sights of his AK. "Okay, I have my target."

JC didn't speak. Seconds later, Danny heard the rifle crack. POP! He quickly followed suit. POW! JC's target dropped instantly, but Danny's was still alive. He could see the guard looking to where the shots had come from. The man looked right at Danny's position, just as he took another shot. POW! The man fell to the ground. Danny had hit him in the chest. JC took another shot, hitting the man in the head. Three more men ran out of the front door with their weapons ready to fire. Danny and JC opened up on them, killing all three before they could take aim on JC and Danny's position.

JC patted Danny on the arm. "Go, get back to the truck. I'll be there in a second."

Danny nodded, staying low as he descended from the roof. He was shaking like a leaf from the adrenaline. He was extra careful with his steps so he wouldn't slip. He heard JC unleash a barrage of gunfire as he removed his AK and got back into the cab of the truck. Danny tried to keep count of the rounds being fired from JC's AR so he would know when his magazine was empty, but he couldn't. JC was shooting too fast. Soon, he heard JC's weapon cease, but gunfire continued to ring out from the direction of the convention center. A horrible thought crossed Danny's mind. What if JC had been shot? What would he do? There was no hope of him pulling off the mission by himself. He would have no choice but to return to the compound. The seconds seemed like hours as he contemplated how long he should wait for JC. Danny quickly changed the magazine of his AK and folded his stock in case he had to shoot his way out of the airport parking lot.

A loud thump hit the top of the cab, followed by the sound of JC landing in the bed of the truck. He was still alive. Danny let out a sigh of relief as he sped off across the runway, and back out the gate of the flight school.

Danny focused on breathing, checking the rearview for pursuers, and maintain the maximum safe speed for the next several miles. After fifteen minutes he allowed himself to think they might actually get away. Ten miles more, and he continued to check the rearview. Still no sign of Schlusser's goons. He reached the end of 292 and pulled to the side as directed by JC. Danny watched as JC jumped out of the bed of the truck and came around to the passenger's side. He still didn't know if JC had been hit, but judging from the way he moved, he was okay.

JC opened the door. "We did it, kid!"

Danny looked him over. "Are you okay?"

JC jumped in and closed the door. "I'm fine, but let's keep moving. No point in taking unnecessary risks."

Danny smirked as he mumbled, "No unnecessary

risks." It seemed like quite a departure from the doctrine JC had held only minutes before.

After a short period of solitude, JC said, "We need to make sure we've got our cover stories down. We'll say we've been traveling together for a couple days for security sake, but we don't really know much about each other. My story is, I'm a NYPD cop who had enough supplies in my house to get through the winter. I hunkered down in my house in Queens and headed south on my bike as soon as the weather broke.

"What about you? What's the farthest north you've ever visited?"

"I've visited Cami in DC a few times."

"Good, your story is that you and your girlfriend went to visit her parents in DC. The EMP was on a Thursday, you were going to hang out for a few days. Her parents were stocked up, maybe they started keeping more food on hand after Snowmageddon or Sandy. Anyway, supplies were getting low, tempers were getting high, so you loaded up a bag, stole a gun and a bike from her house and headed out on your own."

"Wow, you make me sound like a real creep." Danny furrowed his brow.

"These guys ain't lookin' for boy scouts. They'll have higher appreciation for someone who does what needs to be done."

"Isn't it dishonest to be lying?"

JC looked over. "What are you talking about?"

"Lying, the Bible says not to lie."

JC rolled his eyes. "The Bible says not to bear false witness. That's like telling a lie in court in order to get someone locked up. It ain't talkin' about this type of thing."

Danny wasn't convinced. "In Revelation, at the end, it says all liars end up in the lake of fire."

JC looked over the top of his glasses as he sighed. "Okay, what about Rahab? She's listed as one of the heroes of the faith in Hebrews 11."

Still being a relatively new Christian, Danny wasn't very familiar with this particular character. "What does that have to do with lying?"

"When the Israelite spies went to recon the city of Jericho, they ended up at this hooker's house, named Rahab. The authorities hear about some spies bein' in the city and come lookin' for 'em. She hides the Israeli spies on her roof and tells the authorities they're already gone. She cuts a deal with the spies and they spare her life when they sack the city."

Danny nodded as he listened. "Okay, go on."

"She lied to the authorities in order to save the lives of the Israelite spies and ends up in the Hebrews 11 hall of faith. God ain't up there with some rule book waitin' to squash you like a bug if you step out of line. He still expects you to use common sense. That was warfare, and saving the lives of the spies trumped honesty in that situation.

"Same thing for us, we're goin' in as spies, and we have to have a good cover story so we can save the lives of our families. Understand?"

Danny nodded. It made perfect sense to him after JC took the time to explain it. "Yeah, thanks.

So where to?"

"There's a coal-fired electrical plant right across

the river from Schlusser's headquarters. I can't think of a more useless location than an electrical plant in a post-EMP world. It has about the same utility value as a roll of wet toilet paper. That makes it a good place to stash the truck and the rifles. From there, we'll ride our bikes across the bridge and try to get a job."

"You make it sound so easy. But we still have to get to Schlusser's base without getting killed for our bikes or our packs."

"We'll have pistols. If anybody comes at us, try to get away. If we can't get away, ride to a place where you can lay the bike down behind cover before you try to engage."

"How far is Schlusser's after the bridge?"

"He's set up at the National Guard Armory. It's about eight miles, but it's all along the backside of the airport. We won't have to ride through any neighborhoods. Most of the gangs who are still alive have probably taken over upper-class subdivisions and only leave to go on raiding missions to places they are likely to find food or other resources."

"This guy really likes setting up near airports, huh?"

"Douglas International is a completely different animal than the little puddle-jumper landing pad in Greenville. It's enclosed by ten-to-twelve-foot-high fence, with lots of storage and open land. There's a train yard that sits right between the two main runways; that was probably chock full of goods. And he's got an extensive supply of jet fuel."

"What good will that do him?"

"Jet fuel is very similar to diesel. All the military vehicles Schlusser has at the armory probably run on diesel. Diesel has a little more lubricant than jet fuel, but you can easily fix that by mixing 2-cycle oil or vegetable oil in it. But even without adding anything, you could get away with running straight jet fuel in a diesel engine for a pretty good while before it starts causing problems."

Danny put his sunglasses on and lowered the visor of the old truck as the sun rose over the horizon. He continued east along the backroads toward Charlotte. Danny didn't have to ask if they were getting closer, the familiar scent of death and the circling carrion birds in the sky above told him he was approaching a large metropolitan area. "It's been roughly eight weeks since the EMP. I would imagine all but the most resilient people in the cities are dead."

JC nodded in agreement. "Resilient and violent. The next few months will winnow out most of the holdouts." JC pointed to the right. "We're going to take a left over here. We'll be driving through some neighborhoods, so stay alert." He positioned his rifle so that it was ready to fire at any potential hostiles they might encounter.

Danny continued driving down South Point for about two miles. The neighborhoods became increasingly spread out and the landscape looked more rural.

As they crossed a short bridge, which went over a canal, JC pointed to the left. "That's it. Plant Allen Road. It'll take us straight to the electric plant."

Danny followed the directions and drove past the abandoned guard house. He continued on the road for just under a mile. "Where do you want to hide the truck?"

JC pointed toward the employee parking lot. "Right there. Pull in between those two trucks."

"We're going to leave it right here in the open?"

"Yep. I'm going to switch out two of the spark plugs so anyone who tries to start it will hopefully assume that it was taken out by the EMP. It'll look like it's been sitting here since doomsday, right alongside the rest of the vehicles."

"But it will still turn over, even if it's missing two spark plugs. A car that's been disabled by an EMP won't even turn over."

JC nodded. "Yeah, but most people are too stupid to figure that out, and the rest are looking for low hanging fruit. There ain't gonna be trouble shooting some junker in a parkin' lot."

Danny thought about the logic of JC's reasoning. While not the course of action he would have chosen, Danny realized that attempting to conceal the truck would be a sign to passersby that it was a vehicle worth hiding. He pulled into the parking space and cut the engine.

JC exited the truck and walked to a nearby vehicle which had already been broken into. He opened the door, popped the hood and took his multitool from its pouch on the side of his belt.

Danny followed him and watched as JC removed two spark plugs from the vehicle, and then broke off the ground electrode. "You're going to replace two plugs from our truck with those. Then, if someone pops the hood on our truck to check, it will look like it has all the plugs intact. Is that right?"

"Exactly." JC shut the hood to the other vehicle and returned to the old truck.

Once the task was finished, they retrieved the bikes and rifles and headed out to explore the grounds of the electrical plant. Danny pointed to the giant mound of coal to the right. It extended for over a hundred yards and looked to be about forty feet high at its peak "How is that for a place to bury the rifles?"

JC looked over. "It's probably a good place, but I'd rather find a place inside some trees, in case we need cover when we're retrieving them. That's the river bank straight ahead. Let's check that group of trees for a place to stash the rifles."

A fence enclosed the electric plant, separating it from the river. JC began cutting the fence in an area concealed by shrubs and trees on the plant side of the fence with his multitool. "This thing ain't really made for cuttin' fence, so I'm making a hole just big enough to crawl through."

"That'll work." Danny pulled back tightly on the fence as JC cut to make the task move as smoothly as possible.

Once the cuts were made, JC held the cut section of fence so Danny could wriggle under it.

Danny stood up and continued into the wooded area between the plant and the Catawba River. He kicked the dirt beneath his feet. "It's pretty sandy. As long as we can find a place that isn't too dense with tree roots, we should be able to bury the PVC pipe here."

JC called out from the other side of the fence. "Good. Find a spot and I'll bring the pipe."

"What are we going to dig with?"

JC looked around. "There's a utility shed over there. I'm sure I can find a shovel. You stay here with the bikes and the gear."

"Sure thing." Danny continued to walk around the trees, looking for an easily-identifiable location.

Minutes later, JC called to Danny. "I found a shovel."

Danny walked back to the fence opening. "Great. I think I have a good spot. I'll start digging if you want to get the pipe from the truck."

JC passed the shovel through the opening in the fence. "Be right back."

Danny began excavating a long shallow trench to bury the pipe. JC returned minutes later with the PVC pipe. He removed the threaded drain clean out plug from one end of the pipe and placed the rifles, magazines, and ammo inside. "Make one side a little lower than the other. If the clean out end is lower than the capped side, any water that leaks in can leak back out, just as easily."

Danny watched as JC placed his AK-47 in the tube. "I can't stand the thought of my AK getting wet."

JC nodded. "Hopefully, it won't. And hopefully, we ain't here long enough for it to hurt it, even if it does get wet. Anyway, I'll stuff the extra MREs and dehydrated food in the bottom so it will push the rifles and ammo further up the pipe."

Danny continued digging, creating a thirty-degree incline to keep his AK up higher and reduce the odds of it getting wet.

The pipe was soon loaded and buried. JC dusted off his hands. "Let's eat a big lunch before we head out. I don't want to show up with a pack full of food, but we don't know if they'll feed us today or not."

Danny crawled back through the hole in the fence as did JC. They ate a quick meal of cornbread, deer jerky, and trail mix. The trail mix was Danny's own concoction. Much of the food Danny had stored up prior to the EMP consisted of dried bananas, pineapple, mango, and papaya, as well as peanuts, cashews, pecans, almonds, and raisins. He found that a container with a mix of each ingredient made a delectable trail mix which he often kept with him for a snack when he was on security watch.

After eating, JC slung his backpack over his shoulder, picked up his bike and led the way toward the train tracks, which ran between the river and the power plant. "We can take the tracks most of the way to the bridge. Hopefully, the tracks will keep us away from other people."

Danny tucked his .32 revolver in the simple in-the-pants holster JC had given him, put his pack on, picked up his bike and began following JC.

JC turned to look at Danny as he waited. "That was your grandfather's pistol, right?"

"Yeah."

"You know they're probably going to take it. You might not get it back."

Danny shrugged as he pushed his bike. "I know, you told me. The only other pistol I own is the

Glock. I couldn't afford to give it up. Utility takes priority over sentiment in these times."

"I hate to see you lose it." JC shook his head and paused. He pulled his .38 out of his waist. "I was going to stash this in the bushes, right before we hit the bridge. You take this to hand over when we hit the checkpoint."

"And you're going to tell them you don't have a gun?" Danny took the snub nose pistol from JC.

"Nope. I've got to hand over my Glock. They'll never believe I was a cop who didn't keep his service pistol when the lights went out."

"Ouch. That's gonna hurt."

JC snorted. "Yep."

They continued walking with the bikes as the terrain was too rough to ride. After two miles, they came upon a fork in the tracks. JC pointed to the right. "The train bridge over the Catawba should be right around this corner."

Danny paused to find a deep spot of gravel at the point where the two sets of tracks converged. "Then I suppose this place is as good as any to stash the .32."

JC pulled a Ziploc baggie from his pants. "This ain't the best thing to be burying a gun in, but it'll help."

Danny took it and placed the pistol inside. "Thanks. At least the gravel drains well if it does rain." He proceeded to suck as much air out of the bag with his mouth before burying the heirloom. He covered it over with gravel and smoothed the area out so it wouldn't be obvious that something of value was buried there. He stood up and stared at the spot as if to say goodbye to an old friend. Danny had lost so much since the EMP, this pistol shouldn't be such a big deal, but it was the last memento he had to remind him of Pop, that's what he'd always called his grandfather when he was alive.

JC paused for a while, as if he were giving Danny time to think then said, "Okay, we better get moving."

The two of them slowly walked around the bend to the river. Danny looked down at the bike he'd been pushing. "Maybe we could just stash the bikes here also. We could leave them in the woods. Then if we had to make it back to the truck in a hurry, we'd have them."

JC shook his head. "These are our props. They are the primary things I'm relying on to throw them off the scent that it was us who hit Greenville this morning. If it works, the bikes are a small price to pay."

Danny wanted to ask, *and if it doesn't work?* But he already knew the answer to that question. And he'd receive no comfort from hearing JC's coarse response. Danny tried to push the thought out of his mind, but he could still hear JC's articulated reply to the unspoken query. He smirked as the answer played back in his head, communicated with a thick New York accent. *They'll cut us up into little pieces and feed us to the friggin' fish. That's what'll happen if it don't work.*

They reached the bridge and JC paused to look across to the other side. "I don't see any guards on either side. I thought this guy had Charlotte pretty well locked down."

Danny peered into the foliage on the other side of the river. "Maybe they're hiding in the bushes, like snipers."

JC continued to peer across the bridge. "Could be. I'll walk halfway out with my hands up. Hopefully, they don't shoot. You stay here. If they start shooting at me, lay down a couple rounds of cover fire until I get back to this side of the bridge."

Danny sighed as he considered where the line fell that differentiated bravery and stupidity. Nevertheless, he wasn't going to argue. He drew the .38 and waited behind cover as JC ventured out onto the trestles.

JC walked slowly, with his hands held up near his head. As he reached the halfway point, he called out, "Anybody there?" No one replied, and JC kept walking.

Danny noticed he hadn't taken a breath. The suspense had made him forget about his need for oxygen. He took in a large gasp of air, careful not to lose his focus on JC.

JC reached the other side and turned to Danny. He waved for Danny to cross over and join him.

Danny figured they'd be coming back for the bikes, after all, JC surely didn't expect him to cross the bridge with two packs and two bikes. Danny holstered the pistol and walked out on the bridge to meet JC.

When Danny had crossed, JC pointed down river a few yards. "That house has a boat, a jet ski and an inner-tube float. If you have to get back across the river and this bridge is guarded, you can take one of them. The river flows back toward the power plant, so all you need is something to use for an oar to paddle toward the other side. The river will do most of the work."

Danny nodded as he surveyed the dry dock. "If I just want to float, the inner-tube float is probably best. I can use my hands or feet to get to the other side."

"Yep, and if it ain't there, the jet ski is your second best choice. I'm sure none of them work, otherwise they wouldn't be there, but all we need is something to float.

"Anyway, we ain't crossin' here. We'll walk on up to the next bridge. That's probably the US-29 Bridge up there."

Danny looked at the bridge roughly half a mile away. "What's the difference?"

"If we show up from out of town and they ask how we got here, they'll realize they've overlooked this bridge and lock it down. My guess is that when we get to the US-29 Bridge, we'll run into Schlusser's welcome wagon."

Danny nodded. "Yeah. We might want the train bridge open when it's time to leave."

"Exactly." JC walked back across the bridge, found his bike and led the way.

Danny followed as they made their way around the tracks and to a road which would lead them to the US-29 Bridge. They soon hit the intersection of Catawba Street and US-29. Long before they reached the bridge, Danny could see the two military vehicles being used as roadblocks on the other side of the bridge. The next few minutes could go either way. Danny's heart pounded as he anxiously thought, *the guards will believe our story, or they'll cut us up into little pieces and feed us to the friggin' fish.*

CHAPTER 3

And they took strong cities, and a fat land, and possessed houses full of all goods, wells digged, vineyards, and oliveyards, and fruit trees in abundance: so they did eat, and were filled, and became fat, and delighted themselves in thy great goodness. Nevertheless they were disobedient, and rebelled against thee, and cast thy law behind their backs, and slew thy prophets which testified against them to turn them to thee, and they wrought great provocations. Therefore thou deliveredst them into the hand of their enemies, who vexed them: and in the time of their trouble, when they cried unto thee, thou heardest them from heaven; and according to thy manifold mercies thou gavest them saviours, who saved them out of the hand of their enemies.

Nehemiah 9:25-27

Danny's knees shook and his stomach churned as he walked toward the guard on the other side of the river.

One of the guards yelled at them. "Leave the bikes, you can go back and get them in a minute. Keep walking toward me with your hands up."

Danny laid his bike down and slowly stood back up, keeping his hands high as he approached the roadblock.

JC seemed much less nervous. "Everything is fine. This is exactly how they should be treating people trying to enter their territory."

Danny took little comfort in the words, but at least it was going according to JC's plan.

Four guards walked out from behind the two large, green Deuce and a half parked in the middle of the road. Two of the guards had AR-15 style rifles at low ready. The other two wore sidearms. One of the guards with only a sidearm said, "Get down on your knees and interlace your fingers behind your head."

This did nothing to put Danny at ease.

"Do you have weapons?" asked the guard who had been addressing them.

JC complied with the man's demand to get on his knees and put his hands behind his head. "Pistol, knife, and a multitool."

"Okay, we're going to have to take those for now." The guard slowly approached JC.

JC nodded toward his waist. "I've got a Glock in a holster, front, right side, waist."

The guard took the pistol, knife, and multitool and patted JC down before putting his hands in zip-tie restraints.

The other guard without a rifle looked at Danny. "What about you?"

"Yeah, revolver in a holster, same place. And a knife in my back pocket."

The other guard cleared Danny, zip-tied him and helped him to his feet. "What are you fellows doing here?"

"Looking for a job. I was in DC with my girlfriend when the lights went out. Her family got to be less and less friendly as their food stores got lower and lower."

The guard nodded and looked at JC. "What's your story?"

"Held out in New York until winter passed then headed south."

"They let you have guns like this in New York?" the first guard asked.

"If you're a cop."

"You got ID?" the guard asked.

"Back pocket."

Danny's heart jumped yet again as he remembered that JC was retired.

The man took JC's wallet out of his pocket and opened it up. "I'll be danged. I guess you're lookin' for a job, too."

JC replied, "If you're hirin'."

The man folded the wallet and stuck it back in JC's jeans pocket.

The guard nodded. "We might be, but not today. The city is on lockdown. We had an attack against one of our outposts early this morning."

"No kiddin'! What happened?" JC sounded convincing.

The guard cut JC and Danny's restraints. "Squad of eight to ten heavy hitters basically pulled a drive by. Shot up a couple guys and took off before we could get organized enough to pursue. They had AK-47s and AR-15s."

"When will the lockdown be lifted?" JC asked.

"At least not until tomorrow morning," the guard answered.

JC rubbed his wrists. "Okay, I guess we'll come back tomorrow."

The guard handed JC's knife and multitool back to him. "We have to hang on to the guns. They're under a temporary ban until we can restore order. This morning is a prime example of why. This isn't the first time we've had insurgency activity from Greenville."

"Yeah, well, I guess we're on our own to survive overnight with no firearms." JC let it be known that he was annoyed by the policy, but limited his protest to a harsh scowl at no one in particular.

"You guys will be fine. You made it this long, you'll make it through one more night." The guard waved as they began walking away.

Danny and JC picked up their bikes and headed back the way they'd come.

JC pedaled close to Danny. "You know where to?"

"The fork in the tracks?" Danny was sure JC would want to retrieve the .32 for protection until morning.

"Yep." JC kept pedaling.

Once they'd turned back onto Catawba, Danny glanced over at JC. "Eight to ten heavy hitters. How do you like that?"

JC smirked. "If you're responsible for the security of an outpost, it's a natural instinct to tell your superiors that you were up against an unbeatable force."

"Well, I guess their denial is working in our favor."

JC smiled as he continued pedaling. "Yep. For now, anyways."

They reached the fork in the train tracks and Danny got off his bike long enough to excavate the revolver from beneath the gravel. "Where are we going to make camp?"

JC looked around then up at the sky. "No clouds, but I'd rather have a roof over my head than not. The sign at that building right before the train bridge said it's a micro-brewery. Hopefully, we can find a vehicle to sleep in."

Danny nodded. "Maybe we'll find a delivery truck that's not locked. We could sleep in the back, and keep our bikes in there with us so they don't get ripped off. I haven't seen anyone around yet, but that doesn't mean no one's lurking in the shadows."

"Good thinkin'. And I'd say the odds of finding an empty beer delivery truck two months after apocalypse is pretty close to 100 percent."

Danny laughed. "Yeah, I'm sure beer trucks were some of the first things to get cleaned out."

They walked the bikes along the tracks to the brewery. They found a row of three box trucks parked near the loading docks. The doors to the cargo areas were all wide open and the trucks were completely empty. A hand full of empty beer bottles were strewn about, some broken. Danny was careful not to get the tires of his bike near the shattered glass.

JC pointed toward the truck in the middle. We'll take this one. We'll close the doors of all three so the one we're in doesn't stick out as being the only one with something in it. Theoretically, if someone were to come around checking inside, they'll start with one of the trucks on the outside, which will give us a little warning when we hear them open the other door."

"What if they pick the middle truck to start with?"

JC hoisted his bike up into the truck. "Anyone still alive after two months probably has a methodical thought process. The eeny-meeny-miny-moe type have mostly died off. Methodical people start at the beginning and work their way through."

Danny found JC's reasoning unsettling, but figured he was most likely correct. He lifted his bike up and handed it to JC who positioned the bike on the opposite side of the truck from his own.

The two of them took out their sleeping bags and positioned them in the back of the box truck. Afterwards, they ate some of Danny's remaining trail mix, more deer jerky, and shared a can of mixed fruit cocktail that JC had in his pack.

JC sipped the last of the juice from the can. "We'll take this down to the river along with a few of those beer bottles and fill them all up."

"Nick told me that if water is really muddy, like the Catawba, I should let it settle for a while before trying to run it through the hand-pump filter."

JC nodded. "That's exactly what we're going to do. Finish off your canteen and we'll fill it back up with the pump filter from the beer bottles and the fruit cocktail can."

Danny followed JC down to the river bank. The gently flowing river was serene. Danny drank in the picturesque landscape of the tree-lined river bank, dappled with spring blossoms. A patch of white spider lilies was in full bloom, growing up in the shallows near the bank where Danny stood. *Alisa would love to see these lilies, to pull up an easel and paint. I wish I could bring it all back for her. She hasn't painted anything since the EMP.* He loved her for being able to adapt, for being strong enough to do what needed to be done, but an artist was who she was, it wasn't just something she did. Danny missed the days where they were all free to chase dreams and to imagine a future, full of hope and optimism. He sighed as he muttered to himself, "Now we just dream of staying alive for one more day."

JC's voice shattered Danny's daydream. "You okay, kid?"

"What? Uh, yeah. I'm alright." Danny looked down at the dirty beer bottles in his hand and resumed his burdensome task of staying alive. They returned to the box truck and allowed time for the sediment to settle at the bottom of the water containers.

JC pulled out a small spool of fishing line from his pack. "We've got a couple of hours before dark. Do you feel like throwing a line in the water?"

"Got any bait?"

"Couple of plastic worms and a plastic frog. We'd be better off if we could catch some bugs. I'm just thinking of something to pass the time more than anything."

Danny nodded. "Yeah, that's a good idea. I'm going to look for a straight, sturdy branch for a pole."

JC retrieved the multitool that the guards had so generously returned. "Take this with you; it's got a little saw."

"Thanks." Danny took the tool and set out on his quest for the perfect fishing pole. He tromped through the high grass along the bank of the river, inspecting each low-hanging limb of every nearby tree. Danny chose a slender branch and used JC's multitool to separate it from the stock. Next, he whittled away the twigs and leaves with his own pocket knife. The mere task of preparing his pole to fish relaxed him, freeing his mind from the apprehension of infiltrating Schlusser's camp.

JC spent less time worrying over his fishing pole, choosing a nearby stick. He soon had his line tied to the end and tossed a plastic worm into the river.

Danny laughed. "You'll never catch anything

like that. You don't even have a float."

"You're probably right." JC smiled as if he had no intention of getting a fish anyhow.

Danny scowled in disapproval. If he was going to fish, he was going to make a full effort of it. He noticed a soda straw lodged in the grass at the edge of the river. He paused to think. "It floats." Danny stooped over to retrieve the straw. "I'll be right back."

"I'll be here." JC had found a comfortable reclining position on the bank.

Danny walked back to the box truck and retrieved his lighter from his pack. He opened the pliers on the multitool of which he was still in possession. Danny slowly ran the lighter beneath the straw until he could observe the thin plastic becoming soft. Then, he pressed the softened section with the pliers of the multitool. He pulled the straw out and examined it. The clamped portion remained closed. Danny stuck it between his lips and blew on it. "Air tight." Danny repeated the process at the other end of the straw then tied the end of his fishing line to the straw. He tied a hook to the end of the line, roughly six inches below the straw, and searched the area for any type of bug, but none were readily available. Danny relented. "Can I have a plastic worm?"

JC snickered as he rolled over to one side to pull a lure from his pocket. "So you're not an absolute purist, huh?"

Danny pursed his lips. "I guess not."

"That's okay. You tried."

Danny threaded the plastic worm on the hook

and tossed his line in the river. His straw float worked well, but with no reel its direction was at the mercy of the wind and current. He let his mind drift, also with no particular direction. And as it had done since long before the EMP, his mind went to thoughts of Alisa. He wondered how she was, and when he would see her again. The obvious question of if he would see her again, reared its ugly head, but he forcibly evicted the notion from his brain.

"I think you've got a fish!" JC sat up quickly.

Danny hadn't even been looking at the straw floating aimlessly in the river. He felt the green branch in his hand bend and he looked down. "No kidding!" Danny pulled up on the limb to set the hook then pulled the line in by hand. The small fish on the other end was no more than eight inches long, but Danny couldn't have been happier if it were twenty inches.

JC watched as Danny extracted the hook from the fish's mouth with the multitool. "Looks like a bass."

"Should we keep it?"

"I'd throw it back. We sure can't afford to be lightin' no signal fires to let everybody in the neighborhood know we're here, especially with nothin' but a five shot revolver for defense."

Danny was disappointed. "We can't eat it raw?"

"Fresh water fish is full of parasites. You just got over being sick; you don't want to get a tape worm."

Danny looked at his prize. "What about a Dakota fire pit? That puts off almost no smoke."

JC patted him on the back. "If we were further

out, I'd say go for it, but the neighborhood is right up the street from here. Cooking fish is going to carry a scent, even if you're not puttin' off any visual smoke. If it were a bigger fish, maybe we'd risk it, but you won't get five bites out of that thing."

"Okay." Danny lowered his head and tossed the fish back into the river. He cut the line from the stick, rolled it up and handed it back to JC. Danny was done with fishing for the evening. Besides, it would be dark soon.

JC, likewise cut the line off of his make-shift pole and rolled it up on the small length of a twig. He stuck the worms, hooks, and line in the small Altoids mint container which he had in his pocket.

The sun was getting low by the time they had stowed the gear, so they closed the door to the cargo box on the back of the truck, lay back on their sleeping bags, and retired for the night. The floor of the box truck was hard and cold, and it took Danny quite a while to get comfortable enough to go to sleep, but he eventually drifted off.

Danny was disturbed by an annoying mechanical racket. A stream of metal-against-metal squeaks overridden by the occasional echoing bump, reached into his dream state. Groggily, he became aware that the sounds were emanating from the real world, rather than the realm of slumber. He opened his swollen eyes slowly. A steady beam of morning light was creeping into the cargo area of the truck as the door was being pushed open by a slight figure, silhouetted by dawn's glow. Danny's drowsy mind quickly associated this image with imminent danger and shot a quick dose of adrenaline rushing through his veins. He grabbed the revolver and pointed it toward the intruder. "JC, wake up!"

JC turned over with lightning speed and sat up. "Hey!" he yelled at the being.

The thin, ghost-like specter screamed with a shrill, piercing screech and disappeared like a vapor into the early morning shadows.

"What was that?" JC asked.

Danny shook his head as his shaking hand placed the pistol back by his side. "I don't know. It had like gray skin, sunken eyes, and its limbs were as thin as rails. I thought maybe I was dreaming."

JC took a deep breath. "Then I just had the same vision as you. That's exactly what I saw."

Danny considered the creature he'd just seen. "It had long hair, I think it was a young girl. Maybe 12, or maybe 17. I don't really know; she didn't look human."

JC looked down at his hands. "She's probably on the verge of starving to death. Have you ever seen pictures of people rescued from Nazi concentration camps after the war?"

"Yeah."

"That's what she looked like to me, only she still had her hair."

Danny went from being frightened of the unusual creature to feeling sorry for the poor girl. She was human, just like him. "Do you think we could find her? Perhaps give her something to eat?"

JC's eyes showed his pain. "No, we have to stay on mission. Besides, if she's managed to stay alive this long, it has probably been by avoiding other humans. She ain't gonna let us get near.

"Let's pack it up and roll out."

"Okay." Danny rolled up his sleeping bag and attached it to the bottom of his pack.

JC rolled his bike to the entrance of the box and opened the cargo door the rest of the way. "Looks like a beautiful day."

Danny didn't reply. *How can it be such a beautiful day when we are surrounded by pain and death?* He knew JC had likely only said it for his benefit; to cheer him up. But it didn't work. Danny ran his arms through the straps of his backpack, pushed his bike to the opening, and handed it down to JC.

JC said, "I'll be right back," and headed off to a group of trees to answer nature's call.

Danny took off his pack and retrieved the bag of trail mix. He placed it in the corner, behind the trucks roll-up-door rail. *Maybe she'll come back*, he thought. He wouldn't mention the gesture of good will to JC. *I'm not going to have a discussion about it. Besides, doesn't the Bible say not to let your left hand know what your right hand is doing?*

JC soon returned. "We still have to stash that pistol before we head back to the check point."

Danny nodded and they walked their bikes back down to the railroad tracks. The two men buried the pistol in the same fashion and in the same location. They returned to the road and pedaled the bikes toward the bridge.

When they arrived, JC stopped his bike and got off. "You know the drill."

"Yep." Danny followed JC's lead.

The first guard who approached them was the same man they'd spoken to the day before. "Good news, the lockdown has been lifted."

"Good to know." JC interlocked his fingers behind his head as he knelt down to let the man frisk him.

Once the two of them had been searched, the guard said. "Get your bikes and follow this road. Take your first right on Dowd. That will end at the airport, on Wallace Neel. Take a right on Wallace and follow it around the airport to West Boulevard. That will take you around to the armory, where you'll fill out an application and get a medical exam. You've got til sundown to either get a job or get out of town. We're recording your information and if we catch you wandering around instead of going straight to the armory, you'll be shot on sight. We have to be firm until order is restored then things will return to normal."

"What if we get lost?" Danny asked.

The guard's tone lost all of its pleasantries. "Don't get lost."

"We're not gonna get lost." JC patted Danny on the back as if to tell him to shut up then got on his bike.

Danny took his cue to be quiet and mounted his bike to follow JC. Old Dowd Road took them through a sparsely developed section of town, dotted with a mishmash of trailers, modest homes, and businesses.

When they'd traveled roughly a mile, they crossed railroad tracks. JC pointed to the right. "If you ever need to get out in a hurry and undetected, these tracks lead straight to the railroad bridge."

"And the gun," Danny added.

JC smirked. "And the gun." The two men continued towards the airport. They turned right on Wallace Neel, as instructed.

Danny felt vulnerable as they rode unarmed through the streets. He didn't see anybody, but he felt like there were people watching them, sizing them up as they pedaled through. He thought about the frail creature he'd seen earlier that morning and imagined colonies of such beings lurking in the tree lines, hiding in the houses, following them and waiting for an opportunity to strike. He'd read stories of cannibalism in the Bible and heard rumors of such atrocities on Pickens radio. He figured the two travelers would make quite the feast for such a band of miserable survivors.

He looked up the road and to the left. Behind the fence that ran around the perimeter of the airport was a mound of dirt. The mound ran adjacent to the fence, about eight feet inside. Sitting atop of the mound, about a quarter-mile ahead, was a military vehicle. Two guards stood on watch with AR rifles. Another surveyed the area with binoculars. Danny could see the man looking in his direction and instinctively waved. He knew the man saw him, but the guard didn't return the visual salutation. *At least he isn't shooting. You gotta count your blessings these days.*

They eventually reached the guards and continued riding past. Danny kept his head down and kept pace with JC. Before they'd left the sight of the first vehicle, Danny could make out yet another vehicle. As he got closer, he could see that it also had three guards, two with rifles, and one with binoculars.

JC said, "I guess they don't plan on letting someone slip up behind them here."

"Yeah, I guess not." Danny looked around. The stunt they'd pulled in Greenville would have never worked here. There were too many fences, too many obstacles and the perimeter road would give Schlusser's men ready access to any would-be assailants.

Turning onto West Boulevard brought a shocking change of scenery. The vehicles with guard posts were closer together and the airport perimeter fence was decorated with decaying corpses, tied by their hands to the top pole of the fence. Every twenty feet or so, were dead bodies in various stages of decomposition, like a morbid décor of human bunting.

JC glanced over at the flesh-lined fence row. "Looks like Schlusser is big on public service announcements."

"The more you know," Danny said.

After they'd traveled what Danny guessed to be around six miles since the bridge, they arrived at the armory. It was heavily guarded with various obstacles like vehicles and concrete blocks to keep anyone from driving right up to the door. A guard stepped out from behind a vehicle with one hand on his rifle and the other held up in the air, signaling them to halt.

Danny and JC stopped the bikes.

The man wore the same version of Schlusser's uniform as the guards who'd been with Gorbold, the first of Schlusser's goons they'd encountered. Unlike the guards at the bridge and the ones positioned around the perimeter of the airport, he had on a black polo shirt with camo pants.

Danny figured it was some failed attempt at public relations. As if the men in the black shirts were more civilized than those in the mismatch green and camo shirts. *I guess I'm supposed to believe that these guys aren't capable of stringing dead people up on the perimeter fence like a popcorn garland.*

The guard asked, "What's your names?"

"Walker," Danny replied.

"Castell," said JC.

"Okay, applications are in the green tent over by the main building entrance." The guard pointed toward the military tent erected in the parking lot.

"Thanks." JC walked his bike and led the way.

Danny stayed close behind. They leaned the bikes against a handicapped parking sign. Danny looked up at the sign and considered how unfair this world was, and how tough it would be for a handicapped person to survive. *If it's ever going to be a planet worth living on for anybody, it has to start here. We have to take down this warlord before we can think about anything else.*

"Leave your packs outside." Another black-shirted guard handed them both a clipboard, a pen and a blank piece of paper. "You'll have to forgive us but we're having trouble with the copier."

Danny looked at the man to see if he was

cracking a smile so he'd know if he should laugh or not. The man didn't smile, so Danny didn't laugh.

The guard pointed at a blackboard sitting on top of one of the foldable tables, propped up against a tent pole. "All the information we need from you is listed on that chalkboard. Print everything except your signature and make sure we can read it."

JC walked over to a table, sat down and began writing. Danny did the same. Minutes later, Danny's heart skipped a beat when he looked up. *No way! How is he alive?* He saw a man who looked just like Sergeant Gorbold, the first of Schlusser's goons to show up at Nana's farm. Danny shook off the thought. He looked at the man's wrist. *I saw JC shoot his hand off, string him up in the barn, and kill him during his interrogation. I helped put him on the wood pile, lit the fire and watched his body burn with the rest of Schlusser's men.* Danny stared at the man, he was the same height, wore the same black shirt, the same black tie, khaki pants with a black drop-leg holster, just like Gorbold. The man walked over to JC and picked up his application. Danny continued to watch, studying his facial features, which as best as he could remember, looked a lot like Gorbold. *Is this another nightmare? Am I dreaming again? How else can I explain it? I know Gorbold is dead.* Danny strained to picture Gorbold's face in his mind. He tried to remember what the man had looked like, before JC's inquisition, of course. *Maybe it's his brother. If it is, then we've got another Gorbold.*

The man continued to examine JC's paper. "You

have a fairly desirable skill set, especially in these trying times."

JC nodded, but said nothing in response.

The man looked over the top of the paper at JC. "Some fellows with similar qualifications stopped by our Greenville outpost yesterday morning."

"Yeah, I heard." JC pursed his lips.

The man stared at JC for a moment without speaking.

Danny's heart began to pound. He looked back down at his own paper, observing JC's reaction out of the corner of his eye. If the man were quizzing him in the same way, Danny was sure he'd see the panic in his eyes, both because of the Greenville attack, and because of the way he'd burned his brother, if it was indeed Gorbold's sibling. But JC looked as cool as a cucumber, as if he had no idea what the man was pondering as he glared at him.

The man broke his concentration on JC. "You'd have to have stones the size of Texas to come waltzing in here after shooting up one of our outposts."

JC laughed. "Yeah, or a brain the size of a peanut."

The man nodded as he chuckled. "Yes." He didn't look as if he were ready to totally dismiss the subject, but JC's acting job had certainly put the man at ease.

Danny wondered which of the two explanations were the true reason JC had attempted such a stunt. *And I wonder why I went along with it?*

The man extended his hand to JC. "I'm Sergeant Gorbold."

JC stood to shake the man's hand. He feigned excitement, smiling from ear to ear. "It's a pleasure to meet you, sir."

Danny considered what a career JC could have had in acting. *He missed his true calling. He sure knows how to sell it.* Of course, there were likely no survivors in Hollywood. So perhaps JC was performing on the right stage after all.

Gorbold had to pry his hand from JC's overly exuberant greeting. "Yes, well. You'll report to basic first thing in the morning."

JC saluted Gorbold. "Yes, sir."

Gorbold picked up Danny's paper and glanced over it.

Danny held his breath as Gorbold stood next to him. If he didn't breathe he couldn't hyperventilate, giving away his involvement in the Greenville attack and the killing of the man's brother.

Gorbold quickly shuffled Danny's application beneath JC's. "Same thing; basic training tomorrow at 5:00 AM. Spyder will get you two settled into the barracks." Gorbold quickly turned and exited the tent.

Danny gasped for air. Had his interview lasted any longer, he probably would have passed out. Danny stood and walked toward the tent entrance, where he was met by four more men coming in to fill out applications. He offered a smile and a nod. They looked rough, skinny, dirty, and they did not return the smile nor the nod. *I can't blame them. They've probably lost all trust in their fellow human beings. And I would imagine it's been a while since they had anything to smile about.*

JC asked the guard handing out paper and pens to the newcomers, "Where do we find Spyder?"

The man pointed toward the back of the building. "Walk around back, there's a hole cut in the fence. You'll see two soldiers guarding the opening. They'll point you to the hanger where your barracks are."

"Thanks." JC exited the tent.

Danny followed, collecting his bag and his bike on the way out. They approached the men guarding the opening in the fence at the back of the National Guard building. Danny tried to moderate his politeness as it had not been well received up to this point. "We were told to find Spyder."

The guards stepped out of the way. One of them turned to point behind him. "Follow the dirt footpath up the mound and onto the runway. Look straight across, and you'll see the big DHL warehouse. That's your barracks, and that's where you'll find Spyder. You can't take your bikes in the building. The regent doesn't want them tracking in dirt and cluttering the place up. If you've got locks, lock them up. As the base continues to expand to further parts of the airport, bikes are becoming more and more of a commodity."

Danny pushed his bike through the small opening. "I'd recognize my bike if I saw someone else on the base riding it around."

The guard laughed. "Yeah, but if it's a superior officer, you ain't going to say anything to him."

Danny scowled and continued pushing his bike up the dirt path without responding. Once out of earshot of the guards, he turned to JC. "I guess that tells us what to expect from the corporate culture."

JC nodded. "It's about what I expected; somewhere between prison and the military.

"You're sure you remember throwing Gorbold on top of that fire pit back home, right?"

Danny's heart skipped a beat. "Yeah, why? That guy is his brother or something, right? There's no way he came back to life!"

JC laughed. "Yeah, somethin' like that. After what I did to him, he'll be the last one to wake up on judgement day. But still, that was creepy seeing that guy. He's a dead ringer for the Gorbold I killed. Maybe I'll get a chance to see if he's as tough as his brother, before this is all over with."

Once they reached the top of the mound, they rode the bikes across the runway to the DHL tarmac, which was roughly three quarters of a mile behind the National Guard compound.

JC got off his bike near the row of bikes by the cargo bay entrance. Most of the bikes were secured by a lock or a chain. "We ain't got no locks. You got any ideas on how to keep the bikes from gettin' jacked?"

Danny flipped his bike over on the handle bars. "Can I borrow your multitool?"

JC handed him the tool and Danny proceeded to remove the front wheel. "The man didn't say anything about not being allowed to bring a wheel in the barracks. The bike isn't much good without the front wheel."

JC flipped his bike over and did the same. "Good idea. How did you think of that?"

"Alisa and Steven both went to SCAD in

Savannah. Most of the students rode bikes. They'd chain them up out front of the buildings where their classes where, but if they didn't lock the front wheel also, sometimes thieves would take just the front wheel, leaving a completely useless bike."

JC shook his head as he completed his task. "Society was already depraved. That's why I'm not shocked by what I see people doing to each other since the EMP."

Danny walked into the cargo bay door and looked around. It was filled with rows and rows of various cots, mattresses, and sleeping bags; but no cargo. "I'm sure clearing out the cargo was Schlusser's first order of business."

JC surveyed the area. "Heck yeah. He ain't about to let the grunts get a hold of any of the good stuff. We have to be happy with fighting over the scraps."

Danny made a rough estimate of the number of filled sleeping spaces. He guessed there were about 200 men staying in this area. He saw two men at the end of one of the rows. "I guess we can ask these guys if they know where to find Spyder."

JC nodded. "Sounds good."

Danny walked down the row. "Are either one of you guys Spyder?"

"No. He's in the front office." The man pointed to a door leading out of the cargo area.

Danny followed the man's directions. The door led to a hallway with several doors.

"Can I help you?" A tall thin man with a shaved head and a spider web tattoo on his neck came around the corner.

"I guess you're Spyder." JC said.

"How'd you guess?" Spyder didn't crack a smile.

"Sergeant Gorbold told us to see you about getting settled in." Danny politely stepped in before JC's abrasive manner landed them on Spyder's bad side.

"Follow me." Spyder led the way back into the warehouse area. "Pick a spot, in either of these two rows. You can mark off an area six feet wide for your space. Most of the guys come back around 6:30, chow is at 7:30, lights out is at 9:30 and breakfast is at 5:30. You'll head out at 6:30 tomorrow morning. You'll be on Duane's team tomorrow. Chow is in the warehouse at the end of the tarmac. Walk out the cargo bay doors and it's to your right. Any questions?"

"Is there any chance we can get a mattress or a cot?" JC asked.

Spyder rubbed his chin. "What do you have to trade?"

"What are you looking for?"

Spyder smirked. "I ain't lookin' for nothin', but I can facilitate trades for a percentage. If you've got cigarettes, alcohol, weed, pills, silver, gold, or canned meat, I might be able to find someone willing to give up a mattress. Otherwise, get used to the floor."

"Thanks." JC's face did as much to convey his sarcasm as did his tone. He walked away from Spyder without another word.

Danny followed JC to a spot at the end of the row, near the place they'd seen the other two men setting up. He and JC pulled out their sleeping bags and positioned them on the floor.

Spyder walked by as they were getting situated. "As a matter of fact, you'll both be on Antoine's team tomorrow." He walked away wearing a grin which told Danny that his situation had not improved.

Danny sighed as he looked at JC. "Antoine's team. I wonder what that means."

"It means we're getting the worst job on the base."

Danny waited to see if there would be an apology attached to JC's reply. There wasn't. "So maybe we should see if we can start catching more flies with honey."

"We ain't lookin' to catch flies. At least not right now. We're lookin' to get in with the guys who are least satisfied with their current work environment and compensation packages. And if I was a bettin' man, which I ain't, I'd bet Antoine's team is exactly the place we want to be. If you want to cause an insurrection, you don't tap the guys who are fat and happy, like Gorbold."

"Okay." A smile grew on Danny's face as JC's plan slowly became clear to him.

"We've got a couple hours before dinner, let's take a walk." JC tucked his backpack under his sleeping bag.

Danny did the same. "Out of sight, out of mind."

"Yep." JC led the way toward the door.

"Where are we going?"

"Test the fence. We'll see how nosey we can be, before someone tells us to quit being nosey."

Danny gritted his teeth. *Yet another one of JC's*

plans that I'd rather not be a part of. But, here I am, going right along with it.

The two men walked out on the tarmac and followed the runway north for about a mile. The airport was massive. To the left was building after building, cargo hubs for American Airlines Cargo, Fed Ex, UPS, and several other freight companies. Planes sat dormant in the positions they'd been in when the EMP struck, as if someone might throw a switch and bring the entire facility back to life again. But Danny knew that would never happen. To the right were small private jets, the airport fire station, and the Air National Guard buildings. Five massive C-130s sat on the tarmac, like lifeless monuments, tombstones marking the burial site of a culture that had allowed itself to become too dependent on modern conveniences.

JC broke the silence as he pointed ahead and to the left. "That's the main airport way over there. Regular commercial jets wouldn't even use this runway. It's sobering to see this giant airport completely shut down. I use to drive by JFK on my way home from work every day. That place never slept. Planes were always taking off, landing, taxiing around the runway, it didn't stop. Then, 9/11 hit. I remember driving by JFK when the planes were grounded, nobody could fly except military. It was surreal, but I knew they'd lift the ban in a day or two. Not this time. They're grounded for good."

JC surveyed the area. He nodded toward the left. "Look right over there."

"What am I looking for?"

"Two big tanks, over by the Air National Guard

hanger. That's their fuel tanks."

"For the whole airport?" Danny asked.

"No. Just the Air National Guard, but if that's the way we decide to cripple Schlusser, we'll have to take those out also. That's enough fuel to keep him rolling for quite a while."

A camouflaged Deuce and a half drove down the runway, stopping right by Danny and JC. The driver leaned out the window. "You boys lost?"

"No, sir." JC put his hand above his eyes to shield them from the sun as he looked at the man who was addressing them. "We were just trying to get a feel for the layout so we'd know where things are if we're told to go somewhere."

"Which barracks are you in?" the man asked.

Danny pointed to the DHL warehouse. "That one."

"Who checked you in?"

"Gorbold gave us a job, Spyder told us where to sleep," Danny replied.

"Spyder didn't tell you to stay close to your barracks?"

"No, sir," JC answered.

"Well, he should have. The regent doesn't like new people wandering around. You guys get on back before you get in trouble."

"Yes, sir." Danny turned to lead the way back to the barracks.

JC followed. "Take it slow. He said to get back, but he didn't say to hurry. I want to see where he's going and what he's hauling."

"Okay." Danny took a deep breath. He didn't enjoy testing the fence quite as much as JC seemed to. The camouflaged truck pulled up to the far building where Spyder had said chow would be served. Danny and JC watched as people got out of the back.

"Looks like all women," Danny said.

JC stared for a while. "My eyes ain't what they used to be, but the best I can tell, I think you're right. They probably have them staying somewhere else in the airport. I'd imagine they truck them in to take care of chow for the men."

"Did you notice where the truck was coming from when you first saw it?"

JC turned around and pointed. "It came from around the back of that US Airways terminal. They're probably using the commercial terminal for female housing."

The two men moseyed back to the barracks as they were told, but they remained outside to observe whatever comings and goings they could see. As the afternoon progressed, they watched as a group of men came from the armory, following the same path through the cut fence that Danny and JC had taken. They proceeded toward the Air National Guard buildings. These men all wore various types of camouflage, like the men who had attacked the farm. Unlike the men they'd encountered at the farm, none of the men had weapons.

JC commented, "I guess Schlusser makes them check their guns in when they're off duty."

"That's good to know, if we ever wanted to hit the barracks."

"Yep, it'd be like shootin' fish in a barrel."

A few minutes later, another steady stream of

men returned to the barracks where Danny and JC had been assigned. These men all wore dirty work clothes. It was obvious that their task had not been military in nature. Danny and JC waited until several other men walked over to the dining facility before they made their way over. Once inside, they followed the other men through the line. Each man received two scoops of rice and one scoop of beans on a styrofoam plate.

Danny reached the water bucket but saw no glasses. He approached one of the women working the food line. "Excuse me, can I get a cup for water?"

She motioned with her head to a plastic milk crate by the kitchen door. "There's probably some over there. Get one for each of you and don't lose it. That's your cup, you're responsible for cleaning it and keeping up with it."

"Thanks." Danny retrieved two cups, bringing one to JC.

They filled their plastic cups with water and found a seat at a foldable plastic table and ate what they'd been given.

"No fancy fixin's here." JC mixed his beans in with his rice.

"I guess that's why Spyder said canned meat was such a valued commodity." Danny took a bite and finished chewing. "Is it just me or do these plates look used?"

JC nodded. "Yeah, I bet they rinse them off and reuse them as long as they can. No sanitation services and no resupply for styrofoam plates. Once they run out, they'll have no trouble scavenging regular dinner plates, but they'll be a lot heavier to lug around for whoever has to wash them."

Once everyone had gone through the line, one of the women who had been serving called out in a loud voice. "Line up for seconds."

Danny looked at JC. "Are you going back for more?"

"I don't think so."

"I'm going to get some more rice. I doubt we'll get a midnight snack."

"Go ahead. I'll be here."

Danny reached the rice, just as it ran out. He lowered his head and started to walk away.

The woman who had been serving said, "She's bringing some more out in a second, if you want to hang on for a moment."

"Oh, thanks." Danny turned around and waited. A younger girl, pretty, but no makeup and plain hair, early-twenties maybe, came out of a back room carrying a large pot. Danny looked at the girl closely as she walked closer. *Why does she look familiar?*

The girl placed the full pot on the table and removed the empty one.

Gwen. Danny hoped she wouldn't recognize him, but there was no chance of that.

She looked up curiously. "Danny?"

"Hey, Gwen!" Danny acted surprised.

"Keep moving!" the man behind him said grumpily.

"Come down to the end of the table, we can talk there." Gwen smiled.

Danny walked over, out of the way. "How are

you?"

"Alive. This isn't the best gig, but you gotta take what you can get sometimes. What are you doing here? How is Alisa?"

"She's fine. I'm sure she'll be happy to hear you're doing well. It's a long story as to why I'm here. The short version is I'm on a mission. I'll tell you more when I can. For now, my story is that I'm a refugee from DC." Danny gave her his full cover story, in case anyone asked. He was taking a chance telling her this much, but he really didn't have a choice. If she were to accidently say something about him being from Anderson to the wrong person, it could get back to Gorbold, and he'd be fish food for sure.

Gwen looked puzzled, but didn't pry. "Okay. I can go along with that. Are you here all by yourself?"

"Not exactly." Danny looked back toward JC.

"Oh. He's here." Her face lost all of its excitement.

"Well, I better get back. I'll see you around."

She forced a smile. "Yeah, see you around."

Danny took his plate back and sat down. "You'll never guess who I just ran into."

JC's eyes lit up with surprise. "Who could you have possibly ran into here?"

"Gwen."

"You're kidding. Don't play around like that, Danny."

"I'm not joking. She's working in the back kitchen area. I guess she was one of the women that came in on that Deuce and a half from the terminal."

"That ain't good. What if she rats us out?"

"She won't rat us out. If for no other reason, just because she really likes Alisa. And by proxy, she likes me." Danny hadn't seen JC get so rattled over something since he'd met him. No matter the peril, JC always managed to stay totally cool.

"Yeah, but she friggin' hates me."

"She can't stick it to you without hurting me, and thereby disappointing Alisa."

"I hope you're right. What did she say?"

"I told her my cover story so she wouldn't accidentally get us in trouble."

JC ran his hand over his face. "Ay, ay, ay. You didn't tell her anything else did you?"

"No, but I had to tell her that."

"You're right. You did what you had to do. I just wish she wasn't here. Does she know I'm here?"

"Yep."

JC pursed his lips. "Great."

Danny finished his rice then they returned to the barracks. The other men were very standoffish, so Danny and JC kept to themselves until lights out. The sleeping bag directly on the hard concrete floor of the warehouse seemed even less comfortable than the floor of the box truck where Danny had slept the prior evening. He didn't trust the men around him either. The fact that they were still alive, two months after the EMP, and that they were employed by a brutal warlord, meant they were carnivores, capable of the most treacherous of deeds. *It's like trying to sleep in a pit of snakes and scorpions, or a den of jackals.* Nevertheless, exhaustion eventually overtook Danny and he fell asleep.

CHAPTER 4

Behold, I send you forth as sheep in the midst of wolves: be ye therefore wise as serpents, and harmless as doves.

Matthew 10:16

Danny awoke to the irritating sound of someone banging something like a metal spoon against a large metal pot. He sat up with his forehead knuckled in disapproval of the obnoxious alarm. He looked over at JC who was also awake.

JC yelled out at the infernal racket. "Alright, alright, we're up!"

The banging soon stopped with no other accompanying announcement. A single high-wattage bulb screwed into a clamp light was the solitary source of light for the entire warehouse. It was powered by an extension cord, which ran out from the front of the building. Danny said, "I haven't seen any solar panels, do you think that Spyder has an inverter connected to a battery bank? I wonder how any components survived the EMP?"

JC looked at the glowing light that did little more for the vast space than create silhouettes of men scurrying to get ready for work. "Most of these hangars are all metal. If the doors were closed, they could have acted as a faraday cage, protecting whatever was inside. You've got all those metal containers over in the train yard. They'd provide similar protection for whatever was inside them. Spyder probably has a battery bank that's being recharged periodically by a functioning generator."

Danny and JC got dressed, tucked their packs under their sleeping bags and slowly made their way over to the mess hall.

Like the barracks, there was a single clamp light and the tables each had a lone candle. Danny could hear excited murmuring amongst the men. The room was abuzz with muted chuckles and laughter. JC nudged the man in front of him in the line. "What's going on?"

The thin, middle-aged man turned around to reply. "We usually get rice for breakfast every day except Friday. Friday is pancake day."

JC looked curious. "I don't get it. Today is Thursday, it ain't pancake day."

The man shrugged. "I know, but whatever that smell is, it ain't rice."

Two women eventually emerged from the back room carrying two plastic bins and placed them on the table. They uncovered them and the smell of fresh baked bread wafted through the room. Danny eventually made it to the head of the line and took a plate. He smiled at the woman portioning out the meal. "It smells great! Biscuits?"

"Yeah, we got a load of flour. I don't know how much, so don't get used to it." She returned the smile cautiously, as if it had been a while since anyone had shown her any courtesy or gratitude.

Danny and JC made their way to the table and sat next to the man JC had asked about the biscuits.

JC bit into one of the biscuits. "They ain't nothin' like Miss Jennie's biscuits."

Danny nodded. "A cup of coffee would sure make them taste better.'

The man sitting at the table with them chuckled. "The only people who get coffee around here are the men in black shirts. Once in a while you might get some sugar or something, but if you want to eat good, you have to work your way up to a black shirt."

Danny wanted a little more clarification. "You mean the guys with the black polos or the ones with the black button-down shirts and ties?"

"They both eat better than we do, but if you've got a black tie, you get most anything you want. They live in houses, eat meat at every meal, coffee, candy, servants, the whole nine yards."

"Houses?" JC seemed to be fishing for as much information as he could get.

The man paused to wash down his biscuit with a drink of water. "Yep. When they first set this operation up, it was just Schlusser and a handful of men. The National Guardsmen started leaving, one by one, to go take care of their families or try to survive. The police and sheriff's department came in to back up the remaining National Guardsmen, with the intent of trying to hold the armory."

"Why? Who was trying to take it over?" Danny asked.

The man continued. "Local gangs. Schlusser owns one of these private jet companies in the airport. From what I hear, he had some government contracts, transporting military contractors to places you couldn't really buy a ticket to on US Air, if you know what I mean.

"So I reckon he was in cahoots with some of these mercenary types, and all his drinkin' buddies were into guns and stuff. He put a group together, about fifty of them, and they volunteered to help the sheriff and the National Guard hold down the fort. Being the upstanding citizen that he was, the sheriff accepted. Of course, soon after, Schlusser exerted himself as the alpha male. The sheriff wasn't havin' that, though. He put Schlusser in his place. Schlusser waited for the sheriff's men and the National Guard to thin out a little more then he brought in a case of fancy whiskey as a peace offering and got 'em all liquored up. Later that night, Schlusser and his henchmen killed the sheriff, every one of his deputies and the remaining National Guardsmen. Since then, he's been taking a little territory at a time. But it all started right over there in the armory."

"Night of the long knives." JC commented.

The man shook his head. "Nope, they shot 'em

all . . . with guns."

Danny held back a grin as he looked to see JC rolling his eyes. He figured it was a bit much to expect the man to be well versed enough in history to make the connection.

The man sipped his water and continued speaking. "Schlusser moved back into his big house over on the river; he has his lackeys holding this operation together for him. Most of the ones wearing ties were part of that original bunch that took the armory. They all live over in them houses along the river, next to Schlusser's. He cleaned out that whole neighborhood to make room for his friends. Of course, there weren't too many people left over there to clean out; a couple holdouts and a house that a gang had taken over."

"He's got that neighborhood secured?" JC kept digging.

The man took another bite of his biscuit before continuing. "Yep. Several of the houses are designated as bunk houses. The men staying there are security for the neighborhood. They don't have black shirts, but they eat like it. They're bunked up ten or fifteen men to a house, but they all sleep in beds. I wouldn't complain if I was living like that."

"And who told you all of this?" JC asked.

"Seen it with my own eyes. I was part of the work crew who moved the mattresses and extra furniture over to the bunk houses. It's about as close as anybody will ever get to living a life that looks anything like what we had before the lights went out. I'm Sam, by the way."

"I'm Danny, and this is JC. Nice to meet you,

Sam."

"Good to meet you too, Danny. What are y'all going to be doing today?"

Danny shrugged. "I don't know. We're supposed to be on Antoine's crew."

Sam knuckled his forehead. "Wow. I thought I had a lousy job. But, I guess it's a livin'. Lots of folks out there haven't eaten in weeks."

"Why don't they come get jobs here, then?" JC asked.

Sam replied, "Some of them thinks it's too much like slavery, some of them are too old, or too young, too sick, too thin; lots of reasons. Schlusser won't take nobody with kids younger than twelve. I got in here right when he was taking over the airport, so he needed men real bad then. Otherwise I'd be too old. I'll be fifty this year. He ain't in to nursin' nobody back to health neither. If people wait too long and try to come after they've already lost too much weight, he'll turn 'em away."

"I haven't seen any kids at all," Danny said.

Sam nodded. "Oh, they're here. They're all over in the refugee center, up in the main terminal. They're the ones working the gardens."

"Gardens?" JC crossed his arms and leaned in on the table.

"Yep. There's probably 2500 acres inside the airport fence. I'd say three quarters of that is grass. Plenty of room to grow crops." Sam stood up, clearing his plate and napkin. "I best be getting on over to work. You boys take care."

"Have a good one." JC waved to Sam and picked up his plate as well.

"I guess we better get to work, too." Danny took his plate to the bin where everyone else was dropping theirs.

They walked back to the barracks and found a group of men who looked like they were gathering together for work. JC approached them. "You guys know where we can find Antoine?"

One of the men pointed. "That's him; big black guy right over there."

Danny looked. He couldn't miss him. The man towered above everyone else around the barracks. "Big dude! What do you think? Six nine, six ten?"

"Every bit of it. And probably pushing three hundred pounds."

Danny and JC made their way over to the colossal being.

"Antoine, Spyder said we're with you." Danny said.

Antoine looked down. "Lucky you. Ya'll got rubber boots?"

"No." JC answered.

Antoine looked down at his clipboard and held his pen. "Okay, I'll see if I can scratch some up for you. What sizes do you wear?"

"Nine," Danny said.

"Same." JC added.

"Two pair of nines. I'm not gonna lie, the odds ain't good on that one." He wrote on the pad then pointed to the side of the building with the end of his pen. "Y'all go look around the side of the building. Grab a spade shovel and a transfer shovel each. We're going to be doing some digging."

JC looked at Danny. "You've got gloves in your

pack, right?"

"Yeah, you had them on the list of stuff to bring."

"Good. I think we're going to need them." JC led the way inside the barracks and to their sleeping area. The two men retrieved their work gloves and returned to get their shovels. Next they reported to the corner where they'd been told to wait.

"Y'all with Antoine?" A thin but muscular black man lit a cigarette. He then proceeded to write the word *Friendly* on a length of duct tape with a Sharpie. He tore off the tape and applied it to his chest.

"Yeah," Danny replied.

"Okay, then." He handed the duct tape and the pen to Danny.

Danny took the tape and the pen. He looked at the tape on the man's chest and waited for more instructions.

"You write your name with it, man. That's my name, Friendly. What? Did you think we all write how we're feeling for the day, or our general disposition?"

"Oh." Danny printed his last name on the tape, tore off the section and placed it on his chest.

Friendly continued to laugh as he handed the cigarette to the other black man beside him, who was also laughing. According to the tape on his chest, his name was Sly. Danny figured it was short for Sylvester.

JC took the tape next and wrote *Castell*.

A man with a name tag which read *Javier* looked at JC's tag. "That explains why you're on our team." Javier looked at Danny's name tag. He spoke clear English, but with a thick Puerto Rican accent. "Walker. How did you get on the shovel brigade?"

Danny shook his head. "What do you mean?"

"Look around." Javier waved his hand toward the ten men standing around with shovels. "You're the only white boy."

Danny looked around. "Oh."

Sly took a long drag from the cigarette and passed it back to Friendly. "But don't get us wrong, Schlusser isn't prejudiced. He's just as happy to make a white man into a slave as he is a black man or a brown man."

Antoine soon made his way back over to the group with his clipboard tucked under his arm, carrying two pairs of rubber boots. "I've got a pair of eights and a pair of elevens."

Danny looked at JC. "I think I can squeeze into the eights."

JC nodded. "Good. No way I could wear eights. I'll stuff some paper into the toes and make the elevens work."

They changed their shoes, stashing their regular shoes behind a piece of plywood leaning against the side of the building.

"Let's move out." Antoine led the way.

JC kept pace with Antoine. "What are we going to be doing?"

"We're digging a trench from the river to the perimeter fence. It's not that far. A leg of the Catawba comes to within about 2000 feet of the airport. Then, there's a shallow creek which comes right up Old Dowd Road. We just have to dig out a trench to bring it under the I-485 overpass. Then, we'll bring the trench into the airport. Once all of that is done, we'll be mucking out that creek to increase the water flow."

"That's for drinking water?" Danny asked.

"Drinking, washing, irrigation to the crops. The good news is, as long as you can dig, you'll never be out of a job. We've got plenty of work to do." Antoine smiled.

They continued walking. It was nearly two miles from the barracks to the northwest corner of the airport where they would be working. As they crossed the two main runways, Danny saw the workers planting crops in the green spaces between the massive strips of concrete and asphalt. He looked at the faces of the workers. No one looked happy. They were mostly women and girls. A few early-teenage boys were mixed into the group, but not many. And like Sam said, there were no little children, and no one over fifty.

Several rows were planted, and Danny could see green shoots sprouting from the earth. He tried to identify the plants in the rows closest to where they were walking. *Corn, green beans, squash . . . hmm. I'm not sure what that is.*

They finally arrived at the gate which was manned by a six men and a Humvee. The guards opened the gate without acknowledging Danny or the other men with shovels.

"This area is all secured?" JC quizzed.

"Yep." Antoine pointed west. "The regent has all of this area patrolled. Straight ahead is the leg of the river which connects to the creek where we're working. That leg of the river connects to the main river, which forms a peninsula. That's where the regent's house is; Plantation Ridge Road." Antoine let out a short chuckle filled with disdain. "Aptly named."

Antoine pointed along the side of the road. "We'll keep the trench about eight feet from the side of the road. We'll start out at two feet deep then go deeper once we get the initial line cut."

"You gotta be kidding me!" JC looked at the long stretch of road where they had to dig. "They can't get a dozer?"

Antoine shook his head. "If they ain't military, they weren't hardened against EMP."

"Why don't we hit up one of these farms around here; find an old tractor with a back hoe."

"You'd have to talk to Gorbold about that."

JC let out a grunt and began digging.

Danny worked on a section of the trench with JC. All the men on Antoine's crew worked steadily for the next couple hours, including Antoine. Danny doubted that the big man was expected to actually be digging as his position was much more akin to an overseer, but he thought it was commendable.

After a while, a Humvee drove up and a man with a black shirt and black tie got out to inspect the work. He instructed one of the other men in the vehicle, who wore a black polo, to bring a cooler of water out of the back.

As the man brought the water and set it down, he looked toward Antoine. "If it were up to me, I'd make y'all dig that ditch and get your own water."

"You're hard core, Darrel." Antoine pursed his

lips and turned away from the man.

The man with the tie talked to Antoine for a few seconds. Danny figured it was something about the trench, as he pointed toward the freshly dug canal while he spoke. Then, he and Darrel drove away.

The men lined up at the cooler and took turns getting water.

JC wiped the sweat from his head and took a long drink of his water. "I'm going to need a little bigger breakfast if I'm going to be working like this."

Danny sipped his water. He was running low on energy. "I know what you mean. I'm going to have to pace myself with the digging if I'm going to keep going all day."

JC finished his water. "But as long as Schlusser keeps treating his men like garbage, it'll be easier to sow dissension in the camp."

They finished work without eating lunch. Danny noticed that Antoine and some of the other men had brought balls of rice, wrapped in plastic wrap, or pieces of bread wrapped in paper. Each of them carried it in a small backpack or shoulder bag. He determined that he would do the same from here on out. As it was, he barely had enough strength to get back to the barracks. Sly was right about one thing, Schlusser was exploiting them all like slaves.

Antoine led the way toward the creek. "We'll wash up down by the river. Otherwise, you only get a half gallon for washing back at the barracks."

Danny followed sluggishly. "So I guess that's one perk to being on your work team."

Antoine laughed. "Yeah, well, that's about the

only perk."

Danny looked at the man whom he'd found to be so intimidating at the beginning of the day. Despite his size, Antoine seemed rather easy going, almost kind. Danny asked, "So, what did you do before you got here?"

Antoine stopped walking and looked blankly into the distance, as if Danny were asking him about a distant dream that he couldn't quite recall. "Before I got here. Hmm. Where do I start? I grew up here in Charlotte. Went to UNC on a football scholarship. I was going to go pro after college. And it wasn't just me. Coach, all my friends, everybody knew I was going pro. It was like my destiny. Then, I ripped the heck out of my ACL during a game in the beginning of my junior year. I had reconstructive surgery but didn't get cleared in time to play my senior year. Then, it was like my window of opportunity just closed. The dream of going pro faded away. So I got a job as a football coach at the high school where I'd gone. Took me a while to deal with the change of plans," Antoine started laughing.

Danny was puzzled. "What's funny?"

"Change of plans. I thought missing my shot at the NFL was the worst thing that could ever happen to me. But look at me now. Look at all of us. Once the lights went out, none of that stuff mattered one bit."

"Yeah, I guess we all got a change of plans." Danny walked with the rest of the men down to the river. They reached a shallow lagoon, where the river terminated. The men rinsed the sweat out of their shirts and washed off. The clear waters were soon muddied by the activity.

JC spoke Spanish with Javier and Jorge as they walked back. Danny caught the gist of the conversation from his limited comprehension of the language. He gathered that Javier was filling him in on the layout of the peninsula, just across the river.

On the way back, JC walked close to Danny. "According to these guys, Schlusser is about to start moving his military men over into this neighborhood. Classic example of trying to hold too much territory with too few men. Greed and arrogance may prove to be our best allies."

Danny looked around to make sure no one else was close enough to hear. "I like the fact that Schlusser is digging his own grave, but that might take a while. I don't think we have much time before he strikes back against the farm."

JC continued to wring the water out of his shirt as he walked. "Yeah, you're probably right. We've got at least a couple days though. We'll take it easy and see which opportunities present themselves."

Once back at the barracks, Danny changed into some dry clothes and laid the wet ones on one of the cars in the parking lot to dry in the sun, like the rest of the men. His stomach was growling, but he still had a while before dinner would be served, so he went to rest on his sleeping bag. He had almost drifted off for a quick cat nap, when the sound of Spyder's voice rattled the quietude.

"Everyone on Ryan, Oliver or Duane's work team, pack it up. Congratulations, you're getting promoted to security and an upgrade for your living quarters. You guys are all transferring to the office buildings over in the Air National Guard Complex. You'll be two to a room, so pick a roommate and head on over there. You can eat dinner with us and move after, or you can move now, and try to make it to dinner in time to eat at the recruiting center. If it was me, I'd try to make it to the recruiting center. They're probably having more than beans and rice."

Danny watched as more than half of the men in the warehouse scurried to get their belongings packed up. In less than fifteen minutes, nearly 120 spaces opened up in the sleeping area. Spyder directed another thirty new men to take their places.

JC lay on his sleeping bag next to Danny. "This operation is growing pretty fast."

"Yeah, and the caste system is becoming more defined. It's not just brass and grunts anymore, the grunts are being subdivided into tiers."

"As long as we stay at the bottom, that's fine with me."

"Are you thinking about tapping anybody from Antoine's team?"

JC crossed his hands behind his head and lay back. "Not unless I have to. And I won't know that until we get a plan. I have to figure out where those other fuel tanks are then figure out a timeline to light them up."

"We could ask Sam. He seems pretty knowledgeable of the layout and more than happy to talk about it."

"I'd rather get someone talking; see if they'll volunteer the information without me having to ask. Sam might be our guy, but I don't want to send up any red flags by asking if I don't have to. We can't trust anybody in here. They're all lookin' to move up."

"Do you have a deadline in mind? What's the longest you're willing to wait?"

JC glanced over at Danny then back up at the ceiling. "A week, tops. Trust me, I want to get out of here as bad as you do, but we have to take our time and do it right. Alisa will never forgive me if I don't bring you back alive."

Danny didn't reply. His mind began to drift back to Nana's farm. He wondered how they were all getting along, especially Alisa.

"Chow time, let's go." JC nudged Danny, pulling him out of his daydream.

Danny got up and followed JC. "I want to see if one of the food service women will give me a piece of plastic wrap so we can wrap up some leftovers for lunch tomorrow."

"Sounds like a plan." JC replied. The two of them hurried to get near the front of the line.

Danny politely asked the woman serving the rice, "May I have that plastic wrap?"

She squinted her eyes. "We're supposed to reuse it."

"Oh, okay." Danny thanked her for the rice and moved to the woman serving the beans.

The rice lady wadded up the plastic wrap and looked at Danny. "Hey."

"Yes?"

"Since you asked so nicely." She handed the plastic to Danny with a wink.

He grinned from ear to ear. "Thank you so much." It was a small piece of trash, but it meant that he would be able to store food for lunch the following day.

Danny and JC sat at the table with Sam, Jorge, and Javier.

"I wonder what the security teams are eating for dinner," Javier said.

"MREs." Sam replied.

"And you know this how?" Javier asked.

"Saw the boxes stacked up in the recruiting center. We've been over by the Air National Guard section of the airport all day. We hauled out all of the office furniture and put beds and dressers in all those office buildings."

"Where do ju get it de otra furnitures?" Jorge asked in his broken English.

Sam finished chewing. "We cleaned out the Barry Hill neighborhood."

Javier lowered his brow. "I thought the black polos were moving in there."

"Nope. They're moving into the Vineyards, on the peninsula."

"Barry Hill's not good enough for them?" Javier kept the questions going.

Sam shrugged. "I think the regent wants them close by, in case his place ever gets hit."

"Please, don't give me any ideas." Javier continued eating.

Danny glanced over at JC to see his reaction to Javier's statement. JC didn't flinch, he maintained his poker face.

"Why ju don't bring it de mattress over here?" Jorge asked.

"It ain't up to me where they go. I just move 'em

where I'm told." Sam cleared his plate in a hurry, as did the rest of the hungry men. All of them went back through the line when the call for seconds came. There were just over 100 men in the chow hall due to the recent vacancies, so there was quite a bit of rice left over.

Danny filled his plate with rice again after he'd eaten his second portion then balled it up into six small portions, wrapping each one with a torn piece of the plastic wrap. He gave three to JC and kept three for himself. After dinner, he returned to the barracks. He stashed his rice, took his small New Testament out of his pack and read with his flashlight for a few minutes before falling asleep.

The next morning, Danny and JC repeated the process of waking up to the sound of someone pounding a metal pot with a metal spoon. This time, Danny was able to identify the culprit. "Spyder!"

"He gets a kick out of being a jerk." JC covered his ears until the banging subsided then rubbed his eyes and got dressed.

As Danny got dressed, he remembered what day it was. "Pancake day!"

JC fought back a smile. "Don't get too excited. We ain't going to be here long enough to be making a ritual celebration out of pancake day."

Danny rushed to finish getting dressed. "Still, I'm celebrating it today."

JC had to move quickly to keep up with Danny who was determined to be near the front of the breakfast line. Five more new men arrived for breakfast, but there were still plenty of leftovers.

Once again, Danny ate as much as he could then wrapped up several more pancakes in his remaining plastic wrap for later.

Next, it was off to dig the ditch. Antoine led the men across the runways, to the northwest corner of the airport, just as he had done the day before. JC and Danny stayed close to Antoine as they walked. An olive drab green military fuel truck drove down the runway, toward the barracks.

Nonchalantly, JC said, "What is he doing coming from that direction? All the fuel tanks and vehicles are back behind us."

Antoine shook his head. "No. Those are just the Air National Guard tanks. The main airport tanks are up the road, on Dowd."

JC replied matter-of-factly, "Dowd? Isn't that where we were working yesterday? I didn't see any tanks."

"You wouldn't have. Dowd curves around the north side of the airport. The fuel tanks are about a mile from where we're working, over by the rental cars."

"Oh. You said something about irrigation yesterday. Are we going to be digging the channels for that eventually?" JC changed the subject.

Danny just listened. He knew that JC had no intention of being around long enough to even come close to completing the job of digging the canal into the airport, much less the next project. He took note of how JC quickly redirected the conversation into a direction which would make Antoine believe that JC planned on being around for a while.

Antoine went on to explain what he knew about

the plans for irrigation. "Schlusser wants the airport to be as self-sufficient as possible, while at the same time using it as a base to take over more and more territory."

Danny feigned a look of disappointment. "When we signed up, we were under the impression that he was trying to put the pieces back together. We were told that he intends to relinquish power to the state or federal government, once it's back up and running."

Antoine laughed. "The only reason he calls himself the regent is because he's waiting to see how much power he can seize. If he calls himself mayor, that's too small for his ambitions. If he calls himself president, it seems like too big of a stretch when he only has an airport and a couple of small outposts which can't even defend themselves against the local gangs and militias. Regent is a little more flexible as far as titles go. It leaves the man with plenty of room to grow.

"But believe me when I tell you, he ain't giving up anything to anybody. Not that I expect there to be a state or federal government that can contend with the regent anyways."

Danny looked at the teenagers and women working in the gardens. He continued his naive ruse, playing the part of someone who was trying to stay positive. "But all of these people are alive. The regent sort of stepped in to fill the void. If it weren't for him, none of us would have jobs."

Antoine patted Danny on the back. "That's exactly what he wants you to think; that he's your knight in shining armor, and without him, you'd be dead. But you managed to stay alive for two months. We all have.

"Everybody here is only around because they can't find a better deal. But the second that changes, they'll all high-tail it out of here. And you better be ready to bug out when the time comes too."

"Why is that?" Danny was genuinely curious now.

"Lots of folks don't share your appreciation for the good regent."

"Like who?"

"For one, the Sheriff of Cabarrus County, the next county to the northeast. He's up in Concord and he's been pushing back against Schlusser anytime the regent tries to send patrols into his county."

"Wow. Sounds like complex politics. Are you worried that he'll try to attack?"

Antoine shook his head. "I don't think so. The man is kind of the live-and-let-live type, a good man from what I've heard. But people like that don't stand a chance in the long run. He'll be content to keep the regent out of his county. Not the regent, though. He won't stop until he rules the world or somebody kills him. He's addicted to the pursuit. It'll never be enough for him."

They soon reached the work site and set in for another hard day of digging. Danny brought his meager lunch and a canteen to keep himself hydrated; it wasn't nearly so rough as the day before had been. Nevertheless, he paced himself so not to get overly exhausted before the day was finished.

Shortly before noon, the Humvee came around, with the man who wore the black tie. As before, he instructed Darrel, the man with the black polo shirt, to bring out the water cooler.

"Here's my bath water from last night. You boys enjoy it." Darrel set the cooler right by the tire of the Hummer, which was directly in the sun. "You know, y'all look about like a bunch of pigs down there wallowing in the mud."

"You should get down here in the mud with us." JC kept digging as he delivered his snide remark. "Maybe if you did a little work, you wouldn't look like such a pansy."

Darrel stopped cold in his tracks. "What did you say?"

JC threw his shovel in the mud. "You heard me, I called you a pansy. And you're gonna turn around, get in your little truck, and leave without doing anything about it, because you're a pansy."

Darrel looked around at the rest of the work crew who was now laughing and jeering him. "Come up here and say it to my face."

JC stood still. "Listen, I'm not going anywhere. If you're anything but a pansy, you'll take off that pistol belt and come down here."

Darrel released the clip on the strap keeping his drop leg holster attached to his thigh. Next he unfastened the belt clip and placed his holster in the Humvee. "At least come up here out of the mud, little pig."

JC marched up out of the mud. "Okay, I'll meet you halfway, and I'll give you the first shot. But make it count."

Darrel reared back and right hooked JC in the jaw.

JC rolled with the swing, tucked low and came up with an upper cut that knocked Darrel off of his balance. He followed it up with a right jab to the face. Darrel shielded his face, and JC took a left hook straight into Darrel's ear. JC continued the assault, finally getting a hold of Darrel's arm and taking him to the ground. He got on top of him and began to pummel him in the face, head, and throat while Darrel fought to turn over in an attempt to shield himself from the relentless attack.

The man with the black tie drew his pistol and fired three rounds in the air. "Stop it! Stop it right now!"

JC let up and slowly stood to his feet.

"Darrel, get up!" the man yelled.

Darrel struggled to get up on his knees. He turned around on his hands and knees to face the man in the black tie.

"Stand up, man!"

Darrel labored to stand, stumbling backwards as if he had just come off the tilt-a-whirl at the county fair.

"Look at you!" the man scolded him like a child. "You're a bloody mess. Don't pick a fight with someone if you can't win. Especially your subordinate. Now no one in the entire camp will have any respect for you. Take off that black shirt, you've disgraced it."

"But sergeant!"

"You heard me. Take it off." The sergeant still held the pistol in his hand.

Darrel took off his shirt.

"Now put it in the back of the Hummer. On the floorboard. I don't want it getting the seats dirty."

"What about me?" Darrel wiped the blood from his face with the shirt as he made his way to the Hummer.

The sergeant looked at Antoine. "Looks like you've got another white boy on your team. That should quell the rumors about the regent being prejudiced."

Antoine just nodded, but didn't look very convinced by the statement. He watched silently as the man drove away in the Humvee, leaving Darrel on the side of the ditch, bloody and humiliated.

Sly waved as the Humvee drove out of sight. He performed his best Gone-with-the-wind accent. "Yasa massa, you sho nuf done showed us. Ol' Massa Schlusser, he likes him da white slaves, jes' much as da black and brown ones." He turned his attention to Darrel and continued his routine. "Say der, white slave, yous is ready to pick some cotton?"

Everyone on the team got a chuckle out of Sly's impression. Antoine pointed to JC. "Why don't you let Darrel use your shovel? You look like you could use a break."

JC wiped the sweat from his forehead. "Yeah, thanks."

Once the commotion had died down, Danny returned to digging, along with the rest of the men. He couldn't wait to get JC off by himself so he could ask JC if the fight was somehow part of his plan, or if he'd just snapped on Darrel. Danny kept looking back toward the base to see if the sergeant would be sending a security crew to pick up JC, but none came.

The retelling of the incident by the other men on Antoine's work team constituted the entertainment for the rest of the afternoon. With each rehashing of the fight, some important element was brought to light that had been previously overlooked. The men had no reservations about building JC into a legend, right in front of his eyes. Danny found it amusing, and while JC concealed it, Danny suspected he was enjoying the attention. Darrel, however, looked like he wanted to crawl in a hole and die.

That evening, the story spread around the dining hall, bringing a welcome distraction to the mundane existence of the men on the various work crews. Darrel sat by himself, while Danny had to keep scooting over to make room for additional people who wanted to sit at the table with them. It all seemed like a scene from high school.

Then the mess hall fell silent. Danny looked to see why everyone had become so quiet. Gorbold had just walked in the room. Danny turned to look at JC. "Uh oh."

JC shrugged coolly. "Que sera, sera."

Javier, Sly, Antoine, Jorge, Sam, and Friendly all sat at the table with Danny and JC. They collectively stopped eating, talking, and moving. They were so motionless, so noiseless, Danny thought for a moment that perhaps they'd stopped breathing.

Gorbold's boots echoed with each step in the

soundless room. His face held no expression to hint at his intentions. He stood next to the table and stared at JC.

JC glanced up at him then back down at his rice. JC waited for a moment then began eating. Antoine also resumed eating. Soon everyone at the table had gone back to their food, as if Gorbold wasn't really there. Danny looked over at Darrel, sitting by himself at the table in the back corner. He was watching, on the edge of his seat as if he were waiting to hear the fate of his assailant.

Gorbold finally cracked a smile. "I heard you had a little incident at work today."

JC washed his rice down with his water. "Yes, sir."

Gorbold looked over at Darrel who quickly turned away. "Darrel was relatively feared around here. You weren't the first to tangle with him, but you were the first to lick him."

"Yes, sir," JC said.

Gorbold patted JC on the shoulder. "We'll need some men to fill in for sector four gun confiscations, starting tomorrow. The regent is sending 100 men to Greenville to root out the insurrection down there. Once that has been contained, there's a group of farmers causing trouble down around Anderson that I have to take care of. They killed my brother, so . . . it's personal."

Danny tried to figure out if JC was getting a reprimand, a job offer, or if he'd been somehow found out for killing Gorbold's brother. This time, he did hold his breath as he waited for Gorbold's next words.

JC looked up. "Can I be of assistance to you with any of that?"

Gorbold nodded with the even steadiness of clock gears. "I hope so. You'll be part of a team, going house to house tomorrow, over in Pine Crest. After you get the feel for the way we work, I'll be assigning you your own security team. You'll be searching for guns and other contraband items in the various neighborhoods; helping us to restore order in Charlotte."

"Happy to serve, sir." JC said.

Gorbold gave JC a key. "You've got your own room over in the Air National Guard barracks. It's the building with the teal roof, right behind the main hangar. You'll find a bed, a dresser and a stack of black polo shirts. Let me know if you need anything."

JC took the key. "Thank you."

Danny half expected JC to ask if he could come along, but he knew it would be pushing Gorbold's good graces.

Gorbold left and they finished their meal amongst the well wishes and congratulations from the other men to JC.

Once finished, Danny walked back to the barracks with the town hero. JC looked around. "You know I would have tried to get you on my squad, but I don't know what I'll have to do to keep my cover."

Danny knew JC wasn't the type to blow smoke, but he didn't really understand why he couldn't be on JC's team. After all, he'd proven himself militarily over and over. Danny was better trained than most of these yahoos at the airport. "What is that supposed to mean?"

JC looked around to make sure no one was listening. "They're sending me into the neighborhoods, to kick in doors. I might happen upon some good citizens that don't feel like giving up their guns. I might have to do something I don't want to do to keep my cover. I don't want you to have to live with anything like that."

Danny stopped walking. "Oh."

"Yeah. I mean in the long run, I'm softening this guy up so they can take him, but there might be some collateral damage."

"If you hit trouble, couldn't you take out the men with you and say that the hostiles killed them, and let the people in the house run away before backup arrives?"

JC arrived at his sleeping bag and began rolling it up. "That sounds easy, but think about all the firefights you've been in. It's mass confusion, everybody is freakin' out and they ain't gonna know what's goin' on. Let's say that happens and I'll kill my own guys. Once it's just me, the hostiles will take me out."

Danny gritted his teeth. Suddenly he greatly appreciated the fact that JC had not made a bid to get him on his team.

"But don't worry, I'll stay in touch."

"I'll keep my ear to the tracks, and let you know if I learn anything else that can help us."

JC fastened the belt to secure his sleeping bag. "I have a feeling I'm going to be able to get a hold of some items that would be of value to these guys. If I can bring back a few extra mattresses for the guys on Antoine's work team, they'll be loyal to me forever. You just keep needling them about what a rotten deal they're getting."

Danny nodded. "Okay, so I'll see you tomorrow?"

"Yeah, I'll walk down after dinner. You take care of yourself." JC picked up the sleeping bag and held it beneath one arm.

Danny chuckled. "I'm just digging ditches tomorrow. You're kicking in doors with potential hostiles. You take care!"

JC waved as he walked away. "Will do."

CHAPTER 5

The LORD is my shepherd; I shall not want. He maketh me to lie down in green pastures: he leadeth me beside the still waters. He restoreth my soul: he leadeth me in the paths of righteousness for his name's sake. Yea, though I walk through the valley of the shadow of death, I will fear no evil: for thou art with me; thy rod and thy staff they comfort me.

Psalm 23:1-4

Saturday started out pretty much like every other day at the airport, except that JC wasn't around. Danny felt a little less confident about his undercover abilities when he was on his own. As he got dressed and made his way to the dining facility, he whispered to himself, "I'm not alone. God is with me. I guess that's idolatry if I feel safer around JC than when it's just me and God." He looked up to address his Creator. "I'm sorry about that." Danny continued to the mess hall and recalled the story of David and Goliath. *David found confidence to fight the giant because he knew God was with him. Plus, he'd already killed a lion and a bear with his slingshot. I guess God was warming him up for the grand finale. But he did it. He walked right out on that field, all by himself, with only a sling and a stone; and God of course.*

I haven't killed any lions or bears, but I've seen my share of action. Danny suddenly noticed he didn't have a ready number for the times he'd been in firefights, nor could he recollect exactly how many men he'd sent to meet their Maker. *I don't have the experience JC has, but I am what you'd call battle hardened.*

He reached the front of the line feeling much more up to the task than when he'd walked out the door of the barracks only moments before.

There was a second woman standing next to the lady serving rice. "Sugar?"

"What?"

"We've got a little sugar today. Would you like a spoon of sugar on your rice?"

"Yes, please!" Danny was excited to have anything different. He figured if someone wasn't assigned to spooning it on the plates that one of the men would probably take it all, by dumping it into a Ziploc and squirreling it away for himself.

Danny took a seat at what had become his regular table, along with Sam, Antoine, Javier, Jorge, Sly, and Friendly.

Antoine said, "Sunday is the closest thing we get to a day off. We work half day. That's for the whole compound, which includes the kitchen. There's no breakfast in the morning, so you should plan accordingly."

"Oh. What about dinner tomorrow?" Danny asked.

Sly replied. "No dinner either, but we usually get something nice for lunch on Sundays. Don't get your hopes up. You ain't getting' fried chicken or grilled pork chops, at least not in this dining room. But sometimes we get pasta with tomato sauce; we had tortillas one time. You never know, but it will be different."

"That's cool. What did you have with the tortillas?"

"Beans and rice, but wrapping them in a tortilla made them taste completely different," Javier answered.

"We go to work at the same time tomorrow and we're supposed to knock off at 1:00, but all the other crews start coming in around 12:30. Lunch is at 2:00." Antoine continued eating.

Danny finished eating then went back to the serving table for seconds. He wrapped up several balls of rice for Saturday's lunch and Sunday's breakfast.

After dinner Saturday night, Danny saw JC walking down the runway, coming from the direction of the Air National Guard base. He didn't wave as he had no desire to bring additional attention to the meeting. It wasn't prohibited for security personnel to converse with the workers, but it certainly wasn't a common practice. Danny walked over to a stack of empty wooden pallets, near the corner of the building and took a seat.

JC eventually made his way over to the pallets and sat next to Danny. "How was work?"

"Less exciting than what you did, I'm sure. Javier and Sly rode Darrel all day about getting his tail whooped. What about you?"

"Pretty good actually." JC pulled a brown paper bag out of the side pocket of his cargo pants.

"What's this?" Danny picked up the bag.

"Cheeseburger and a pistol."

Danny wasn't sure what kind of answer to expect, but it certainly wasn't that. "What am I supposed to do with them?"

"Cheeseburgers, you generally eat, and pistols, they're for killin' people."

Danny cracked a smile. "Okay."

JC said, "I've got five twin mattresses sitting inside the main hangar. Get Antoine and give him the first mattress. Let him know that anyone who has a problem with you guys having a mattress in the barracks will be sent to him to deal with. That should quell any jealous discontentment amongst the other men. You take the second then the other three can go to whoever. Maybe Javier, Sam, and Sly.

"In case I can't get back down here tomorrow night, I'll stash some toilet paper and some more goodies up in the front wheel well of that C-130 closest to your barracks."

Danny slid the burger out of the bag and took a bite then held the rest of the sandwich low by his leg. The cheeseburger was euphoric. He had to fight not to let out any sounds of ecstasy that might betray his exquisite feast. "So how are you planning to destroy the fuel tanks?"

"I watched them top off one of the military fuel trucks from the tanks over by the Air National Guard. It looks like Schlusser has had them reconfigured to operate solely on the pressure from the fuel in the tank rather than pumps. The only thing stopping the jet fuel from flowing all over the place is the manual shut-off valve. From what I can tell, he has both tanks feeding into the main dispensing outlet."

"Thanks for the burger. I've never tasted anything so good." Danny closed his eyes as he chewed the extravagant epicurean delight. "Did you get to drive by the other tanks?"

"Yep."

"How many?"

"Four huge ones, and six smaller ones, about the size of the two at the Air National Guard. But from what I can tell, Schlusser has them all feeding into one outlet, like the ones near my bunk house."

Danny finished chewing. "How long will that take to drain all the fuel from ten tanks?"

JC shrugged. "I don't know. All day probably."

"Couldn't we get drills and puncture all ten tanks to speed up the process?" Before JC could respond, Danny added, "I know it would make a lot of noise, but what if we shot holes in the tanks?"

JC shook his head. "Those tanks are double walled with lightweight concrete between the two steel walls. To drill it, you'd have to drill the first steel wall, switch to a masonry bit, drill the concrete, and then switch back to the metal bit and drill the second steel wall. You'd have to drill with a small bit to start a hole, then switch to a larger bit to get any kind of flow going. And you'd have to do all of that ten times."

"Twelve, if you count the tanks at the Air National Guard." Danny added.

"Yeah, twelve. You could shoot holes in them, but you'd need a .50 cal to penetrate both walls and the concrete filler. We'll have to take out the guards and open up that manual valve. All we need is enough time to drain a couple hundred gallons. Then we can light the fire. Once the fuel starts to burn, no one will be able to reach the shut-off valve to close it. Those tanks are probably fire rated for two hours. That fire is going to burn all night, with no way to put it out. The tanks will eventually weaken and fail, resulting in any undrained fuel being consumed in the fire."

Danny pointed across the runway. "What about the firehouse?"

JC shook his head. "Fire trucks aren't military. They weren't hardened against EMP."

"Yeah, but they've got fire extinguishers."

"That might work if they put the fire out within the first few minutes of the valves being open, but we won't even strike a match until we've got a couple hundred gallons on the ground. Then forget about it. There ain't enough fire extinguishers on earth to put that fire out."

Danny furrowed his brow. "You said take out the guards. How would we do that?"

JC nodded toward the paper bag. "Shoot 'em."

"I've found that tends to draw unwanted attention. Especially if we're going to have to hang around for several minutes, waiting for enough fuel to drain out for a good fire."

"Unless we can silence the shots."

"I'm guessing you've got an idea on how to do that."

"That's a .38 snub nose in the bag. Stick an oil filter over the barrel. It's going to obstruct your front sight, but it will keep it quiet for a couple rounds. You'll have to get close if you can't see that front sight. If I could get a couple AR-15s with reflex sights, we'd be able to see over the oil filter, but that's going to take some conniving."

Danny looked toward the parking lot. "No shortage of oil filters, although they may be slightly used."

JC chuckled. "Yeah. You might want to get a couple filters ready. Let them drain out for a day or two. Maybe even try to wash them out with water. There's a good chance the muzzle flash will ignite the residual oil inside the filter if you don't clean them out. And get some duct tape. You'll need a way to secure the filter to the muzzle."

"So, theoretically, you would attack one set of tanks, and I'd attack the other set. We'd coordinate our time to light the fires simultaneously then rendezvous back at Catfish's truck?"

JC rubbed his beard. "I haven't thought that far ahead yet. We need to take out the guards simultaneously. If any of them have a chance to return fire, that will alert the other security forces and we won't have time to drain the tanks.

"Plus, when we hit the Air National Guard tanks, we have to take out those fuel trucks. They've all got a valve on the back of them that drains with gravity, so we'll open those valves at the same time. I don't want to leave Schlusser with three full fuel trucks."

"How many guards are we talking about?"

JC raised his eyebrows. "There's actually none at the Air National Guard tanks. I guess Schlusser thinks nobody would be foolish enough to try and pull something right there by the security team's barracks. There's almost always someone walking around."

Danny stuck a finger in the air. "Ah. He has underestimated our stupidity!"

"Yeah. I guess he has." JC laughed. "The main airport tanks have two guys at the front gate, and four on the back side. Since the tanks are on the perimeter, the guards on the back are watching the tanks and the fence. Killing two birds with one stone, so to speak."

"So if the tanks are on the perimeter, does that mean there's another patrol three hundred yards away on each side?"

"Unfortunately, yes. In the dark, with suppressed fire, we could pull it off. We'd have to take the two guys at the gate first, slip inside, take out two more guards simultaneously, and then in quick succession, take out the other two before they could get a shot off to alert the guards on either flank."

Danny shook his head as he rolled his eyes. His tone dripped with sarcasm. "And all of this after we've already lit the fire at the Air National Guard. Sounds easy enough."

JC pursed his lips. "I know. Like I said, I hadn't really thought that far in advance yet."

"The bottom line is that we're going to have to bring someone else in."

JC shook his head. "I really don't want to do that."

"But your current plan has the two of us, lighting two fires, roughly a mile away from each other, and killing six men, in less time than it takes a man to draw a weapon and return fire. I'll give you credit, JC. You've managed to pull off some pretty unbelievable capers, but this scheme is butting heads with the laws of mathematics and physics. We need at least three more people by my numbers."

JC shook his head. "No way. One more, tops. If we had someone else to light the fire at the Air National Guard, you and me could take out the six goons at the main tanks."

"I appreciate your confidence in me, but that's a stretch. Anyway, you admit we have to bring someone else in."

"I didn't say that."

"You said one more."

"I said one more, tops. That means either one or none."

"Semantics. You know we have to bring

someone else in."

JC grimaced. "Who do you have in mind?"

"I don't know, Antoine?"

JC shook his head. "He doesn't strike me as a risk taker."

"And I do?"

JC bobbed his head from side to side. "You're coming along."

"Who would you pick?"

JC shrugged. "I don't know. Javi or Sly. Both of them seem to hate Schlusser and his system."

Danny pursed his lips. "I think Antoine is just more reserved about expressing his discontentment. Besides, whoever you bring in, we'll have to take them back to the farm with us. They'll have nowhere else to go."

"Whoa, whoa, whoa. Now you're bringing more people back to the farm?"

"What are you going to do JC? Leave the guy standing at the electric plant on the other side of the river while we speed off in Catfish's truck? Thanks for risking your life to help us blow up Schlusser's fuel. Hope you don't get caught. See ya, wouldn't wanna be ya."

JC exhaled deeply as he jumped down from the stack of pallets. "There's a lot of moving parts to this thing. Let me think about it tonight. I'll try to get back down here tomorrow after lunch."

Despite the kitchen staff having a short day and there being no breakfast served, Spyder still banged the metal spoon against the metal pot at 5:00 AM on Sunday morning.

"Seriously?" Danny awoke, more annoyed than usual. At least he'd gotten a good night's sleep, thanks to his new mattress. He got dressed, took two balls of rice and three pancakes that he'd saved from Friday and went outside to eat his breakfast on the stack of pallets. It was still pitch black outside; the sun wouldn't be up for nearly two more hours.

Danny used the cover of darkness to steal away to the parking lot across the street where he removed the oil filters from four vehicles. He quickly returned to the barracks before he was missed by anyone.

As he waited for the sun to rise, Danny sat in the dark, rather than use the batteries in his flashlight. Some of the men would collect the candle stubs and wax drippings from the candles in the dining hall. They'd braid and twist threads of cotton from worn out clothing to use for a wick then they'd melt the wax remnants in an empty jar to make their own candles. But Danny wasn't planning to be there long and would be conservative with the use of his flashlight to make the batteries last.

Later, Danny and the rest of his work team made their way across the massive runways toward the ditch. As they approached the garden workers, Javi said, "Hang tight guys. I have to drop a note off to one of the girls to get to my wife."

Danny held Javi's shovel and the team slowed their pace to allow Javi time to make a run with his message. Danny glanced over at Antoine. "Javi's wife is here?"

Antoine nodded. "Yep, she's part of the team that cooks and cleans at the houses over on the peninsula. I think that's the only thing that keeps him here. Javi is resourceful. He'd probably get by out there on his own. But his wife is here and they're both eating."

"He doesn't get to see her?"

"Only on Sundays. He's probably giving one of the women a note to tell his wife where to meet him after lunch."

Danny made a mental note to scratch Javi off the roster of potential accomplices. There's no way he'd be a part of anything that might make his wife a target for retaliation against him. "That's pretty tough, not getting to see your wife all week."

Antoine nodded. "Yeah. It's a different world."

"What about you?" Danny asked.

Antoine lifted one eyebrow. "What about me?"

"Do you have a wife or girlfriend anywhere?"

He shook his head. "I was dating a teacher at the school where I coached when the lights went out. She lived on the other side of town. Took me a whole day to get to her house after the attack. I assumed we'd stick it out together. She had other plans. Her brother was a prepper or something. She set out on a bicycle to his house, up in Pennsylvania. She said he'd tried to warn her to prepare, which she never did. She said he might make a place for her, but she was sure he wouldn't be willing to share with me."

"Wow. That's tough." Danny lowered his head.

Antoine's voice cracked like he was holding back his tears. "Everything about life since the EMP is tough."

Danny dropped the subject and walked slowly

beside Antoine while they waited for Javi to return.

Javier finally ran back to the group and took his tools from Danny. "Thanks."

"No problem. Are you going to see your wife tonight?"

"Yes, we've got some catching up to do." Javi sounded excited.

Antoine looked at Danny. "What about you?"

"What? A girlfriend?" Danny wanted to tell Antoine about Alisa. He missed her so much. The chance to talk about how cute she was, how smart; to tell how she could be such a warrior, yet so feminine would almost make him feel like she was there. But as JC had said, this scheme had too many moving parts. He didn't need to complicate it with his back story. "No. Not right now."

"Well, it's easier to be alone for the moment. Maybe things will turn around and times will get better. We can always hope." Antoine patted Danny on the back.

Shortly after they arrived at the work site, Danny walked down to the lagoon by himself under the pretenses of needing to see a man about a horse. He took a plastic bag from his backpack which contained the oil filters. He removed the filters and rinsed them as best he could in a short amount of time. He washed out the oily trash bag he'd kept them in, and then returned the filters to the trash bag. He tied it off so it wouldn't leak then he put the bag back in his pack. Danny quickly returned to his job site.

No one did much work Sunday. The morning was spent sitting under the shade of the trees near the unfinished canal and reminiscing about the way things used to be.

Danny looked at the pile of shovels. "Won't the sergeant be around to see how far we've progressed?"

Sly looked at Danny like he was crazy. "The brass don't work on Sunday. Saturday is their half day. No threat of anyone coming around today."

Friendly pointed at Darrel. "And the brass better not hear that we take it easy on Sunday neither."

"Not unless you want another beat down." Javier added.

Danny certainly wasn't about to complain about not working. He'd already lost several pounds in the few days he'd been at the airport. He had no desire to lose any more weight.

Jorge sat next to Danny. "Why JC don't get me a mattress? He don't like me?"

"Of course he likes you. He could only get five yesterday. I'm sure he'll get some more. I'll make sure you get the next one."

Jorge didn't look convinced, but Danny couldn't do anything more.

Shortly after noon, Antoine stood up. "We can start heading back if you guys are ready. But let's take our time. We don't want to get back to the barracks before 12:30. If we do, Spyder will snitch us out."

Lunch was canned beef ravioli and apple sauce for dessert. For most of the men, it was the best thing they'd eaten since the EMP. Danny ate hardily then went outside to read his Bible on the pallets while he waited to see if JC would come.

Shortly after 4:00, Danny saw JC walking down the runway. He continued to read his Bible until JC arrived.

JC pulled a few pallets out away from the wall, took off his backpack and dropped it behind the pallets. "Wait til I'm gone to get into that."

Danny tried not to look behind the pallets. "What am I going to find?"

"Canned chicken, can opener, toilet paper, batteries, candy, and duct tape. BBQ pork sandwich. Another gun."

Danny wondered what kind of candy was in the pack. "Should I put the gun in the same vehicle as the other one?"

"Yeah. The less places you have to be seen snooping around, the better. Where did you put it?"

"I stuck it under the hood of that white Honda Pilot over here on the side lot. Spyder's office window looks out to the front lot, so I didn't want to risk being spotted by him."

"Good thinkin'. Did you get some oil filters?"

"Four."

"That should do it."

"Sounds like you had a pretty good day."

JC nodded. "Yeah, we hit the jackpot. We kicked a door over in Arbor Glen. A bunch of delinquents had been looting. Kids about your age. They had all kinds of stuff; jewelry, weapons, liquor, a pretty good stockpile of food. Who knows how many people they'd killed to get it all."

"Firefight?"

JC pursed his lips and gave a slow nod. "Yeah."

Danny knew by the look on JC's face that he'd had to kill and he didn't feel good about it, so he didn't ask for more details.

JC looked back up. "But, I got us a short barrel AR-15."

"You stuck it in the C-130?"

"Nope. Even with the short barrel, it's too big. It would draw too much attention. There's a maintenance building all the way down at the south side of the main runway. Hangar Road is the street that intersects with Yorkmount, right out front of your barracks. Follow it all the way to the end and hook a left, right before you hit that big parking lot. I stashed the rifle and six full mags inside a trash bag and tossed it in the dumpster on the right side of the building. There's a pair of bolt cutters in the dumpsters, also. Ain't nobody digging through the trash yet. They're still working their way through all those containers in the rail yard."

"None of your guys said anything to you about the rifle?"

"I told them to go hide half the liquor while I took the rifle, the rest of the liquor, and the other goods we commandeered down to the armory to turn in. Trust me, they ain't sayin' nothin'. They're all half in the bag by now, anyway. I doubt they'll even remember anything about a rifle by tomorrow. The sergeant at the armory was happy to see me coming in with two cases of liquor, a few guns, and all that jewelry. I'm sure he'll keep one case of liquor and send the other straight to Schlusser."

"Everybody is skimming the till, huh?"

"That's how these types of operations work. As

long as the boss is getting his beak wet, he doesn't care what's going on. If times get lean and he feels he's not getting his fair share, he'll start cracking heads. But for now, the gears are running smoothly."

"Any more mattresses?" Danny asked.

"I couldn't even think about mattresses today. We had so much stuff to load from that hit."

"Okay. Jorge is asking for one, whenever you can."

"Tell him, I'll see what I can do." JC gave Danny a pat on the shoulder and headed back to his barracks.

Danny waited for JC to leave then immediately took the gun, a .357 revolver, to stash under the hood of the Honda. He also put the duct tape there and softly closed the hood. He returned to the pallets and fished around inside the pack for the candy. "Skittles! Awesome!" He ate a few, and then walked inside the barracks. He found Jorge and handed him a roll of toilet paper and one of the cans of chicken.

"Oh, thank you man!"

"No problem. JC said he'd work on getting you a mattress soon."

"He's livin' good over der, no?"

Danny thought that was a curious thing to say, especially when JC was the only person who'd stuck his neck out for any of them. "Yeah, but he's looking out for us, too."

Jorge quickly went back to his bunk to hide his loot.

Danny found Sly and Friendly who were out on

the tarmac, playing spades on a wooded spool being used for a card table. Overturned five gallon buckets served as chairs. He tossed an unopened pack of Skittles on the table and winked as he walked by.

The two men smiled as they waved. "Thanks, Danny," they said, almost in unison.

"Hey!" Danny found Antoine walking by himself along the tarmac, hands in his pocket.

Antoine turned with a forced smile. "Hey, Danny."

"You look like your feeling down."

Antoine bit his lower lip. "Yeah. I know I should be grateful for what I have and stay positive about the future, but it's hard to see ever having anything else but this."

Danny spun the pack around to the front, letting it hang over his chest with the strap over his right arm. He reached inside with his left hand and pulled out a can of chicken and a bag of Skittles. "Will this cheer you up?"

"Candy? No kidding!" Antoine smiled. "Thanks, Danny. Yeah, that helps."

"You never know when something good might come your way. Do you believe in God?"

Antoine looked at Danny. "I used to."

"But what?" Danny walked beside the gentle giant.

"All this."

"So you believed in him before the EMP?"

Antoine chuckled. "You got me. I guess I didn't have time for him before. I was either chasing my football dream or scrambling to put together plan B after my injury."

"Then when the lights went out you had time for him, but you were mad at him for letting the lights go out."

Antoine shook his head with a grin. "When you say it like that, it makes me sound like the bad guy."

"I'm not judging. I'm just asking if that's how it was."

"Yeah, something like that."

Danny looked over. "Did you ever think that he loved us all enough to turn the lights out so we'd have time to get to know him?"

Antoine stopped in his tracks and looked up at the clouds. He was quiet for a moment then said, "No, I guess I never thought of it like that."

The two men resumed their walk, but neither said anything more.

The next morning, Danny awoke feeling rested from a good night's sleep on the mattress and what had turned out to pretty much be an entire day off of work. After breakfast, the men gathered by the tools.

Antoine looked around. "Anybody seen Jorge?"

"I didn't see him at breakfast," Javier said.

"We'll give him a few more minutes. Otherwise, he knows where we're working. He can always catch up," Antoine said.

While they waited Danny asked Javier, "How did it go last night?"

Javier smiled. "Good. It was nice to see her."

"What's her name?" Danny inquired.

"Sylvia. Silvy, I call her." Javier looked over

toward the terminal.

Danny knew how hard it was for a man to be away from the girl he loved. He hoped it wouldn't be long before he was back home with Alisa.

Antoine shook his finger in the air. "Okay, guys. Let's get going. Jorge will catch up."

Danny continued to think about Alisa as they marched off toward the trench.

Danny and the rest of the men were digging, when at roughly ten o'clock the Humvee pulled up. He turned to Friendly who was working right beside him. "Kind of early for his daily inspection, isn't it?"

"You can't never tell with these cats. They'll change it up on you to try and catch you slacking off."

Four guards with black polos got out of the Hummer, along with the sergeant.

"Something's not right." Danny looked at Friendly, who had a look of curiosity on his face.

"Yeah, something's up." Friendly leaned on his shovel.

The sergeant looked right at Danny, "Walker, come with us. Sergeant Gorbold needs to speak to you."

Two of the four guards had rifles and Danny had no doubt that they'd shoot him if he failed to comply. He looked at the surrounding trees to see what his options were for cover, should he choose to make a run for it. He didn't stand a chance.

The sergeant snapped his fingers. "Don't even think about it. We'll kill you in your tracks."

Danny's stomach sank lower as all doubts about the nature of his detainment disappeared with the snap of the sergeant's fingers. He laid the shovel down and climbed out of the ditch. He glanced at Antoine.

"You'll be okay," Antoine said with a nod.

Danny knew that Antoine was just saying that to make him feel better. But it was still a nice gesture.

One of the guards cuffed Danny and another patted him down before pushing him in the Humvee. It was a quick trip to the National Guard Armory where Danny had filled out his application. He thought back to that moment and wished he could erase it. *I should have never come with JC. I knew this was an insane plan from the beginning. I can't be mad at JC. I'm the idiot who went along with it.*

The Humvee drove to the backyard of the armory. Danny was quickly taken out and stuck in one of the smaller shipping containers.

"I thought I was going to see Gorbold."

The guard pushed him backwards into the container. "You will."

"I wouldn't be in any hurry if I were you. You ain't getting a promotion." The other guard slammed the door close.

Danny was alone, cuffed, and in the dark.

CHAPTER 6

I went down to the bottoms of the mountains; the earth with her bars was about me for ever: yet hast thou brought up my life from corruption, O LORD my God.

Jonah 2:6

Danny had no other available pastime besides worrying. His mind could not fend off the gruesome thoughts of how his end might come. He whispered to himself nervously. "Maybe they'll just make me kneel down on my knees, put a gun to the back of my head, and pull the trigger. It will be over with in no time." He paced back and forth as his eyes adjusted to the complete lack of light. The pinhole cracks along the edges of the door gave enough light for him to see where the walls began and ended. He walked to the rear of the container then turned to walk back. "I wonder if they've picked up JC. Of course they have. There's no way they'd pick me up before they had him in custody." Danny recalled what JC had told him about being interrogated. "Never admit you're a spy. Deny, deny, deny; no matter what."

His mind shifted to wondering about what evidence they could possibly have against him and who could have turned them in, but he dared not utter the words aloud. *Maybe Spyder saw me stashing something in the hood of the car. Maybe they found the guns. Even so, that's not proof that we're spies. Maybe Gwen said something. It had to be her. No one else knows anything. But she knows enough to bury us, especially if she told them where we're from. Gwen doesn't know about Gorbold and the assault on the farm. Maybe they haven't put it all together yet. I wonder how bad they will treat us to make us talk.*

Danny's thoughts drifted to even darker territory. He began feeling the edges of the container, looking for a sharp edge. He prayed softly, "God, you know I'd never commit suicide if there is any other way, but what if they torture me? What if it's the only way out? I can't tell them about the farm. I can't give them any information that would give them the upper hand. I can't help them find Alisa. I can't let them hurt Nana, Cami, and everyone else."

Danny heard a still small voice from inside. *Have faith.*

He pursed his lips, leaned against the wall of the

container, and slowly slid to the floor. "Yeah, right. Faith."

He sat quietly as the minutes turned to hours. Finally, the door opened. "Get up!" The silhouette of a guard stood as the only obstacle to the blinding sunlight.

Danny squinted and tried to stand. Two guards stepped in and stood him to his feet. They walked him to the armory and brought him to an empty room with only a chair. They sat him in the chair, with his hands still restrained.

Gorbold walked in. "We heard you and your friend were asking all sorts of questions about our little setup here. Wanting to know about the peninsula."

Gorbold punched Danny in the mouth, sending blood and spit flying across the floor.

Danny's heart raced and his lungs fought to take in enough oxygen. He hadn't expected Gorbold to get so rough, so fast.

Gorbold walked slowly around the back of Danny as he continued to speak. "Asking about the fuel tanks, the fuel trucks, organizational structure."

Danny shook his head as he tried to keep his eyes on Gorbold so he could brace for the next blow.

Gorbold walked around to the front of him, reared back, and struck him right in the nose.

Stars flashed before Danny's eyes. Unlike the punch in the mouth, which had taken the pain a moment to register, the agony of the second strike was immediate.

"Sir, please. With all due respect, I have no idea what you are talking about!" Danny pleaded as his mind fought to figure out where all of this was coming from. *Gwen wouldn't know anything regarding us asking about the fuel tanks or the peninsula.*

Gorbold backhanded Danny again in the mouth, pushing his lips and gums into his teeth, and causing more blood to go flying. Gorbold held Danny's driver's license. "How did you end up in Cabarrus County from Savannah?"

"I told you at the interview. I was in DC when the EMP hit. I wore out my welcome with my girlfriend's parents and I had to leave. I heard there were jobs and food here from another guy on the road."

"You're in Mecklenburg County now, son. I know all about that. I'm asking about Cabarrus."

"I don't know where that is."

"It's the county to the north. Sheriff Parnell is refusing to recognize the regent's authority. He's been hitting our troops every time we try to enter his county and now he's sent you and the cop down here to spy for him."

Danny shook his head. He knew this wasn't coming from Gwen. He strained to think how Gorbold had gotten all of this in his head. *Jorge! He wasn't at work this morning! He was cooking all of this up; trying to move up the totem pole. He was there when JC and Javi were speaking in Spanish about the peninsula. He would have been one of the only ones who could have known what they were talking about.*

Danny looked up with blood dripping from his mouth and nose. "Sir. We are not spies."

"Sure you are. The cop wound up down here from New York somehow and got a job with the Cabarrus Sheriff's Department. Parnell figured that Yankee accent would throw us off the scent and sent the both of you to infiltrate our organization. I can't figure out how you got roped into all this yet, but I will. And if I was a betting man, I'd bet you'll be the one to tell me."

Gorbold hit Danny in the face three more times in quick succession. Once in each eye and once more in the mouth. He took his bloody gloves off while he gave Danny a chance to catch his breath. "Let me explain how we work around here. I'm going to stick you back in the box overnight to think about it. Then, come morning, I'm going to drag you back out of the box and ask you again, only I'm not going to be as nice as I was today."

Danny sat in the chair, arms cuffed behind his back, with blood dripping from his nose, flowing from the corner of his mouth, and now running into his eye from the laceration above his eyelid. He was dizzy and felt sick.

"Of course, if the cop talks before you, I won't need any more information from you and I'll make an example out of you in a public execution." Gorbold squatted down to look Danny in the eyes. "A slow, painful, agonizing, methodical, public execution."

Gorbold stood back up to his feet and looked at the guard by the door. "Stick him back in the box. Send someone in there to clean him up and give him some water. I don't want him dying of infection or dehydration before I figure out what Parnell is up to and how many other men he has in here." Gorbold walked out the door. "But just water. No food. No point wasting resources."

Danny tried to stand as the guards picked him up to walk back to the container, but he couldn't see and he was dizzy, so he kept tripping. The guards gave up trying to keep him on his feet and dragged him by his arms to the shipping container. They dropped him on the ground of the metal box and closed the door.

Danny sighed a breath of relief. At least his interrogation was over with for the day. After a half an hour or so, his heart rate slowed. His face throbbed with pain all over. But eventually, exhaustion from the physical abuse and mental stress caused him to lose consciousness.

Danny awoke to the sound of the rusty hinges on the shipping container and a female voice. "By myself? Is he dangerous?"

A guard's voice replied, "He's had the stuff kicked out of him. He couldn't hurt a fly. I'll leave the door open so you can see what you're doing. If he gives you any trouble, just yell and I'll come in there and soften him up a bit more."

Danny rolled over to see the silhouette of a woman coming in the door. His right eye was nearly swollen shut, but he could still see out of his left eye. "Can I have some water?"

"Yes, just hang on for a minute."

The voice sounded familiar. Danny's good eye adjusted to the light and he could make out the form of the girl's face. "Gwen?"

The girl retrieved a bottle of water from her bin of first aid supplies and looked up. She stared closely at him, as if she knew the voice but not the face. "Danny, is that you?"

"Yeah."

"Oh my! You look . . ."

"Awful?"

She raised her brows as she put the bottle to his lips. "Just drink. I'll get you cleaned up. That will help a lot. What happened?"

Danny had no choice. He was in what is commonly referred to as *a pickle*. He was going to have to tell her everything in hopes that she would take sympathy on him and try to get him out. If she used the information for her own gain, Danny would probably die a worse death. But at the end of his current trajectory, he would be no less dead.

Gwen took a rag and poured some alcohol on it. "This is going to burn. Let me know if you need a break. I'll stop and give you another drink of water."

Danny nodded and proceeded to fill her in on the attack against the farm, and JC's idea to infiltrate the camp. He explained how Jorge had reported their conversations and accused them of being spies.

She continued to clean the blood off of his face with the cloth. "Oh, Danny. I'm so sorry. But they don't know anything for sure. They have to let you go eventually."

"They believe what they want to believe." Danny lip was so swollen, he felt like he had a small potato tucked between his upper lip and his gums. "Gorbold is convinced that we're working for

Sheriff Parnell. If we don't get out of here, he's going to kill us."

She'd cleaned the coagulated blood from above Danny's eye, which had reopened the wound. She held the cloth tight against the laceration to stem the flow. "I wish I could help."

"You can."

"How, Danny? I've got no weapon, I'm staying in the terminal, almost two miles from here, with no vehicle. What do you think I could possibly do?"

"What time is it?"

"About six-thirty. I came down here with the kitchen crew to help serve dinner. I'm on rotation. Sometimes I scrub pots, sometimes I help prepare the food for the security guys, sometimes for the terminal. Wherever they need an extra hand for kitchen work, that's where they put me."

"So you're serving the workers tonight at 7:30, right?"

"I was, but they pulled me to come in here to take care of you."

"They're not going to leave you in here with me for a whole hour. Do you know who is helping JC?"

"I didn't see any other guards standing by the other containers. I don't think JC is here."

Danny thought about that. He wondered where they could be holding him. He was sure JC was still alive; at least he had been up to that point. Could Gorbold have been lying about JC? Danny shook the thought off. For now, he had to come up with a plan. "There's a big black guy in the dining room. He sits at the table closest to the wall on the right, if you're standing behind the serving table. Second row; his name is Antoine."

Gwen held the bottle to his lips to give him a drink. "Danny, I can't get involved in this."

"That's what you said last time. You can't sit on the fence, Gwen. If you refuse to take a stand, it's the same as supporting the crimes Schlusser is committing."

Gwen feigned a laugh. "Ha! The regent is a whole different animal than Travis and Bret and those guys. You can't even compare the two."

"No, Gwen. They're exactly the same. Schlusser is a little better organized, a little better supplied, and significantly smarter, but they're exactly the same. And you're in exactly the same position."

Gwen continued to clean Danny's cuts without saying anything more.

"How many guards are watching my container?"

"One."

Danny decided to start laying out his plan anyway. He knew time was short and she was his only shot at getting out, going home, and seeing Alisa again. "There's a white Honda Pilot in the side parking of the workers' barracks. Under the hood, I've got two pistols, some oil filters, and duct tape stashed. Pull Antoine to the side and tell him what happened to me, and tell him about the guns. You guys come around at like 2:00 in the morning, when most everyone is asleep. Tell Antoine to tape the oil filter on the muzzle of the gun and kill the guard at close range. The filter will suppress the sound of the pistol. You have the second pistol with a filter taped to the barrel, in case someone else shows up."

Gwen gripped the bloody towel in her hand. "Danny, stop. I don't want to hear anymore. I can't do this."

"You can do it!"

She shook her head. "I can't. Even if I did and we got away with it, where would I go? I'm here because there's nowhere else on earth for me to go. Nobody wants me, Danny."

"You'll come back to the farm with me. You and Antoine. Alisa wants you. She's your friend. And so am I."

Gwen dropped her head and began crying. She wiped her eyes with the back of her wrist. "What about JC? He's not going to let me stay there."

"If you rescue me, he won't have any problem with you coming back. He didn't let you stay because he thought you could have done more to help Alisa."

"You don't know that."

"Gwen! I do know that. Besides, I'll make sure you stay. I promise."

"But what if Antoine sells us out? Then we'll both be dead."

Danny shook his head. "He won't. He wants a better life, just like you do."

Gwen gave him another drink. "There's guards all over the place. How am I supposed to sneak out at 2:00 o'clock in the morning?"

"All the guards are facing out, watching for potential intruders. They're not paying attention to what's happening inside the airport."

"How will we get out? There's like ten guys stationed in front of the armory, and they can call for a hundred more in a second."

"They're all facing out. We'll retreat back inside the airport and find another exit."

"Like where?"

"Antoine will know. He's been on the work crew for a long time. He knows this property like the back of his hand. He'll know where to find a weak spot so we can get out."

The guard banged on the door. "You need to be wrapping it up in there. The kitchen needs you back."

Gwen yelled back. "One more minute. I've just got to get a Band-Aid on his head." She took an adhesive bandage and covered the wound above Danny's eye.

"So?"

"So, what?"

"Are you going to help me or are you going to leave me to die?"

She sighed. "If Antoine says no, I can't do this by myself."

"But you'll ask him."

"I'll ask." She held the water bottle so Danny could finish the last swig.

"You promise?"

"I promise." She swallowed hard. "For Alisa. I owe her." Gwen put the rag, the alcohol bottle, and the empty water bottle in her bin and left.

Danny tried to find an agreeable position, but he was still cuffed. He wasn't going to be comfortable, but at least his mouth wasn't parched with thirst. He felt better having had the blood cleaned off of his face and neck. His mind bounced back and forth from wondering about JC to running through his plan to escape. *Is JC still alive? If he is, how will we find him? This place is over four square miles. If he's not being held at the armory, it will be like trying to find a needle in a hay stack. Assuming he is still alive, of course.*

Supposing Antoine goes along with the plan. Then what? Do we just run away without doing anything to slow Schlusser down? That will just prolong the agony. He'll be at the farm soon enough, and then we'll all be dead. Even Alisa.

Danny's brain churned the same things over and over as he waited to see if anyone would show up to effect his rescue.

The hours crept by as Danny sat with his muscles cramping from being unable to move his arms much. There had been no glint of light peeking through the cracks of the container door for some time. He was sure it was well after midnight. Danny heard a heavy thud, like a sack of flour being thrown against the container door. The sound was followed by the slow soft creaking of the rusted hinges.

"Danny!" Antoine's voice whispered through the crack.

"You made it!" Danny whispered his reply.

"Yeah, lets' go!"

Danny worked his way to his feet. "Check the guard. See if he has handcuff keys. Is Gwen with you?"

She peeked in. "I'm here."

"Good. Strip the guard of his rifle, gun belt,

radio, and black polo."

Antoine whispered. "These look like they could be handcuff keys."

"Only one way to find out." Danny turned around so Antoine could try out the keys.

Antoine removed the cuffs. "Okay, let's go."

Danny rubbed his wrists. "I have to go to the bathroom. I've been holding it for a while."

"Please hurry!" Gwen pleaded as she finished removing the items from the dead guard.

Danny quickly found a secluded spot to relieve himself. As he hurried back to Gwen and Antoine, he peeled off his bloody shirt.

"You're gonna have to get dressed while we move." Antoine handed the guard's black polo to Danny and led the way.

Danny took the shirt and pulled it over his head. "Hang on for a minute."

"We don't have a minute. We have got to go." Antoine kept moving with Gwen right at his side.

Danny took the guard's gun belt from Gwen as he hurried along beside them and strapped it around his waist. "Get us to a safe place so we can talk about the plan."

"What plan? There's no plan to talk about." Antoine's voice betrayed his agitation, even at a whisper. "Gwen said we bust you out then you're taking us back to some big farm in South Carolina where we'll all live happily ever after. That plan needs no explanation, as far as I'm concerned." Antoine pulled back the fence where he'd cut another hole for them to access the airport, further from the guards in the front of the armory.

Danny checked the guard's semi-automatic pistol to see if it was chambered after he crawled through the hole. "Yes, that's the plan, but that's the short version."

"And the short version is the version I agreed to." Antoine followed Gwen through the opening and shot Danny a piercing scowl.

"Just hear me out. There's a maintenance building down by the south end of the main runway. JC dropped a rifle and ammo in the dumpster next to the building. It's pretty secluded. We should be safe there for a few minutes. Do you know where I'm talking about?"

Antoine maintained a steady pace as he walked stooped over to lower his profile across the open field. "I know where it is, but we're getting out of here, right now. We've got three pistols and a rifle. That's more than enough weapons if we get out of here without being seen. As a matter of fact, we don't even need guns, because we ain't shooting nobody else. Not according to the version of the plan I agreed to."

Danny realized that Antoine had no intention of being flexible about the plan. "Okay, okay. But we at least have to stop long enough to figure out how we're going to get across the river and to the truck."

Antoine's voice sounded less irritated. "You've got a truck?"

"Yes, on the other side of the river."

"Where on the other side of the river?"

"I have to stop long enough to get my bearings. I'll tell you, but we've got to find a place to stop and figure it out."

"Don't try to pull a fast one on me, Danny."

"I won't. Can you get us to the maintenance building without being spotted?"

"Follow me." Antoine stayed low and hustled toward the trees on the other side of the open field.

Gwen stayed close to Antoine and Danny followed her. Once they reached the tree line, Antoine stood up straight and slowed his pace. "The maintenance building is right through here. Maybe a half mile."

Danny asked, "Gwen, can I have the guard's radio?"

She passed the walkie talkie to Danny. He turned the volume low. "When they figure out I'm gone; we'll hear about it over the radio."

"Once again, in the short version of the plan, we'd already be crossing the river when that happens." Antoine kept moving.

Danny asked Antoine, "Do you have any idea where they could be holding JC?"

Antoine threw his hands in the air. "None whatsoever."

"Maybe we could abduct a guard and make him tell us." Danny strained to think of a solution.

"We don't even know if he's alive. And what makes you think some random guard is going to know where he is, if he is alive." Gwen stepped high to keep from getting her feet caught in the undergrowth of the woods.

"She's right, Danny. That's a major risk that offers very little odds of paying off. I've never heard of them keeping anybody detained anywhere else besides the armory. I hate to break it to you, but

I doubt he's still alive. JC is a fighter. He probably took a few with him."

"You don't know that he's dead." Danny did not want to accept the possibility.

"We don't. But we don't know that he's alive and we sure don't know where he is, if he's alive. I do know that JC wouldn't want you getting yourself killed going on some wild goose chase trying to find him." Antoine's voice had softened.

Danny recognized the wisdom in his words. "Okay, but either way, we can't let his death or capture be in vain. We have to cripple Schlusser before we leave."

"No, Danny." Antoine glanced over his shoulder. "He who fights and runs away, lives to fight another day."

"He's right, Danny. Besides, it's two against one. You're out voted. Just show us the way to the truck." Gwen walked close to Antoine as if it were a sign of their solidarity on the issue of escaping.

Danny held up the radio. "This thing is going to start chirping any minute now. And you know what Schlusser's men are going to do?"

"Yeah, they're going to start looking for us," Gwen answered.

"Where?" Danny still held the radio in the air for effect.

"Where what?" Gwen snapped.

"Where?" Danny restated his question. "Where are they going to be looking for us?"

Antoine took a deep breath. "I know what you're trying to do here, Danny."

"And?" Danny held his hands out.

"And it ain't going to work."

"What are you guys talking about?" Gwen turned to look at Danny.

Antoine answered. "He's insinuating that Schlusser will assume that we have fled from the airport and that he'll be looking outside the airport for us, in all directions."

"Am I wrong?" Danny kept walking to keep up.

"So what should we do?" Gwen asked.

"We should hide out inside the airport until the search has been called off, and then we can slip off into the night, at our leisure," Danny replied.

"Why do I get the feeling that you're still not giving me the long version of the plan?" Antoine sounded suspicious of Danny.

"It's still evolving."

Antoine said firmly, "Well, it needs to stop evolving. We need to find the shortcut to grandma's house and get out of here."

"If you were going to hide out in the airport, where would you go?" Danny was relentless.

"I'm not hiding out in the airport, so it doesn't matter." Antoine's voice was becoming agitated again.

"But if you were, you must have thought about this before. I know you have a spot. Just tell me."

Antoine exhaled deeply. "If I was, which I'm not, I'd lay low in the sleeper cab of one of those semis that stopped in their tracks coming into the train yard cargo area."

Gwen protested. "The cargo area is one of the most heavily guarded spots in the airport. That's where Schlusser gets all of his goodies."

"Yep, but there's two tractor trailers with empty containers on the service road coming in from West Boulevard. Ain't nobody guarding them. Nothing in them."

"You can't see them from the container yard?" Danny asked.

"Nope."

"Then that's where we should hide."

"No, it's not Danny! We should get out of here. We'll all be executed as spies if Schlusser catches us!" Gwen was becoming more frantic.

Danny put his hand on her back. "It's okay, Gwen. Settle down. See, your initial instinct is to run, which is exactly what Schlusser expects us to do. Staying here is counterintuitive. Schlusser's goons would never even consider us hiding inside the airport."

Gwen turned. "Help me out here, Antoine."

Antoine was slow to answer. "He's got a point."

"Don't say that!" She objected.

"What do you guys have in the way of provisions?" Danny quizzed.

Antoine said, "I've got my one-liter water bottle, that can of chicken you gave me, my rice for lunch tomorrow, and most of that bag of Skittles."

"I've got two half-liter water bottles. No food." Gwen answered.

Danny bent back a branch that was obstructing his passage through the woods. "You've got a can opener, right?"

"Yeah. I have a pocket knife with a can opener." Antoine slowed down as the brush was getting thicker.

"We can do it. As long as I'm not moving much, I can go for a while without eating. We can conserve all of the food and eat it right before we leave." Danny stepped over a fallen tree.

Gwen stopped walking long enough to turn and look at Danny. "And when might that be?"

"Tomorrow night. We'll lay low until about this time tomorrow, and then we'll head out."

"That's the maintenance building." Antoine pointed straight ahead.

"Great!" Danny rushed to locate the dumpster. He jumped over the side and quickly found the rifle and magazines wrapped in a heavy duty trash bag. He located the bolt cutters and climbed back out of the dumpster. He unwrapped the trash bag and removed the rifle and magazines. "Can you put some of these magazines in your pack, Antoine?"

"Sure." Antoine took four of the magazines from Danny.

Danny stuck the other two magazines in his back pockets, one magazine in each. "Do you have those other oil filters?"

"No, we only had two guns. I didn't see the need for them." Antoine still held the .357 in his hand with the oil filter attached.

"That's okay. But let's go ahead and tape the two oil filters on the barrels of the rifles. If we get in trouble, they'll serve us much better than a couple revolvers" Danny held out his hand to Gwen.

She gave him the .38.

Danny quickly removed the oil filter and handed the pistol back to her. "What about the duct tape?"

"Oh, I wasn't about to leave that behind."

Antoine dug the duct tape out of his pack. He handed it to Danny.

Danny quickly affixed the oil filter to the barrel of the AR-15 then gave the tape back to Antoine. "Do yours the same way."

Antoine took the tape and used it to secure the filter to the rifle he'd taken from the guard. "How's that look?"

"As long as it's secure." Danny tested Antoine's filter to see if it would jiggle.

The radio sprang to life. "Ethan, I'm in the back of the armory. I don't see Charlie anywhere."

Another voice responded on the walkie. "He probably went to take a leak. I wouldn't worry about it. That guy in the box couldn't hurt nobody, even if he could get out."

Antoine pointed toward the container yard. "That's our cue. We need to get moving, right now."

Danny nodded and followed Antoine as he moved quickly in the direction of the train yard.

Gwen trailed closely behind Danny. "I'm scared, Danny."

"It'll be okay. They aren't even looking for anyone yet." Danny kept the radio close to his ear, listening for the next transmission.

Antoine headed due west. "We have to cross the main runway then we can use those trees for cover, all the way to the truck."

The voice came back over the radio. "Which container is Charlie supposed to be watching?"

The other voice replied. "One of those short tan ones."

"This one has blood all over the front of it."

"Probably the kid's blood. Gorbold worked him over pretty good, from what I hear. Charlie is probably taking a nap somewhere. Just look inside and make sure the kid is still breathing."

Danny ran faster, trying to make it to the tree line before the guard came back on the radio. Antoine and Gwen struggled to keep up as Danny sped across the runway.

"Charlie has been shot! The kid is gone! Charlie's rifle and gun belt are missing!"

The other man called out over the radio in a staticky voice from speaking too loudly and too close to the mic. "Lockdown! Comms relay! We have a prisoner escape. Lockdown! All department overseers, lock down your facilities and get a head count."

Danny turned to look at Gwen and Antoine who probably couldn't understand the radio since the volume was so low. "It's official."

Antoine pointed at the trees only thirty feet away. "Keep moving."

They reached the trees and paused to catch their breath. The voice came back over the radio. "Max, you better go wake up Gorbold. Austin, you and Brody both get a Deuce and a half and circle around the perimeter. Pull three guys from every watch position. I'm sure Gorbold is going to want to send out a search party. And keep your eyes open. You never know, you might get lucky and spot the guy. He's on foot and couldn't have gotten too far."

Antoine was still huffing from the run. "Let's keep going. I want to get to the truck before these guys start moving around."

They continued moving as fast as they could through the brush. Antoine pointed. "We're going to that big white rig."

"It's unlocked?" Gwen was breathing heavy.

"The window is broken, like every other vehicle in the airport." Antoine labored to speak and keep breathing as he jogged toward the white semi.

Danny was the first to reach the rig. He opened the driver's side door, which had the window broken out. He pulled Gwen up by her hand when she arrived then helped Antoine into the truck.

They got into the back of the sleeper cabin and pulled the privacy curtain shut. The three of them sat on the side of the bed and caught their breath.

Minutes later, Gorbold's voice came over the radio. "Ethan, this is Gorbold. Get a search patrol organized right now! Get six Humvees and have three of them patrol the northeast quadrant of I-485. I'm almost positive this kid is headed for Cabarrus County. He can't get there unless he crosses I-485. I want him stopped before he gets to Parnell."

"Yes, sir!" A voice replied.

"It looks like you were right," Antoine said.

"Yeah. Gorbold was convinced that we were spying for the Sheriff in the next county. He never had a clue who we really were." Danny leaned back on the bed.

"Which direction is your truck?" Gwen asked.

"Southwest," Danny replied.

"Totally the opposite direction from the way he is looking." Antoine smiled.

"But we still have to keep an eye out, in case

someone does come to search the truck. We'll sleep in shifts. There's only two beds, anyway." Danny pulled the privacy curtain slightly to the side so he could see out the front window as well as the driver's side rearview.

"One and a half beds." Antoine pointed with his thumb at the bunk over his shoulder. "That shelf up there wouldn't hold me for five seconds."

Gwen chuckled. "I'll sleep on the shelf. Unless you want me to take first watch."

Danny smiled. "No, go ahead. There will be plenty of time for sleeping over the next twenty-four hours."

Gwen climbed up onto the top bunk. "This guy was a mess."

"You don't know that. It could have been the looters who messed everything up. What's up there, anyway?"

Gwen rummaged through the things on the top bunk as she pushed them to the side to make room to lie down. "Tee-shirts, socks, a hat, trash bags, wire coat hangers . . ."

"Hang on to those trash bags, they could come in handy." Danny began looking in the cabinets of the kitchenette, not expecting to find food, but just to check if there might be some other items of value. "Look at this! A half a box of Cheez-Its!"

"Schlusser's men probably weren't taking anything that had already been opened." Antoine opened the mini fridge, the smell or rotten food quickly permeated the cab of the truck.

"Close it! Close it fast!" Gwen demanded.

"Hold on." Antoine took out three cans of ginger

ale, a can of V8, and a jar of grape jelly before closing the fridge. "It'll air out, and all of this stuff is still useable."

Gwen held one of the tee-shirts over her nose to shield it from the rancid scent. "I'm not eating anything that came out of there."

"We'll see if you're still that picky tomorrow night." Antoine winked at her.

Danny continued to search the rest of the cabinets. "And a box of corn flakes; feels like it's about two thirds full."

"That's great!" Antoine exclaimed. "We could eat the corn flakes tomorrow around noon. Then eat everything else right before we head out."

Danny nodded. "Yeah, and maybe some jelly. How much is in there?"

Antoine held his flashlight up to the jar. "Almost full. These finds will help out a lot."

"Guys, I'm really tired. I'm going to sleep. Wake me up if we get attacked." Gwen rolled up several of the tee-shirts to make a pillow.

"Sure you don't want us to let you sleep through it?" Danny chided.

"Shut up, Danny. Don't make me regret rescuing you." She turned over in the top bunk with her back to the guys.

Antoine stretched out on the bottom bunk. "Wake me up in about three hours, and I'll take second watch."

"Thanks." Danny sat in the swivel chair and found a comfortable position where he had a good view of the window and the side view mirror.

Antoine and Gwen were soon asleep and the

cabin of the truck was silent except for the rhythmic breathing of Danny's two companions. Danny wondered where JC was. *What am I going to do? I can't leave him behind, but where would I even start to look for him? If he's still alive, they've got him under heavy guard, especially after my jailbreak. What chance do I have of breaking him out with these two?*

There was no easy answer, but after mulling it over for hours, Danny decided he would have to move on without his friend. It broke his heart, and smothered him in guilt. *There's no way JC would ever leave me here, but I can't think of any course of action that would amount to more than a pointless suicide mission.*

Danny huffed. *But I'm not going to let JC's life or this mission be in vain. I'm taking out some of those fuel tanks, even if I have to do it by myself.*

Danny kept the radio on low and continued to monitor the decreasing chatter about the manhunt. According to one of the voices, Spyder's head count of the workers' barracks had revealed that Antoine was missing. Also, a young woman from the terminal was unaccounted for. Both were presumed to be spies sent by Sheriff Parnell to infiltrate the airport.

Gorbold's men had taken Danny's watch when they put him in the box, so he had to guesstimate the time. He felt himself nodding off and it seemed like three hours had passed, so he gave Antoine a nudge. "Hey, big guy."

Antoine had been sound asleep and seemed to take a while to figure out where he was. "What's up?"

"Can you stand watch for a while so I can get a few hours of sleep?"

"Oh, yeah. Sure. Any news?"

Danny shook his head. "Not really. You and Gwen are officially spies now. Other than that, no new developments. The airport is still under lockdown and the patrols sent out to I-485 haven't returned. I haven't heard anything to indicate that they are looking for us on the property."

Antoine sat up and rubbed his eyes. "You didn't see any coffee in any of those cabinets, did you?"

Danny chuckled. "No, but there's a Starbucks right up the road."

Antoine laughed. "I guess coffee is a thing of the past."

"We've actually got a pretty good stockpile of it at Nana's."

"If you'd have told me that, I'd have busted you out of here a long time ago."

"Just keep that attitude in mind for later."

"Why?" Antoine looked at Danny curiously.

"I have to hurt Schlusser's operation before I leave and I could use your help."

Antoine shook his head. "No. You have to get out of here before you get yourself killed."

"JC and I had a plan all put together to take out Schlusser's fuel supply. Those huge tanks of jet fuel are what is allowing him to spread out his operation. Without that fuel, he's contained to this general vicinity. As long as he has that fuel, Nana's farm isn't any safer for us than this sleeper cab."

"You and JC's plan almost got you killed,

Danny. Quite frankly, if it hadn't been for me and Gwen willing to stick our necks out, you'd probably be dead by tomorrow. I hate to break it to you, but the odds of JC still being alive are slim to none."

"Yeah, I know that. And that's why I can't let this all be for nothing. I have to do what he came here to do."

Antoine kept shaking his head. "You're going back on your deal to take us to a safe place. You know we would have never agreed to any of this."

"I didn't have time to lay out the whole plan, but this was always my intention."

Antoine threw his hands in the air. "I can't even imagine what Gwen will say when you break this cockamamie scheme to her. She's liable to start screaming, giving our position away."

A sleepy voice from the top bunk said, "What cockamamie scheme?"

Danny rolled his eyes. It wasn't turning out the way he'd planned for this to go. He was supposed to convince Antoine then Gwen would have no choice but to go along with it. He explained the plan and rationale behind taking out the tanks. "It's just a matter of time before Schlusser's goons come back to the farm."

"Can't we all just go hide somewhere else?" she inquired.

"Where, Gwen? You've been out there. If you don't have a defendable stronghold, a group to provide security, supplies, water, and farmable land, you're as good as dead. Where else do you think you'll find all of that? And if we let Schlusser have Nana's farm, what makes you think he won't take the next one, and the next one?'

She was silent for a while then looked down at Antoine. "He's right. They do have all of that."

Antoine looked up at her. "So you're willing to risk dying to blow up these fuel tanks?"

She exhaled deeply. "Either we risk dying now or face certain death later. I've seen it out there and there's nothing left except complete chaos or places like this where you're nothing but a slave." She paused for a while. "I'll risk dying for a chance to have what they have at Nana's farm. Freedom, community, love for each other."

Antoine looked up toward her bunk. "You make it sound like the Garden of Eden."

She let one arm hang over the side of her bunk. "Compared to this place . . . it is."

Antoine sat silently as if he were contemplating Gwen's words. Finally, he looked up at Danny. "Let's hear what you have in mind."

CHAPTER 7

But Jesus beheld them, and said unto them, "With men this is impossible; but with God all things are possible."

Matthew 19:26

Danny awoke to the sound of light rain against the top of the semi. He sat up to find Gwen and Antoine playing cards at the small table. "How long have I been out?"

Antoine glanced at his watch. "Six hours."

Gwen played her next card. "We divided up the corn flakes, so you can eat yours whenever you want. I was starving, so I ate half of mine earlier."

"Thanks." Danny pulled the privacy curtain over a bit further and looked out at the rain. "What about the water?"

"We each drank part of one of the half-liters with our corn flakes. A third of it is still left, so that's yours next to the bed." Antoine laid down another card.

Danny was parched, so he unscrewed the cap and sipped the water. "There's gotta be a way to catch some of this rain for drinking water."

"Not without getting out of the truck and being seen." Gwen didn't look up from her cards.

Danny looked toward the top bunk. "Where are those wire hangers and trash bags?"

"I put the trash bags in my pack and the coat hangers are under the mattress on the top bunk," Gwen answered.

"Can you get those trash bags for me? And can I have the duct tape from your pack, Antoine?"

The two of them laid their cards face down on the table.

"Here you go." Antoine handed the tape to Danny.

Gwen gave him the hangers and trash bags.

"Thanks." Danny fashioned a frame from the hangers then taped a trash bag to the frame. He created a small reservoir at the bottom and sat the contraption in the driver's seat with several inches of it sticking out the broken window. The falling rain trickled down the bag and into the reservoir. It was a slow process, but a little water would make a big difference.

The day passed slowly, but night time finally came. Danny went back over the plan one more time to make sure everyone was well versed in the details.

Gwen would have to get through the fence, open the valves of the Air National Guard Fuel tanks, as well as the valves on the fuel trucks. She'd have to light the fire then retreat via the tree line one mile south then two miles west to get out of the airport, through the south side of the train yard. From there, she'd still have another mile to follow the power line clearing, which would take her to the bank of the river. She would wait there for Danny and Antoine.

Danny and Antoine would sneak up to the north side of the airport and take out the two guards at the fuel tanks. Then, they'd slip around to the side and kill the other four guards before any of them could get off a shot. Next, they would open the tanks, let them drain for at least five minutes then light the fire.

They would retreat along the back side of the train tracks to the lagoon then follow the tree line along the branch to the river. Once there, they'd appropriate a boat or flotation device which would take them down river to Gwen's location, pick her up, and then cross the river to the Allen Steam plant where the truck was stashed.

"You know this is impossible, right? I mean, I'm committed to trying, but statistically speaking." Antoine crossed his arms.

"With God, all things are possible," Gwen said.

Danny looked at her curiously.

She smiled. "I've been reading that little Bible you guys gave me. The first night after I left the farm, I was like, I'll never survive. I had all but given up and I opened that Bible. That verse was on the first page I turned to. I took it as a sign that if I'd believe in God, he would get me through somehow.

"I made it here, which isn't great, but I'm still alive. Then I ran into you again, Danny. I mean, what are the odds of that? How else can you explain it?"

Danny thought about how Gwen was choosing faith over fear because of what God had brought her through. He considered everything God had protected him from and it encouraged him as well. He smiled back at her. "Yeah, with God, all things are possible."

Antoine laughed. "If we pull this off, I'll be a believer, too."

Danny winked and pointed at Antoine. "I'm going to hold you to that."

Over the following few hours, Danny drilled with Antoine to get him used to magazine changes for the AR-15. He gave Gwen the semi-automatic pistol that he'd taken from his guard, exchanging it for the .38 snub nose, which would be his backup gun. Danny did the best he could to remember all the basics that JC had taught him. He had Antoine and Gwen both drill with their weapons, dealing with jams, teaching them to remove the magazine, clear the chamber, and then reinsert the magazine and rack a fresh round.

"We've done this twenty times!" Gwen complained.

"Good, then you're halfway done." Danny chuckled.

"Ugh!" she groaned.

"Being a little faster at changing a magazine or clearing a jam could be the difference between life and death. Besides, you've already embarrassed Antoine enough at cards for one day." Danny winked. Once he was satisfied that they were ready, he said, "Let's eat our food then pray. If we're going to pull this off, we'll need all the help we can get."

All the water had been drunk. The jelly and the cornflakes were eaten. They divided the V8, crackers, rice, chicken, and Skittles, giving larger portions of each to Antoine as he had a more substantial caloric need. Each of them had a room-temperature ginger ale to themselves.

After they finished eating, Danny said a prayer asking for safety. Gwen did likewise. Antoine bowed his head as the other two prayed. Afterward, he simply said, "God, I'm sorry I haven't made time for you. If you get us through this alive, I'll make sure that changes."

"Amen!" Danny patted the big man on his shoulder. "Let's roll out."

"It's still raining. Are you sure the plan will work?" Gwen quizzed.

"It's just drizzling. It's not enough rain to put out a jet fuel fire. But make sure you keep your lighter dry." Danny took down the water catchment contraption from the window and removed a piece of the trash bag. He dried it off with one of the tee-shirts from the top bunk, tore it in two and handed half to Gwen. "Wrap your lighter in this and keep it snug in your pocket."

They exited the truck quietly and they were on

their way. They moved slowly, conserving their energy until they hit the open runway. Once there, they sprinted across and into the shadows of the building. The rain was uncomfortable, but it guaranteed them that they wouldn't run into anyone who was simply out for a midnight pleasure stroll. It also meant there would be no glaring moonlight to give away their positions to any of the guards working the perimeter fence. Antoine led them through the least populated path to the Air National Guard base, staying close to trees and shrubs along the edges of parking lots, whenever possible. They finally reached a secluded spot behind the tanks. Danny cut the fence with the bolt cutters and gave them back to Antoine to stow in his pack. "Hide under that fuel truck for fifteen minutes then open up all the valves on the back of all three trucks. Next, go open the valve on the tanks. Let it drain for about five minutes then light the fire. That should give us just enough time to get to the main tanks and do what we've got to do."

Gwen began to crawl through the hole. "I don't have a watch."

Danny pursed his lips. "Okay, one Mississippi, two Mississippi, make tick marks in the dirt or something to track the minutes."

Once through the hole, she looked back. "Starting now?"

"No, as soon as you get under the truck." Danny waved at her. "Godspeed. We'll see you on the river bank."

"What if I get lost?" She sounded nervous to be left on her own.

Antoine shook his head. "You can't get lost. When you come out of those woods on the south side, it's a 100-foot wide clearing for those main power lines. Take a right and follow the power line clearing all the way to the river."

"Okay. You guys be safe." Gwen's face was full of anxiety.

"You, too." Danny gave her one last wave for encouragement and began moving quickly toward the main tanks.

Antoine stayed close to Danny's side, instructing him on the path of least resistance. They moved at a steady pace reserving themselves for the one-mile sprint they'd have to make across the easternmost runway and the main terminal tarmac. Once they reached the open area, Danny began praying, "God make us fast and invisible."

The rain provided some covering, but it would take more than luck for them not to be spotted running across the tarmac with rifles in hand. Danny pushed himself hard, but was careful not to outrun Antoine. They made it to a massive collection of baggage carts on the north side of the terminal, which provided visual cover in the low light and drizzling rain.

"About . . . another . . . five hundred . . . feet." Antoine fought to catch his breath. "Through these trees." He breathed deeply. "And across long term parking."

Danny nodded. He looked back over his shoulder to make sure Gwen hadn't lit her fire yet. Seeing no glow in the sky behind him, he pressed on. They crossed Birmingham Parkway into the rental car lot where they had good cover and were able to spot the guards at the entrance to the main fuel tanks.

"We'll cut this fence, but crawl through, and then shoot both guards from a prone position. As soon as they're down, we have to run to the gate, get inside and locate the four guards on the back side. We have to try to get a visual of all four before we start shooting."

"What if we can't see all four?"

Danny continued cutting the fence. "Then we'll improvise."

"Improvise? Danny, we didn't talk about improvising! Explain to me what you have in mind."

Danny looked back. "If we're not inside that gate when Gwen lights her fire, we're going to have a lot more improvising to do, so let's just get the ball rolling."

"I don't like this, Danny." Antoine scowled as he got down to crawl through the hole in the fence.

"We'll be fine." Danny considered all the times JC had coaxed him through questionable maneuvers. Now it was Danny's turn to step up to the plate and lead. He wondered how many times JC had said, *we'll be fine*, with as little confidence as he had at that moment.

Danny crawled through the hole, switched on the reflex sight, took aim and looked over at Antoine. "Ready?"

Antoine only had backup sights, which barely cleared the top of the oil filter taped to the end of his barrel. He glanced at Danny, took a deep breath and said, "Ready."

Danny counted down. "Three, two, one."

The bolts on both rifles snapped almost in unison, followed by a mild supersonic crack.

The guard on Danny's side grabbed his chest, looked down then straight out at Danny.

Danny pulled the trigger again and the man fell straight down.

Antoine also took out his target in two shots. "Not exactly silent."

"Silent . . . er." Danny whispered.

"Kyle, what was that noise?" One of the guards from the back called out as he and another guard began walking toward the gate.

"They hear us!" Antoine's voice sounded afraid.

"They heard the sonic crack. They probably don't know where it's coming from, though. Let's see if they all come to us."

"Before they get the word out over the radio?"

"Here they come, get ready." Danny took aim at the two guards coming from the back.

Click, crack! Click, crack! Click, crack. Danny fired three rounds at his target.

Antoine did the same, killing the guard on his side.

Danny got up and sprinted toward the gate. As he reached the first downed guard, he heard the man's radio. "All available personnel. We have a fire at the Air Guard fuel tanks. We need everyone down here immediately."

Danny looked past Antoine, who was close on his heels, to see a bright orange glow against the rain clouds above the Air National Guard base.

"Hey, what's going on?" Two more guards were

coming from the back fence. Both were raising their weapons to fire on Danny and Antoine.

Danny's rifle was already leveled. He opened up on the two guards until his magazine was empty. Antoine followed suit. Both guards went down, but each fired off a round or two as they fell.

Danny quickly changed magazines. "We're going to have company pretty soon. You open the shut-off valve and I'll get a hole cut in the back fence. If you see someone coming, just light the fire, regardless of how much fuel has dumped."

"Got it." Antoine turned to let Danny retrieve the bolt cutters from his pack then rushed toward the large round shut-off valve.

Danny worked as quickly as he could, cutting the fence. As soon as he had a hole he felt Antoine could fit through, he yelled, "Light it up!"

Antoine stood back from the gushing flow of jet fuel and sparked the lighter. The liquid had only just begun to flow out of the pipe, but it quickly flashed into a searing inferno. Antoine dashed towards the fence.

"Go, go, go!" Danny held the fence back as he saw headlights from two separate military trucks coming towards them from both directions.

Once Antoine was through, Danny crawled through, stood up and ran to the train tracks.

Rifle fire broke out from the other side of the flames. Men from one of the trucks had spotted them and were intent on killing Danny and Antoine. Several rounds crashed into the gravel near their feet.

"We have to get under the overpass before the

trucks can get to Marshall Drive. Otherwise we'll be cut off and we'll never make it to the river." Antoine pointed to the road going over the tracks as he continued to move quickly.

Bullets continued to pepper the foliage on the side of the tracks. Danny ran as hard as he could, leaving Antoine several yards behind. He figured if he could get under the overpass in time, he could provide cover fire for Antoine, even if his friend was a little slower. Danny finally reached the overpass, but could see the headlights heading up Dowd, in his direction.

He went under the bridge and waited in the trees for Antoine. "Come on! Hurry!"

Antoine soon caught up. "Into the woods. There's a service road on the other side."

Danny followed him and the two of them maintained the fastest pace possible.

"If we can get under I-485 without being spotted, we're home free," the big man said as he ran.

As they came back out onto the train tracks, Danny could see the glow of the headlights on the I-485 overpass. He ducked back into the tree line. "We're cut off."

"Let me think." Antoine followed him and stopped to catch his breath. "We'll go north, to Wilkinson. That will take us under 485."

"And to the river?"

"Yeah. We'll have to move about a mile through the neighborhoods, but there's hardly anybody left over there."

"That will put us in the water way north of where we had planned. Won't we end up floating right by the peninsula, where Schlusser and all of his top goons are living?"

"Yeah."

"We can't do that. You know they'll be watching the water. Especially the ones guarding his house. Can we get past 485 and reconnect with the train tracks? If so, we could cross there."

"Yeah, but I would imagine the train bridge is being guarded."

Danny smiled. "It wasn't when JC and I got here."

"What about Gwen?"

Danny shrugged. "We'll find a way back across to get her after we get south of the peninsula."

Antoine lifted his eyebrows. "Sounds like a plan."

The two men began what was to be about a three-mile detour.

"Let's keep moving as fast as possible. We have to get outside of the 485 beltway. They could have a guard on the Wilkinson overpass if Schlusser expands the search perimeter."

The two men stayed close to the tree line and charged as hard as they could toward the underpass.

"No guard yet." Danny said when they reached the underpass.

"Then let's get going while the going is good." Antoine led the way beneath the highway, stopping before crossing the road to check for a potential patrol.

Once they crossed beneath I-485, they moved quickly, but didn't run. For one thing, they were moving through heavy brush, and for the other, neither of them had the energy to run another three miles.

Whenever possible, they used the shrubs and trees for cover as they moved west on Wilkinson. When no natural cover was available, they moved behind the buildings. It slowed their movement, but they couldn't risk being exposed on the open road. One patrol driving along the street could bring their mission to an abrupt end.

A long string of businesses and commercial buildings lined Wilkinson Boulevard, all of which had tall chain-link fences separating the back lots. Danny and Antoine developed a system of Danny climbing to the top, Antoine passing him the bolt cutters, Danny cutting the top row of barbed wire or concertina and handing the cutters back to Antoine to place back in his pack before climbing over himself.

They finally reached a dirt trail. Antoine paused to catch his breath. "This should take us to the tracks."

"Let's hope they don't have a guard posted there." Danny began walking down the path.

"And if they do?"

"I guess we take them out if we can. We'll approach from inside the tree line. If it is guarded, I doubt there will be more than four men. Schlusser is spread pretty thin. That's the only thing we've got going for us."

Danny and Antoine had less than a mile to walk to the tracks. Since both were growing tired and the immediate danger of capture had passed, they moved at a slightly slower pace. Danny looked back toward the main tanks and felt satisfied by the brilliant orange glow against the low clouds above; evidence that the fire was still consuming the regent's most precious resource. He continued to tread along the passage, turning for a glimpse at the sky above the Air National Guard. While not as bright as the illumination above the main tanks, it too reflected scorching blazes below. "Looks like the fires are still burning. JC said if it keeps burning for two hours, those tanks will probably fail."

Antoine paused to look over his shoulder. "It's not showing any signs of stopping. What happens when the tanks fail?"

Danny turned his eyes back to the pathway. "I guess tanks will crack and the fuel will gush out all over the place."

Just then, a giant explosion lit up the sky and filled the air with the echo of the blast.

Danny turned toward the Air National Guard. "What was that?"

Antoine shook his head. "I don't know, maybe the fuel truck."

Spooked by the detonation, Danny picked up the pace. "There's the tracks. Let's keep a low profile until we can determine if they're being guarded."

Antoine nodded and stepped inside the brush along the side of the path.

The two of them proceeded slowly, being careful not to step on any twigs that might snap and reveal their location. Danny edged ever closer to the tracks. He whispered, "I'll step out first and cross the tracks. If I get all the way across without getting shot at, you follow. If you see trouble, lay down cover fire so I can retreat."

Antoine nodded.

It was the maneuver JC had used before, so it made sense to utilize it again. Danny took a deep breath before stepping out into the open. He knew that if he were to be attacked from the other side his chances were slim, but he was a smaller and faster target than Antoine. Danny walked quickly out onto the tracks. He looked down at the house on the river bank below. He saw the same inner tube on the dock that he had seen a week before. *Has it only been a week? It feels like I've been gone from Alisa for months.*

Then, a thought struck him. *That would be the perfect flotation device to retrieve Gwen from the other side of the river. It's big and cumbersome, but it's not heavy.* Danny turned and sprinted back towards Antoine.

"What's wrong? Did you see somebody?"

"No. I found a flotation device we can use to get Gwen." Danny pointed down toward the bank. "Follow me and give me cover while I slip down to the dock."

"Danny, we've got a couple miles to walk to where we're going to cross the river."

"I know, but it's a black inner-tube float. If we use it to get Gwen, it won't reflect light, and we can stay down in the water, very low profile. I can't think of anything more perfect and I doubt we'll happen upon another one. We better strike while the iron is hot."

Antoine nodded his approval. "Okay."

Danny quickly made his way down to the dock

and retrieved the float. It was bigger than it had looked from the tracks above. He placed the large flotation device over his shoulder and made his way back up to the tracks. He whispered to Antoine, "You lead. If we get in trouble, I'll need you to lay down some cover fire until I can get this stupid thing off my shoulder and get my rifle up to a firing position."

"Alright. I suppose you've already cleared the tracks. If anyone was on the other side, they'd have shot you when you turned around."

"You're probably right, but we'll still go one at a time, just in case." Danny took the float off his shoulder so he could cover Antoine.

Antoine hustled across the tracks and dropped into the shrubbery on the side. Danny picked up the inner tube and scurried across the bridge.

"You know the way from here, right?" Antoine quizzed.

"Yeah, the power plant is straight down these tracks. We walked it twice."

"Then give me the float and you take the lead."

Danny complied, handing the giant float to the huge man. It didn't look nearly as unmanageable on Antoine's large frame as it had felt to Danny. "I've got one quick stop to make." Danny led the way to the place where the tracks split and recovered his grandfather's .32 revolver.

"You guys had this pretty well planned out, didn't you?"

"We thought we did." Danny pursed his lips as he thought about where JC was being held and how he was being treated. "Either way. It had to be done.

Otherwise it was only a matter of time until Schlusser's men came back to the farm to wipe us out for good."

The two men continued down the tracks, moving as quickly and quietly as they could. They finally reached the steam-powered electrical plant and arrived at the location where Danny and JC had stashed the guns, food, and spark plugs.

"Wait right here." Danny crawled under the fence and dug up the PVC pipe. He quickly unscrewed the clean out plug and retrieved the items inside. He passed them through to Antoine and crawled back to the other side.

"MREs?" Antoine looked at the food Danny had handed him.

"Yeah, let's eat one on the way. But first, let's get the spark plugs replaced in the truck. We're not under duress right now, but who knows what can change between now and the time we get back with Gwen."

The two of them hastily moved to the parking lot and changed out the spark plugs in Catfish's old truck. Then, they set out to retrieve Gwen.

Danny looked over at the dazzling red sky just as a second explosion flashed from the direction of the Air National Guard. "Another fuel truck?"

"That would be my guess." Antoine had already opened one of the pouches and was pouring the contents into his mouth. He passed the pouch to Danny. "Spaghetti. Best thing I've eaten in over a month."

Danny took the pouch, and like Antoine, poured some of the contents straight into his mouth. A few noodles didn't quite clear his lips, so he sucked them in and chewed. "Wait til you get to Nana's. You'll eat better than you've ever eaten in your life."

Antoine was now working on another pouch from inside the MRE. "Don't tease a big man about food."

Danny laughed. "It's true. I'd never tease you about food."

Antoine pointed across the river. "That's the clearing. She should be right there. As long as she didn't get caught."

"And as long as she didn't give up on us. We took quite a bit longer than we anticipated." Danny worked his way through the brush to the bank. "Same drill as the tracks. I'll swim across, you cover me."

Antoine nodded. "Yeah, alright."

Danny took his boots off and emptied his pockets into his boots. He looked at the water and considered whether to take off his pants and shirt. He dipped his toe in the water. It was cold, frigid, in fact. *Clothes aren't going to keep me any warmer in the water. If I get them wet, I'll be cold all the way home.* Danny stripped off his shirt and cargo pants, leaving only his boxer shorts. He placed the float in the water and began to wade in. The chilly river sent shivers of pain all through his body. Once he was in knee deep, Danny took a deep breath and let himself fall into the bitter muddy waters of the Catawba. He gasped as the shock echoed up his spine and neck. Danny pushed the float out and began kicking toward the other side. It became obvious that he was drifting south at a swift pace, so he corrected his course to account for the current. Danny continued to kick toward the opposite bank at a steady clip, focusing on keeping his feet below the water so not to make any unnecessary splashing noise. Fighting the current required more energy and time, but Danny eventually reached the other side. Coming back out of the water in the nippy, April, night air was even worse than getting in the water. His teeth chattered as he scanned the edge of the woods for a signal from Gwen.

"Danny!" A loud whisper came from the shrubs.

"Gwen?" He pulled the float from the water so he could rub his arms for warmth.

She emerged from the brush. "Is Antoine alright?"

"He's on the other side. He's fine. We need to get going."

"Is it cold?"

Danny didn't have the patience to answer. Shivering, he said, "Come on, let's go. Antoine is straight across from us, but we're going to let the current push us south and walk back up to his location. Trust me, that will be much easier than fighting the current. Do you still have those trash bags from the semi?"

"Yeah. In my pack."

"If I were you, I'd stuff my clothes in a trash bag, my shoes in another, and my pack in another. Then, I'd double bag them all. You don't want to be riding home all wet."

"Okay, but don't look at me until I'm in the water."

"I'm not going to look, Gwen."

"And don't tell Alisa we went skinny dipping."

Danny rolled his eyes. That was the last thing on his mind. Getting home was his only concern. "We're not skinny dipping. We're wearing our underwear, which isn't much different than a swimsuit. But anyway, this is survival. I don't think she'll care."

"And you're not going to look, right?"

Danny waited out into the water with his back to Gwen. "Just hurry!"

"Oh! It's freezing!"

"Just jump in quick and get it over with." Danny edged out farther from the bank.

"It's too cold. I can't!"

"Okay, I'll tell Alisa you said hi." Danny knew Gwen couldn't see his mischievous grin.

"I saved your life, Danny! Wait up."

"And I can't tell you how much I appreciate it, but I have to get out of here before Schlusser's men show up. Otherwise, your sacrifice will be for nothing."

"Okay! Okay, I'm coming. Hang on! Oh, it's so cold!"

"Just jump in. I'm telling you." Danny waited. He heard her plop into the water.

"Ahhh! I'm freezing!" Gwen came around to the side of the inner tube holding her collection of trash bags.

"Give me your heaviest bag." Danny held one hand up out of the water.

She passed him the largest trash bag. "My pack. Please don't lose it. It's all I have."

"I've got it." Danny positioned the bag on top of the float so that the weight was supported by the inner tube. "Hang on, kick with your legs, but keep your feet submerged."

Gwen rested one arm over the side of the inner tube and began kicking. "Okay, why?"

"Piranha. Splashing makes you look like an injured animal and they'll be drawn to you thrashing around."

"What!" Gwen began swimming harder toward the other side.

Danny fought back a chuckle.

Gwen looked at his face. "Danny! There's no piranha in the Catawba. I should have left you in the box."

The two of them had roughly 1000 feet to swim to the other side. They reached the west bank of the river in much less time than it had taken Danny to cross, both because they weren't fighting the current and because the two swimmers were able to propel the float across quicker than one.

Antoine walked south as they crossed, keeping pace with their southerly drift while the current pushed them down river. He was waiting on the bank when they arrived.

"Antoine, turn around until I get out and get dressed." Gwen instructed.

Danny took all of the bags ashore and left Gwen with the float. "I'll leave your clothes at the water's edge. I'll walk in a little further and get dressed."

"Thanks." Gwen waited to get out.

Danny got out of the water, squeegeeing himself off with his hands. He rung out the legs of his boxer shorts as best he could without removing them.

Antoine handed him his boots and clothes. "How's the water?"

Danny's teeth chattered. "Like bath water. Why don't you go in for a dip?"

Antoine chuckled.

Gwen complained as she came out of the river. "Oh. It's worse coming out that getting in!"

"Just tell us when you're decent. We need to get moving." Danny's feet were still damp as he put his socks on.

Seconds later, Gwen walked up to the men. "You can turn around now. Thanks."

"We've got food at the truck." Antoine carried the rifles and the trash bag containing Gwen's pack.

"Really? Like what?"

"MREs." Danny took his rifle from Antoine as they began walking back toward the truck.

Antoine pointed to the bright glow of fire coming from the airport. "See what you did?"

"Wow." Gwen was still shivering.

"Good job, Gwen." Danny patted her on the shoulder. "You, too, Antoine."

"Happy to help." Antoine smiled.

"Thank you, Jesus!" Gwen exclaimed. "We completed our mission and we're all going home alive."

Danny's face grew more somber. "All except for JC."

Antoine and Gwen were quiet for the rest of the walk back to the truck. When they arrived, Danny passed an MRE to Gwen. "Here you go."

"Thanks!" She tore right into it.

They got in the truck, with Gwen in the middle and Antoine in the passenger's seat. Danny stuck the keys in the ignition and began shaking his head. "I don't think I can leave without JC."

Antoine's voice was soft. "If I knew where he was, I'd say let's go get him right now, Danny. But I don't. And neither do you."

Danny toyed with the dangling key chain but refused to start the engine. "He'd never leave me behind."

"So what do you think he would want you to do?" Gwen was eating her chili-mac MRE. "Would he want you to get yourself killed looking for him or get the information you have back to the farm and try to protect his family? I mean, wasn't looking out for his family the whole reason he came here in the first place?"

Danny couldn't argue. She was right. She was exactly right. He could almost hear JC telling him to quit messing around and get back to the farm, right down to his Yankee accent. Danny looked at her with a subtle nod. "Yeah. That's what JC would want." Danny turned the key and they were on their way home.

CHAPTER 8

Sing unto God, sing praises to his name: extol him that rideth upon the heavens by his name JAH, and rejoice before him. A father of the fatherless, and a judge of the widows, is God in his holy habitation. God setteth the solitary in families: he bringeth out those which are bound with chains: but the rebellious dwell in a dry land.

Psalm 68:4-6

Danny pulled up to the old white farmhouse. Nick and Steven were on watch in the pinnacle and walked out to greet them. The sun was just starting to peek over the horizon in the east.
"Where's JC?" Nick's face showed his concern.

Danny sighed. "You guys remember Gwen, she helped Antoine bust me out of jail. I'd be dead if she hadn't been there." He continued to debrief Nick and Steven on the events of the past week.

The door of JC's trailer opened and Melissa came out holding Annie's hand. The two of them walked toward the truck. Melissa's smile dissipated as she got closer and closer. "She heard the truck and headed straight for the door. She sleeps with one eye open, waiting for JC to come home." Melissa didn't ask where JC was.

Annie, however, wasted no time. "Where's daddy?"

Danny had rehearsed telling Melissa on the way home. He'd played out the scene over and over on the trip back. He'd mentally prepared himself to accept whatever outburst there might be. He'd steeled himself, in case he had to tell Chris or Jack; he was ready to be cussed out, hit, punched, or attacked, by either or both of JC's sons. But to look at this precious little girl and tell her he did not know where her father was, or even if he was still among the living, Danny was unprepared. Tears formed in his eyes as he knelt down beside her. "I don't know, sweetheart. I don't know."

Melissa was fighting back tears herself. "Come on, Annie. Let's go back in the house." She picked Annie up and carted the little girl back to the trailer without waiting for an explanation on JC's whereabouts. It was as if nothing would ease her grief, so why should she bother with the gory details?

"You guys look like you need some rest," Nick

said. "I'll get some water boiling for showers. Steven, why don't you show Antoine and Gwen to an empty trailer."

"Sure thing." Steven picked up his crutches and led the way. "Antoine, you can take the small trailer in the front row, closest to the house. No one has ever used it.

"Gwen, we'll put you in the big trailer behind the barn. It was the Cooks' trailer, but Pauline moved back to her house after Rocky was killed. I don't know if she'll come back or not. But if she does, she'll need some company. She's been having a real hard time without Rocky."

Gwen lowered her head. "Danny told me what happened. I'm sorry you guys got hit so hard."

"It's a tough world." Steven paused to open the door to the small trailer for Antoine then looked back at Gwen with a look of compassion. "But I'm sure I'm preaching to the choir."

"Thanks." Antoine looked at the trailer like it was a mansion and slowly made his way inside.

Steven cut across the courtyard, past the solar shed to the large fifth-wheel trailer behind the barn. He opened the door. "Let us know if you need anything. Alisa and Dana probably have some clothes that will fit you. I'm sure Nana will be making breakfast soon. So get cleaned up, eat something with us, and then you can rest."

"Thank you, Steven." Gwen smiled. "And thank you for giving me a second chance."

Steven patted Danny on the back. "You brought my best friend home. You've earned it."

Danny and Steven left Gwen at the trailer and

made their way back toward the house. Steven moved at a steady pace on his crutches. "I know somebody is going to be very happy to see you."

Danny nodded. "I'll be happy to see her, too. But I want to get cleaned up first. My face looks like a watermelon that rolled off the back of a truck."

Steven took a close look at Danny's black eyes and busted nose. "Yeah, that's gonna take some time. I don't think it's going to wash off."

Danny snickered. "I know, but being all nasty makes it look that much more pathetic."

"Okay, I'll get you a towel and meet you out back by the shower booth."

"Thanks." Danny took the first batch of water that Nick was heating over the fire. He didn't wait for it to get hot. He let it heat up just long enough to knock the chill. Normally, he'd have let Gwen have the first shower, but he hadn't seen his wife in more than a week and that overruled his inclination to be a gentleman. Once cleaned up, he tiptoed up the stairs and opened the bedroom door. He quietly crawled in bed next to Alisa and held her in his arms.

She stirred gently at first. Then, suddenly rolled over. "Danny!"

"Hey." He smiled and ran his fingers through her hair. He'd missed being beside her.

"Danny, you're home!" She looked at him. "What happened to you? Who hurt you?"

"Kind of a rough bunch, up there in Charlotte."

She wrapped her arms around him and pulled him close. "Oh, I'm just so glad you're home, that you're alive. I've been praying every day. You guys got back just now?"

"JC didn't come back."

She pulled back so she could look into his eyes. "What happened? Is he dead?"

Danny shook his head. "I don't know." He told her what had happened at the airport, reliving the nightmare which he would have to tell again and again over the following days.

"So Gwen is here? At Nana's farm?" Alisa looked perplexed.

"Yeah. She's staying in the Cooks' trailer for now."

Nana called up the stairs. "Y'all come on, breakfast is ready."

Danny rolled over. "I'm so tired, but I'm hungry too. I've been eating almost nothing but rice for the last week."

Alisa kissed him gently, as if she didn't want to hurt his bruised face. "You stay here. I'll bring you breakfast in bed. Then you can sleep all day."

Danny smiled. "If Nana will let you get away with it, I'll accept your offer."

Alisa got dressed and scampered down the stairs. Danny looked at the four walls around him. He was safe, he was home, and he should have been happy, but he knew JC was none of those things.

Alisa returned minutes later with a large serving platter that was being used as a tray. "Nana said you could have breakfast in bed, but just this once. She made all of your favorites; biscuits, eggs, grits, country ham, and red-eyed gravy."

Danny was very hungry. He'd expended a lot of calories in the operation and hadn't really been full once over the entire week. Alisa sat beside him and took a few bites from Danny's plate while he filled her in on all the details of the mission.

After he'd finished eating, he yawned. "Being back here, in my own bed with a full stomach, I'm suddenly so sleepy."

Alisa kissed him on the head and picked up the tray. "You rest. I'll see you this afternoon."

"Okay. I love you. I missed you more than you can imagine."

"Me, too." She smiled as she left the room with the tray.

Danny closed his eyes to pray for JC, asking that God would bring him back, somehow. As he was praying, he drifted off into a deep sleep.

Danny was abruptly dislodged from his sweet slumber by the sound of the door being opened all of a sudden. He rolled over to see what the cause of the commotion was.

Alisa entered the room, followed by Dana and Melissa.

Alisa was the first to speak. "Danny, we need you downstairs."

Danny sat up quickly. "Are we begin attacked?"

Dana answered, "No, it's Chris and Jack. They're gearing up to go look for JC."

"Give me a second to get dressed. I'll be right down." Danny shook his head.

"You have to stop them, Danny," Melissa pleaded as she turned to go out the door. "I can't take losing them too."

Danny waved the girls out so he could put his

pants on. "Yeah, I'll be right down." He got dressed as quickly as possible, then grabbed his pistol belt, fastening it on the way out the door.

The girls were waiting at the bottom of the stairs.

"Who are they planning to take with them?" Danny tugged at the tail of his tee-shirt to straighten it.

"Just Christopher's buddy, Clay," Melissa replied.

Alisa crossed her arms. "Don't let them recruit you, Danny Walker! You just got back."

Danny shook his head. "No, there's no way. We'd need an army to attack the airport head on. Anything else is a suicide mission." The second the words were out of his mouth, he wished he'd found another way to say it. He watched as the ill-timed statement found its way to the core of Melissa's soul, knocking the life out of her.

"I . . . didn't mean it like that." Danny put his arm around Melissa's shoulder.

"Yes you did." She looked at the floor. "Anyway, you're not telling me anything I don't already know."

Danny gave her a quick hug then pulled back to look her in the eyes. "And you've tried to dissuade them from going?"

"Yeah. I've pleaded, I've yelled, I've cried, but nothing works."

Danny gave her shoulders a squeeze. "I'll talk to them, but if they wouldn't listen to you . . ."

Melissa looked into his eyes. "I know. No promises. But please, Danny, try to talk some sense into them."

Danny looked at Alisa and Dana. "You two, go find Nick. Tell him what's going on. Maybe since he's former military, Chris and Clay will listen to his reasoning."

Alisa and Dana nodded and took off, out the door.

Melissa crossed her arms. "They're out front. They're putting all their gear in Catfish's truck right now."

"Get Annie. Bring her out to the truck. If they're going to go, make sure they know what they're leaving behind." Danny headed out the door.

Danny jogged over to the truck. "Hey guys."

"Hey, Danny." Jack hoisted his pack over the side of the truck, leaning it up behind the cab. "You coming with us?"

"You know I can't do that, Jack. I've seen the layout. You need a lot more people and a much better plan than you can throw together on the road."

Chris folded up his ghillie suit on the tailgate and stuffed it into a mesh laundry bag. "You guys got in and out. It must be pretty porous."

Danny shook his head. "Not at all. They have a patrol set up about every three-hundred yards. To get in, we had to give up all of our guns. To get out, we had to take out a patrol then outrun the guards on either side before they gunned us down. And all that was in the middle of the night."

"Then we'll hit them at night." Chris situated the ghillie suit next to Jack's pack.

Danny stuck his hands in his pockets. "So, what's your plan?"

"We'll snatch up one of Schlusser's guards and drag him off to a quiet place where we can get to know each other a little better." Chris took a metal ammo box that Clay had just brought from their trailer.

Jack finished explaining the plan. "We'll start cutting on the guard until he tells us where dad is or he quits breathing."

Danny pursed his lips. "He'll probably quit breathing first. I don't think the average guard is going to know where your dad is. Gorbold was convinced that we were all spies for the sheriff in the next county to the north of Charlotte. I'm sure he's got your dad somewhere no one knows about."

"We killed Gorbold." Jack furrowed his brow.

Danny sighed. "There's another one. His brother."

Chris leaned on the side of the truck bed and said matter-of-factly, "Then we'll snatch up Gorbold."

Danny shook his head. "Not a chance. He's surrounded by guards all the time. You'd need an army."

"We have to try." Jack checked the magazines in the front of his tactical vest.

Chris checked the magazine in his .338 Lapua sniper rifle. "He'd never leave us in a pit like that."

Danny took a deep breath and let it back out. "No. He wouldn't. But he'd go in with a feasible plan. If you three run off and get yourselves killed, we'll be short three men when we come up with one. That might be the thing that swings the odds in Schlusser's favor and ultimately causes our mission to fail, leaving your dad to rot."

Jack didn't say anything, but it was obvious that Danny's reasoning was getting through to him. He looked at his older brother as if he were waiting for his reply.

"We're not going to fail. We're going to bring him back." Chris opened the door of the truck. "Let's go guys."

Nick walked up as the others were getting in. "You guys can't take the truck."

"Catfish said we could." Chris said turning the key.

"It ain't up to Catfish. The truck is communal."

"Like heck!" Chris was getting agitated.

Nick leaned in the door to look at Clay. "You think this is a good plan?"

"He's my buddy." Clay looked straight forward. "If he's going, I'm going with him. We've been through a lot together. It was long trip from Texas to here."

Nick continued to lean in the window so Chris couldn't leave without dragging him down the gravel drive. "Your buddy is upset right now. He's hurting and not capable of making a rational decision. He needs you to tell him this is a mistake, that if you guys do this, you're jeopardizing the greater mission. I've always known airmen to be disciplined, to do the right thing, even when it's not the easy thing. Are you telling me I've been wrong about the Air Force all these years?"

"No, sir." Clay continued to look forward.

Nick looked at Jack. "Is this what you believe is the best course of action, or are you going along with it because you want to support your brother?"

"Come with us, Nick." Chris looked over at the man hanging on the passenger's window and put the truck into drive. "I'll let you drive. I'll ride in the bed of the truck."

Nick held on tight as if he half expected Chris to take off with him still in the window. "Chris, your buddy and your brother are both placing their lives in your hands. If you leave, I promise you, they'll both wind up dead. And you'll die knowing that they lost their lives because of your bad decision. It will all be for nothing, because you'll never even find out if your dad is still alive or not. Is that how you want this to end?"

Chris put the truck in park, gunned the engine, and cut the ignition. He jerked the keys out and pointed his finger in Nick's face. "Fine! Then you better start putting together a plan to get my dad back. You've got til this time tomorrow." Chris got out of the truck, and leaving all of his gear still in the bed, stormed off toward his trailer.

Jack and Clay also got out of the truck, grabbed a load of gear from the bed and followed Chris into the trailer.

Danny looked up at Melissa, who was holding Annie in her arms and had been observing from a distance.

She was too far away for Danny to hear what she was saying, but he could tell by her lips as she said, "Thank you." The expression on her face wasn't exactly a smile, but it was pretty close.

Danny nodded as if to say, you're welcome.

Nick walked to the back of the truck, dropped the tailgate, jumped up to sit on it and patted it for

Danny to come sit next to him.

Danny took his cue. He lifted himself onto the tailgate. "Good job."

"It was a team effort."

"What are we going to tell Chris tomorrow?"

"Hopefully, he'll be thinking more clearly by then."

Danny leaned forward and looked at Nick on his left. "What if he's not?"

"I don't know. What's that place look like?"

"It's big. The men are way too spread out, but there's a lot of them."

"How many?"

"Total?"

"Shooters, how many shooters?"

Danny shook his head. "Antoine could tell you better than me, but I'd guess twelve hundred, maybe fifteen."

"All inside the airport?"

"No. Schlusser has a bunch of them on his private peninsula. I'm guessing he has two to three hundred there. Probably around twelve hundred on the base. I saw around fifty men at the armory. He's got patrols with four to six men, every three hundred yards."

Nick ran the calculations in his head. "So that's about two, two-fifty on guard at any given time."

Danny nodded. "Running three shifts, so seven-fifty. Plus, he has raiding parties that go out into the neighborhoods. They shake people down, like Gorbold tried to do to us."

"Big operation." Nick rubbed his chin. "How many non-combatants?"

"I'm not sure. There were two hundred of us in the barracks. I'd see a couple hundred people working the gardens when we'd cut across the runways for work. Again, Antoine would know better than me."

"What about Greenville?"

"It was thin, but Schlusser reinforced it with another hundred men. He was on a hiring spree."

"He must have a lot of supplies."

"I guess so. We didn't get much of it, but he treats his soldiers better. The gardens are coming along nicely, and he's got that whole train yard full of supplies."

"Of course, I'm sure he'll be tightening his belt now that his fuel stocks have been depleted."

Danny grinned. "Yeah. He'll be making less trips to the grocery. That's for sure."

Nick patted Danny on the shoulder. "Good job. JC would be proud."

Danny pursed his lips. "I'm glad we were able to take out the fuel tanks, but if JC is still alive, there is no question in Gorbold's mind that he is a spy after that stunt."

"JC knew what he was walking into. He wouldn't have it any other way. You made his family safer, bought us all some time, that was his goal."

Danny and Nick sat quietly on the tailgate for several minutes.

Jack walked out and stood near them.

"How's your brother doing?" Nick asked.

"Mad."

Nick looked at the young man. "How are you

doing?"

"About the same as my brother. Are you guys coming up with a plan?"

Nick shook his head. "We need a lot more men than we have if we're ever going to hit the airport."

"What about Ranger Dave?" Jack kicked the dirt with his boots.

"We've never even made contact with him," Nick said.

Jack stood still by the truck. "Then let's go find him. Maybe he'll help."

Nick looked at Danny as if he felt sorry for the young man.

Danny shrugged. "All he can say is no."

Nick knuckled his forehead. "Wait. Are you actually considering it?"

Danny smiled at Jack. "We could give it a shot. He'll be on the air tomorrow night at eight. We can be in the area, try to find a hill or something where we can get more range with our little handheld, and hope we can reach him."

Nick twisted his mouth to one side as if he were thinking. "If we're going to do it, we're going to run it right. We'll have a forward team that will try to make contact and an overwatch team. We don't know if he'll be as friendly as he sounds on the radio."

Jack nodded. "So the team that's going to make contact will go in Catfish's truck and the overwatch team will ride in the Humvee we took from Schlusser?"

Nick hopped down from the tailgate. "The Hummer sucks too much gas. Besides, if Ranger

Dave spots an up-armored vehicle with a .50 cal mounted on top, we'll have a tough time convincing him that we're just there to talk. I recommend taking that old Chevy we captured."

Danny shook his head. "Catfish took it over to his place and popped a hole in the gas tank to drain it."

"You're kidding! Somebody remind me to keep Catfish away from the vehicles. That truck was in better condition than this heap of junk." Nick kicked the hub cap of Catfish's old truck. "The windshield is shattered on the white F-150."

"If you scrunch down and lean forward, you can still see out the bottom," Danny replied.

"Do you think you could drive all the way to Pickens, hunched over like that?"

"I could," Jack interjected.

"Okay. You, Clay, and Chris will be on overwatch." Nick turned to Danny. "You, Antoine, and myself will try to make contact. We'll roll out tomorrow evening at five. That will give us an hour to get there, an hour to find a high spot to transmit from, and an hour before he goes on for his evening broadcast. That's our window to try to catch him on the radio. Go tell your brother, Jack."

"Okay, see you later." Jack sprinted toward the trailer.

"I better go tell Alisa what's up. She'll want to know." Danny headed toward the house.

"She'll want to come along." Nick laughed.

Danny huffed. "Yeah, another long *discussion*."

"It's not an inherently dangerous mission, if all goes well, that is. Maybe you should let her tag along. You have to pick your battles."

"If all goes well. That's a big if." Danny glanced back at Nick.

"Better to let her go with us on this one and ask her to stay home when we have to hit the airport." Nick raised his eyebrows.

"I wish it was that easy." Danny threw a hand in the air to wave bye. He knew Nick was probably right. It was a relatively safe mission, and he couldn't keep her pinned up on the farm all the time.

Danny found Alisa and Dana upstairs going through their clothes, picking out several items to give to Gwen. He explained the general outline of the plan.

"Danny, I want to go." Alisa's tone was just south of demanding.

"You'll have to be ready for a fight, but you can't look like it. We have to try to get Dave to trust us."

A smile slowly grew across her face. "Are you serious? I can go?"

Danny bobbed his head from side to side. "If everything goes as planned, you can come along."

"I'm going, too." Dana almost shouted.

Danny raised his arms, palms facing out. "It's not a trip to the mall."

"I survived the journey here from Savannah. I've been on a rescue mission, and I killed people when we were attacked. I think I'm qualified to go places besides the mall." Dana placed her hands on her hips.

"I'll have to talk to Nick." Danny crossed his

arms. "We can't have too many people in the truck.

"I'll sit in the bed of the truck. I don't care," Dana added.

Danny turned to go back down the stairs. "I'll make sure I tell Nick."

When he got back outside, Chris was pulling up in the F-150.

"We're rolling out now." he yelled.

"What?" Danny was confused.

"It's six-thirty. If we leave now, we'll get to Pickens before the broadcast."

Danny looked at Chris who still appeared angry. "You said you were giving Nick twenty-four hours to come up with a plan."

"Yeah, a plan to hit the airport. We don't even know if this Dave guy will help us. If he's going to be part of the initiative, we need to find out tonight, so we can figure that into the plan. I'm not dragging my feet on this."

"Have you talked to Nick?"

"I just sent Jack to tell him to get ready. Listen, Danny, I don't care what Nick says. We're going up there right now. Otherwise, my dad is sitting in a cage while I sit around here waiting to see if the people up in Pickens will even consider lending us a hand on this. And pack some food because we're not coming back until I get an answer."

Danny sighed. He still wasn't rested up from his trip to the airport, but he totally understood Chris's reasoning. "Hang tight. Let me go talk to Nick."

"Okay, but hurry. I want to be on the road in fifteen minutes."

"Can you grab some extra MREs from your

dad's trailer? There's no way everybody can pack food, weapons, and ammo in fifteen minutes."

Chris nodded. "I'll take care of the food. You just convince Nick that we need to move now."

Danny jogged to Nick and Cami's trailer.

Cami opened the door and gave her little brother a hug. "I'm so glad you made it home. I wanted to come see you this morning, but Nick said to let you rest."

Danny kissed his sister on the cheek. "Thanks. I could have slept all day if this crisis hadn't popped up." He nodded toward Nick and Jack who were sitting on the couch having a deep discussion.

Danny walked over to where the two were talking. "Chris is all fired up. I don't think we're going to convince him to wait until tomorrow to go up to Pickens."

Nick crossed his arms. "Rushing into things is a good way to get killed. Besides, he's going to have to learn that I'm making the tactical decisions for the compound in JC's absence."

Danny sat next to Jack. "I don't think that would be a problem if it weren't JC's life at stake. He has a point about moving quickly. Even if we make contact with Ranger Dave and he agrees to help us, we'll still have a long, drawn-out process to come up with a plan to hit the airport. If we don't go, Chris is going by himself, and he's in no position to be negotiating for assistance."

Jack stood up. "He's not going by himself. If Chris goes, me and Clay are going."

Nick looked at Danny then at Jack. He sat silently with his hands crossed and his elbows resting on his knees for several seconds. Finally, he looked up. "Okay, tell everybody to gear up. The contact team wears civilian clothes with concealed pistols." Nick turned to Jack. "Overwatch team wears full battle rattle. Minimum of 200 rounds of rifle ammo each, sidearms, and at least 120 rounds of pistol ammo."

Jack headed out the door. Danny turned to follow him.

Nick caught Danny before he cleared the door. "Bring that new AR-15 you picked up in Charlotte. We'll have rifles tucked under the seat. You're not wearing a chest rig, so you'll be depending on overwatch to give you ammo if we get in trouble. No one else is running an AK."

"Okay." It made Danny nervous to go into a potentially hostile environment without his AK. He knew what the AK did in a firefight. He'd trained with ARs, but he'd never tested one in battle. When he reached the house, he hustled up the stairs to where Alisa and Dana were. "We're rolling out in ten minutes. If you girls are coming, wear civilian clothes with a small pistol concealed on your person."

"Ten minutes? I thought we were going tomorrow?" Dana protested.

"You guys are welcome to sit this one out," Danny said.

"Oh, no. I'm ready to go right now." Alisa took the old .32 revolver and tucked it into a small clip-on, concealed-carry holster which she stuck in the back of her jeans. "I'm going to get Gwen."

"Gwen?" Danny dropped his pistol belt,

removed his Glock and stuck it in an inside-the-waistband holster.

"Yeah, she already feels like she's not wanted around here. Can you imagine what it would be like for her if Dana and I leave her on the farm by herself?" Alisa bounded down the stairs.

Danny aired his grievance as Alisa was descending the stairs. "She's not alone. Cami, Melissa, Nana, lots of people are here."

Dana answered for Alisa, since she was already gone. "You know what she means. Gwen is our age. She'd feel like an outcast; more so than she already does."

Danny rolled his eyes. "It's just that the numbers keep growing."

Dana followed Danny down the stairs. "You never know; a little feminine charm might help you boys strike a deal."

Everyone rallied around the two vehicles, and Nick gave a quick overview of the mission. "Overwatch team, you'll stay close until we make contact. After that, you'll stay back about a quarter mile. You'll be listening in on all our radio transmissions with Ranger Dave once we make contact, so you'll know where we are at all times. If you hear me say my funny bone is itching, that means we're in trouble and you need to come in with guns blazing. Got it?"

"Got it, let's get this show on the road." Chris still sounded anxious as he put the F-150 into drive and pulled away from the house.

Nick took the driver's seat in Catfish's truck, and Antoine rode shotgun. Nick was a substantially sized man, and Antoine was huge, leaving a very slim space between them. Danny opted to ride in the bed of the truck with the three girls rather than up front.

It was far too windy for conversation, so Danny just enjoyed the scenery. Nick purposely avoided going through Anderson or any other populated areas on the way to Pickens.

They arrived in Pickens without incident, in just under an hour. Nick drove to an open area on the side of a high hill, on the north side of Pickens. He got out and tossed a tennis ball connected to a long string over a nearby tree branch. Nick then tied the string to a length of wire which he used for an antenna extension and pulled the string, running the wire up to the top of the tree branch.

Nick pressed the talk button on the handheld UHF/VHF radio. "This is Nick from Anderson, calling Ranger Dave."

"That's not how the other hams talk," Danny advised.

"I'm not a ham. I'd rather not come off as someone putting themselves out there as a ham. It would sound disingenuous."

"Point taken." Danny nodded.

"Ranger Dave, can you read me? This is Nick, from Anderson."

"This is Ranger Dave, I can barely hear you, Nick. Are you in Anderson?" Ranger Dave's voice was clear, but his system was transmitting with a lot more power than the small handheld.

"No. We're on the north side of Pickens. I'm on a handheld."

"It sounds like you said you're near Pickens. Are you on a handheld?"

"Affirmative."

"What was that?"

"Yes."

"Nick, if you can hear me and you know where the Pickens Flea Market is, I think we'll be able to communicate a little better if you can get there with your handheld. I'll do my news program, then hopefully, we can chat afterwards."

"Roger." Nick set the radio down. "Anybody knows where the Pickens flea market is?"

"I do." Gwen said. "It's on Walhalla, which turns into Main Street in town. They used to have a fall festival there. A bunch of us from my high school would go every year."

"Can you get us there?" Nick asked.

"If you can take me to Main Street."

"Pickens is a small town. It certainly wouldn't be as bad as going through downtown Greenville, but I'd still rather avoid Main Street if we can help it. What side of town is it on?"

"The west side."

"So Main Street, or Walhalla, runs east and west?"

"Yeah."

Nick paused. "We must have crossed it coming here. How far outside of town is the flea market?"

"Not far. Maybe a mile."

"Okay, I think we can find it. Gwen, you ride up front with us."

Danny raised his eyebrows as he glanced at Alisa. Gwen was very petite, but it would still be a tight fit between Nick and Antoine.

Nick addressed Chris. "When you see us pull into the flea market, keep driving for a quarter mile and pull off to the side of the road. Try to find some cover so you don't look suspicious."

Chris nodded. "Got it."

Everyone loaded back into the trucks and headed towards the flea market grounds.

When they arrived in the parking lot, Danny was surprised to see activity. Four heavily-armed men stood at the gate of the entrance. A series of open-air booths were set up beneath rudimentary shelters constructed of 4-inch-by-4-inch wood posts, staked in a concrete slab, and holding up a pitched tin roof. The roof was rusted but not dilapidated. The tables were all hand built and made of wood.

At the entrance, a large hand-painted, plywood sign read, *Admission: Quarter ounce of silver or equivalent. No Guns. Firearms transactions must be conducted in the gun tent.*

Danny looked at the old army tent in the parking lot area, outside of the perimeter fence. Two more heavily armed men stood guard at the entrance of the tent.

One of the guards, an older man, walked up to the truck to speak to Nick. "Sorry, we're not letting anyone else in. Gates close at sunset, which is in about fifteen minutes. You'll have to come back tomorrow."

Nick asked the man, "What items are you trading?"

The guard pointed to the main flea market behind him. "Clothing, shoes, food, tools, soap, fuel, most anything you'd want except flat screens and laptops."

Nick chuckled. "What about the green tent?"

"You have to be vetted by a member of the community to trade guns and ammo. We've had some bad folks rearing their ugly heads. Gangs, warlords, and such. We're all about the Second Amendment, but as a private endeavor, we also reserve the right to do business with whom we choose."

"That makes sense. We actually just need to make a quick call, and we'll be on our way. But now that we know you're here, we'll plan a trip up to trade."

The old man glanced behind him. "Pay phone is out of order and cell service ain't what it used to be, so unless you've got a couple soup cans with some fishing wire ran between them, you'll have a tough time making a call."

Nick laughed and held the radio up. "Ham radio call. Ranger Dave told us to come here. He thinks we'll have a better chance of reaching him on our handheld from here. I suppose he's nearby."

"Oh, Ranger Dave. Hold on one second." The man picked up his radio and began walking. "Trading Post One, calling Dave."

Danny tried to listen to what the man was saying as he walked away, but couldn't make it out.

The man walked back over to the truck seconds later. "He's gonna start his show in ten minutes. Go ahead and call him."

"Thanks." Nick got out of the cab and stood in the bed of the truck to get the best possible reception and transmission. "Ranger Dave, this is Nick, from Anderson."

"Hey, Nick. How can I help you?"

Antoine and Gwen got out so they could hear what was going on.

"We ran into some trouble with one of the local warlords that you warned us about. A guy named Schlusser sent what amounted to an extortion team down our way. We fought him off, but we know it's only a matter of time until he comes back. We're looking to team up with some folks and take him out for good."

"That's a tall order, Nick. I've heard about this guy. He's pretty well set up. We're focusing on keeping our little corner of the universe clean. We'd be stretching ourselves pretty thin if we tried to do more than that."

Nick pressed the talk button. "I'm sure you know how close Greenville is to your little corner, and I'm certain that you're aware Schlusser just sent a hundred reinforcements to Greenville. Taking care of your corner only works when everybody is on the same page. When you've got a malignant element like Schlusser, the cancer spreads until all the healthy cells are dead."

Dave was silent.

Nick pressed the button. "Look, I've got a guy with me who has been inside his compound. He can tell you all about how he operates, his strengths and weaknesses. We'd be happy to share the intel with you if we can meet in person. No obligations on your part. We're just happy to share the info so you can be better prepared for when he comes to

Pickens. You've got a nice little operation here, and I can promise you that Schlusser will want a piece of this pie, sooner rather than later."

Dave's voice came back over the radio. "I'm going to put you in contact with a man from the Pickens militia. All the info you're talking about needs to go to him. And he's the only one who has the authority to put together any type of coalition. You guys just sit tight where you are. His name is Ben. Thanks for driving up here and reaching out. I've got to start the broadcast."

"Roger, Thanks, Dave." Nick let his hand drop, holding the radio at his side. "And now we wait."

Danny looked up. "I guess Ranger Dave lives within a half mile of this place if we're able to reach him from here on the handheld."

"Not necessarily." Nick pointed toward the trees behind the flea market. "There's a wire running horizontally between those two trees in the back. I think they have a repeater over there."

Danny focused on the area Nick was pointing to. "Hmm. You know, if you wanted to set up, supply, and fund a militia, running a trading post would be the perfect way to do it. You'd have a line on all the gossip, the support of the people because you'd be providing safety and provisions, and a recruiting center since you could offer a job to people who didn't have any other way to get by."

Gwen looked over at Danny. "That's basically what Schlusser is doing, except that whole *support of the people* thing."

Antoine added, "This strikes me more as a capitalistic model. Schlusser's looks more like a dictatorial communist model."

Nick nodded. "You're right. This does seem more capitalistic, at least on the veneer."

Alisa shrugged. "You've got to give the Pickens folks some credit, Schlusser didn't even bother putting up a veneer."

Another older gentleman walked out of the gate, accompanied by two heavily-armed guards. He had a neatly trimmed grey beard, weathered skin, and the pronounced crow's feet at the corners of his piercing grey eyes showed a life of adventure and experience. His olive drab BDU shirt was clean and pressed as was his trousers. He wore a matching OD green cap, and his pistol belt held a classic 1911 pistol. "I'm Ben." He offered his hand to Nick who had climbed out of the bed of the truck to meet the man.

Nick shook his hand. "I'm Nick. It's a pleasure to meet you, Ben."

"Dave tells me you folks have some information you'd like to share."

"Yes." Nick introduced the rest of the team to Ben. "Danny infiltrated Schlusser's base in Charlotte."

"By yourself?" Ben looked impressed, and he did not seem like a man who often was.

"No sir, I went with our team's tactical commander, JC. He was captured and didn't make it back. In fact, I was captured also, but Antoine and Gwen busted me out."

"Wow! I'd like to hear all about this. Why don't y'all follow me on over to the mess hall. Have you eaten?"

"Not yet, but we brought MREs, so we don't mean to be a burden," Nick replied.

"Nonsense. You'll be my guests."

Nick walked next to Ben. "Also, for full disclosure, we're all armed."

Ben turned his attention to Danny. "I wouldn't be much of a host if I didn't respect your right to defend yourselves, would I?"

Danny smiled. "Yes, sir."

Ben led the way through the crowd to a large tent in the rear of the compound. Danny could tell by the way the other people at the flea market spoke to Ben and looked at him, that he was more than just the head of the militia. He was in charge of everything that went on at the flea market.

Danny took note of the number of vendors inside the flea market. He guessed there were at least thirty. They were all packing up for the day, so he couldn't see everything they'd been offering at their booths, but he saw a few vendors with canned goods, two with some produce. He guessed it consisted of either early crops or food that had been grown, or at least started in a green house. Others offered hand tools.

Alisa tugged on his shirt. "Look, jewelry!"

Danny turned to look at the man taking a selection of shiny objects off his table.

"It's just like the mall!" Dana exclaimed.

Gwen winked. "I don't know what mall you were going to, but it's not like the malls I remember.'

"It's the new mall. We have to take what we can get." Dana laughed.

"They need a Cinnabon. It would smell more like a mall," Alisa joked.

"We could open one!" Dana said excitedly. "I doubt we'd get sued for copyright infringement."

"You know, that's not a bad idea." Alisa looked half serious.

Danny shook his head as he tried to keep up with Ben. "We're not opening a Cinnabon. At least not until we've got the apocalypse under control."

"I'm going to start working on the recipe as soon as we get back." Dana slapped Danny on the back playfully.

They soon reached the mess tent. An aroma of roasted meat filled the tent.

Antoine shook his head as if he were in awe. "I don't know if I can handle this. Miss Jennie's breakfast was the best thing I've eaten since the lights went out. And now this? It's too much for one day."

Danny reached up and patted him on the shoulder. "I'm sure Ben will understand if you tell him you're not hungry."

Antoine laughed. "Oh no. That ain't gonna happen."

Ben directed everyone where to sit. "They'll bring plates out in a moment. They'll be small portions, but you're welcome to seconds. We just don't allow for any waste, whatsoever."

Danny took a seat at one of the picnic tables in the huge tent. There were three rows of picnic tables, each with five tables pushed flush up against each other. He estimated there were about forty men eating in the tent. He figured they most likely ate in shifts, so there were probably at least another forty men on the grounds.

Ben sat next to Danny. "So let's hear about this wild adventure of yours."

"I guess I should start with our first contact with Schlusser at Nana's farm."

"That would be fine." Ben instructed the women bringing the food out to serve Danny and the others first. "Would you folks mind if I ask a blessing over the food?"

"Not at all. Please do." Danny bowed his head.

Ben said a quick, heartfelt prayer for the meal then looked up. "Please enjoy."

Danny and the others dug into the roasted pork, rice and red beans, and green beans. It was a true feast. As he ate, he told Ben of the attack against the farm. He also told how JC and he had pulled a hit and run against the Greenville outpost.

"That was you?" Ben's soulful eyes showed a mixture of amusement and astonishment. "Son, you've got guts."

Danny rolled his eyes. "I don't know about that. I was scared out of my wits."

Ben smiled and shook his head. "We all get scared, son. It's whether or not you let that fear control you that determines if you are a man.

"Then you went straight from there to Charlotte to infiltrate his main base?"

"Yes." Danny continued the saga, explaining how Gorbold has mistakenly assumed they were spies for the sheriff in Cabarrus County and how Gwen and Antoine had sprung him from the box.

"You don't have any idea where they're holding

this other fellow JC?"

Danny crossed his hands and looked down at the table. "None."

Ben furrowed his brow. "Well, that ain't good. But I'm sure I'm not telling you anything you don't already know. Would your outfit be willing to help us take down the Greenville outpost?"

Danny looked at Nick. "We'd like to try to get JC back first."

Nick nodded his approval. "Danny's right. We've got an overwatch team a quarter mile up the road. Two of JC's sons are on that team. They were ready to take off on their own to try to get him back."

Ben shook his head. "That would have been suicide."

"We told them." Danny pushed his empty plate back. "The only way we were able to talk them down was by agreeing to rush out here and try to put something together."

Ben stroked his beard. "I've got just over eighty men. I might have another twenty or thirty that I could call on for a one-time strike. Antoine, do you concur with Danny's assessment of the airport, fifteen hundred shooters and another five hundred non-combatants?"

"I guess that sounds about right. Although, I've never been in the area they call the refugee center." Antoine looked at Gwen.

"All I know is that the kitchen planned for two thousand a day, and that was just for people inside the fence. So add everyone on the peninsula to that. You're talking at least another three hundred."

Ben looked at Nick. "Ballpark, twenty-five hundred. We simply don't have the numbers to go up against that kind of a force. But if you'll commit to helping us shut down Greenville, I give you my word that I'll help you put together a viable plan to find more men and get inside the airport. I can't say how long it will take, but I want to put this son of a buck out of business just as bad as you do.

"Any way you slice it, you're going to have to take out Greenville. From what Danny said, it sounds like Gorbold will be on your doorstep before he comes my way looking for trouble. He's wanting vengeance for his brother. And as long as Greenville is operational, he has a forward operating base to launch that attack."

Nick sighed. "You're absolutely right. I hope I can sell it to JC's boys."

Ben nodded. "I understand. But they need to realize that Greenville is our immediate problem, and my men aren't going to leave their post unattended until that threat is eliminated. I'll have the kitchen wrap something up for your overwatch team. Maybe they'll get their belly full and get a good night's sleep. If so, they might think a little more clearly in the morning."

Nick stood and shook Ben's hand. "Do you have a timeline in mind for an assault against Greenville?

Ben looked down at the table. "If they just sent those reinforcements down there on Saturday or Sunday, they're still getting used to the place. Now would be the time to hit them, before they can get settled in. We should send a recon team in for a day or two, but that gives them more time to get organized. Could your team be ready to roll at sundown, tomorrow?"

Danny exhaled deeply. He was tired. "I guess so. Nick, what do you think?"

"We can be ready."

"Good. Be up here for supper, we'll iron out a plan after we eat and we'll run a few drills before we roll out. How many shooters are you bringing?"

"Seven," Nick replied.

"Seven?" Ben asked.

Nick nodded. "Yeah, Steven is still walking on crutches. He'll be sitting this one out."

"Can he drive?" Ben inquired.

"I'll ask him, but I don't know for sure."

Alisa pointed her finger at each of Danny's group as if she were doing the math in her head. "Nine, counting me and Dana. We've seen our share of action."

"Make that ten," Gwen added. "Remember, I'm a professional saboteur."

Danny's face showed his displeasure. "Someone will need to watch the farm."

Alisa was quick with her response. "Cami and Melissa can hold the farm. As long as we eliminate the Greenville outpost, there won't be anyone to give them any trouble. If we don't, none of us are safe, anyway."

"She's right, Danny." Ben's deep voice was soothing.

"Okay. We'll be here tomorrow by six." Danny began heading toward the tent exit.

Nick walked beside Ben. "We've got a Humvee with a .50 cal mounted on top, but no diesel."

"You bring that Hummer. I'll make sure you go home with a full tank of diesel. Do you have ammo for the .50?" Ben turned to Nick.

"Some."

"I might be able to get ammo, but no belt."

"We've still got the belts with the spent rounds. I can bring those in case you come up with some ammo."

Ben patted Nick on the back. "It was good meeting you folks. Y'all have a safe trip home, and we'll see you tomorrow."

Danny and the others said goodbye to Ben and returned to the truck. Nick called Chris on the radio. "We're rolling out, and I've got a little peace offering for you boys if you're hungry."

"How did it go?" Chris's voice came over the radio.

"Good. We'll discuss it when we get back to the compound," Nick replied.

Nick rendezvoused with Chris's vehicle and handed off the food which Ben had sent. "Stay close, but not too close. Give us a call if you get any company from the rear."

Chris took the food and passed it over to Clay and Jack. "Roger that. See you back at the farm."

The two teams arrived safely back at Nana's without incident.

Nick got out of the cab of the truck and helped Dana and Gwen as they jumped out of the back. "Everyone get a good night's sleep. We'll run some training drills in the morning after breakfast then have a big lunch before we go back to Pickens."

"Okay, we'll be ready." Danny jumped down

then helped Alisa out of the truck.

"Good night." Antoine waved as he headed toward his trailer.

"Sleep tight, Antoine. I'll come by and make sure you're awake for breakfast." Alisa waved back.

Steven came out of the house, hobbling on a cane rather than crutches. "How did it go?"

"Not bad." Danny looked toward the back row of trailers where he saw Catfish coming out of his camper.

Chris parked the F-150 and came over to where Danny and the others were congregated. "So, did we strike a deal?"

Clay and Jack walked over, carrying the food Ben had sent for them.

Nick put his hand on Chris's shoulder. "We did. It might be a little bit of a longer process than what you had hoped for, but I'm hoping you'll see the logic in it. Either way, it's how it has to be."

Nick continued to explain the short-term and long-term goals to take out Greenville then use the credibility of having accomplished that task to build a larger force with which they could attack the airport in Charlotte.

Chris looked angry. "My dad will be dead by then."

Danny wasn't about to say it out loud, but he and everyone else knew that JC was probably dead already.

Nick looked at Chris and Jack. "You understand why the Pickens militia isn't going on a suicide mission to Charlotte until they've dealt with the problems in their own backyard. Right?"

Chris nodded with his head held low.

Danny had seen the pain in JC's eyes before Chris had returned from Texas, as he wondered when and if his son would ever come home. Now, he saw the same pain in Chris's eyes, as he agonized over his father. Jack looked sad, also. But Chris's pain looked different; as if he, being the eldest son, felt responsible to bring his father home.

"So are you guys with us?" Nick inquired.

"Whatever Chris decides." Clay crossed his arms, a symbol of his unyielding determination to stand by his friend.

Jack stepped closer to his brother's side as if to show his solidarity. "Yeah, me too."

Nick nodded that he understood then stared into Chris's eyes. "These two men are placing their lives in your hand. So how are you going to repay them for their loyalty? Will you be the leader that JC raised you to be or will you throw their lives on the altar of your own vengeance and watch them burn for nothing?"

Chris bit his lower lip which was quivering. "We're in." He quickly turned away from the group and walked off toward his trailer. He turned and pointed at Nick. "But I know what you all think, and my dad is not dead. So don't plan on dragging your feet. I won't stand for it. We're going to do things your way, Nick. But I'll be on your heels every day, barking like a mad dog, until you finish it and bring my dad home."

Danny watched the exchange, wishing it wasn't like this. He wished JC was still here, that there was no Schlusser, wishing that the power would come back on, and everything could just go back to normal. He sighed as he took Alisa's hand to lead her back to the house. Despite his vain hopes, this was reality, and they all had to live life on life's terms.

CHAPTER 9

Blessed be the LORD my strength, which teacheth my hands to war, and my fingers to fight: My goodness, and my fortress; my high tower, and my deliverer; my shield, and he in whom I trust; who subdueth my people under me.

Psalm 144:1-2

The next morning, Nana, Cami, and Melissa served breakfast for the compound while Tracey Reese watched little Annie Castell, along with her own children. All, except for ten-year-old Jason Reese, of course, who had become Steven's shadow since his father was killed.

After Steven had asked God to bless the food,

Danny spooned a large helping of red-eyed gravy over his biscuits and passed the bowl to Antoine. "Is it all I said it would be?"

Antoine smiled as he took the gravy. "Everything and more."

Alisa passed the eggs to Danny and looked across the table at Gwen. "You still look tired. Did you sleep okay?"

Gwen sipped her coffee. "Once I finally got to sleep, I did, but it took a while. I'm used to sleeping in that big open terminal with all those people around. It was weird being in the trailer all alone."

Dana reached over and put her hand on Gwen's. "If Pauline doesn't move back in tonight, I'll come sleep in your trailer with you."

"It will be like a slumber party!" Gwen squealed. "Alisa, why don't you come?"

"Oh no! I just got my man back. I'm not letting him out of my sight again for a long, long time." Alisa laughed and put her arm around Danny.

Danny pursed his lips. He was glad to see the girls smiling, but he wondered if they were being delusional. They'd all committed themselves to a firefight which would be going down that very evening. He looked at Tracy, a young widow with three small children, and remembered how heartless and unforgiving war could be.

After breakfast, everyone geared up and gathered behind the barn.

Nick inspected everyone's weapons and the load-carrying vests of those who had them. He looked at Steven who was wearing a vest which had been taken from one of Schlusser's men who had attacked the farm nearly three weeks earlier. "You think you're up for the fight?"

"You guys are already outnumbered." Steven was still babying his injured leg.

"That's not what I asked."

"I can't run any marathon, but my trigger finger is in the best shape of my life."

Nick fought back a grin. "Can you drive a stick?"

"I can drive anything."

Nick patted him on the shoulder. "Good, you're gonna be my driver. Lay back on training for the morning. Once I get everyone else squared away, we'll practice some maneuvers with the Humvee. I want you to get a feel for driving with another person standing up in the back, manning the .50."

"You're going to run the .50 cal yourself?" Danny asked.

He nodded. "Clay and Chris are probably the only other people, besides me, who have ever shot one. A mounted, belt-fed weapon has a little different feel than an AR or an AK."

Danny let his AK rest against the wall of the barn. "Did you tell Cami that you're running the .50?"

"No, Danny. I didn't. And I hope you won't either. Excuse me, I need to try to get Antoine and Gwen set up with rifles." Nick ended the conversation by walking away.

"What was that all about?" Dana asked.

Danny watched Nick as he entered the barn. "Remember the assault on the farm?"

"How could we ever forget?" Alisa placed her

AR next to Danny's AK.

"Where did we center all of our fire?" Danny turned back to face the others.

Alisa lowered her brow as if she were thinking. "Oh, the machine gunner."

Dana's face showed her heavy concern as she looked at Steven. "And you'll be right beside him."

Steven took her hand. "I'm not going anywhere until it's my time to go. And if it's my time, it doesn't matter where I'm at."

Dana pulled her hand away from his and draped her arms around him. "Don't talk like that, Steven."

Alisa stood next to Danny. "You sounded like you were questioning Nick's judgement, on manning the .50, I mean."

"With JC gone, he's all we have for a leader." Danny gave Steven a half smile. "Militarily, that is. You're growing into a real fine preacher."

"Thanks." Steven smiled back at Danny.

Catfish made his way over to Danny's group. "Got me one of them AK-47s. Took it off one of 'em that I shot." He proudly held up his rifle for all to see.

Danny chuckled. "Nice going, Catfish. You look good with it."

Catfish had curiously attached two Molle magazine pouches to the straps of his overalls. "If our boys woulda had these in Nam, things mighta turned out different. You can drag these things through hog slop and they'll keep on tickin'."

Dana rolled her eyes. "If you can drag it through hog slop, then it's the perfect gun for you."

"You best watch your mouth, youngin'. I'll have

Miss Jennie get after you with a switch!"

Alisa inspected Catfish's awkward looking magazine pouches. Each one held three AK-47 magazines. "Have you practiced changing mags from those?"

Catfish quickly raised his rifle, pointing barrel up, hit the magazine release switch, and in one fluid motion tossed the magazine that had been in the rifle to the ground, pulled the Velcro flap from the pouch on his overall strap, retrieved the magazine from inside, and rocked it into place, giving it a good shake to ensure it was snuggly seated within the magazine well. He looked at Alisa. "What do you think?"

She put her hands up as if to surrender. "I guess you have."

Nick returned with Antoine and Gwen following close behind him. "Danny, your team is Gwen, Dana, Alisa, and the Fish."

"Now listen here!" Catfish shook his finger in protest at the moniker Nick had borrowed from JC.

Nick paid no attention and turned to Antoine. "Antoine, you'll be on the fire team with Chris, Clay, and Jack. We'll go over some basic troop movement drills, both to freshen up and for Gwen and Antoine's sake, since they haven't trained with us before. I also want to see Gwen and Antoine practice magazine changes and drill for weapons malfunctions. Both of those things are so much easier to practice when you don't have some jerk on the other side shooting at you."

Danny nodded with a smirk. He wished he didn't have such a vivid understanding of that concept, but it was one that was all too real for him.

Nick pointed to Steven. "Pull the Hummer around. I'll get these guys started, and we'll do a little driving."

Danny worked with Antoine on magazine changes while Dana and Alisa did the same with Gwen. He'd hoped to have the big man on his team, but that would have required Catfish or Gwen to go with Chris. Danny knew that didn't make sense. Chris and Clay, and even Jack had more military training than anyone on Danny's fire team, which effectively meant Danny had been relegated to the B team. He sighed as he looked at Catfish and the girls. "I'll take this crew any day. They've got heart; every one of them."

Danny's fire team and Chris's fire team practiced working together as a squad. They worked on bounding overwatch, which allowed one fire team to provide cover fire while the other team moved. Once the moving team was in position, they could then provide security so the other team could move. This leap-frog maneuver would be the primary method the two teams would utilize to advance, reposition, and retreat during the attack later that evening.

The squad also drilled advancing on a target while using the Humvee as a shield. Steven and Nick would keep the Hummer close to the squad, both so it could be used as an evac vehicle in case someone was injured and so that a ready replacement would be available for Nick, if he were to be taken out. Additionally, the Humvee would have a large supply of fully loaded magazines for the AR-15s and the two AK-47s. Nick had told everyone that this could turn out to be a long, hard fight and they were likely to expend thousands of rounds of ammunition.

All the talk of injury and filling the gap when someone was shot brought a heavy cloud of despair over the group. Everyone on the team had seen action in one form or another, but they'd all tried to stay light hearted about the mission, at least up until now.

"Great work, soldiers!" Nick announced. "Let's go eat, then we'll do a final inspection and roll out to Pickens."

Being on Chris's fire team, Antoine sat with Chris, Jack, and Clay. The big man looked at Danny with a shrug as if to apologize for not sitting at the table with him.

Danny smiled and waved to let Antoine know that he wasn't offended in the least.

Nana, Cami, and Tracey made fried chicken, instant mashed potatoes, biscuits, and green beans for lunch. It was a meal that they usually only got on Sunday. Danny was sure that the three cooks had prepared it for the members of the team who wouldn't be coming home. For them, whoever they were, this would be their last meal at the farm. The thought choked Danny up, causing a knot to form in his throat. He excused himself to go to the restroom, where he sat quietly and prayed for a while. "God, I know this world is not our home. It was never meant to be our final destination, but I love all these people so much. I don't want to see any of them die. It was hard enough to watch Korey and Rocky die.

Wondering what happened to JC is even tougher. Please, God, watch over all of us, especially Alisa. Please don't let me be left behind on this forsaken planet without her. God, if you have to take her, please take me also."

Danny returned to the table to finish his lunch.

"Are you okay?" Alisa whispered.

"I'm fine." He smiled at her and took her hand. "I love you, Alisa."

She smiled back at him. "I love you, too, Danny Walker."

After lunch, everyone geared up and waited by their respective vehicles. Nick walked from person to person, having each person jump up and down to check if their gear was rattling or if anything looked like it might fall out. He checked each person's magazine pouches to make sure the magazines were all facing the right direction, everyone's, except for Catfish's, that is. He couldn't seem to get his head around how Catfish was reloading. Nick shook his head as he walked away from the old man. "I guess you know how it works. That's all that matters." He looked up at the rest of the group. "I've got four spare AR-15's in the Hummer in case your weapon jams up and you can't get it running again. Catfish, Danny, I'm sorry, but if either of your weapons fail, you'll have to transition over."

Catfish shook his AK-47. "These don't jam. That's why we've got 'em."

Nick sighed. "Let's hope you're right, Catfish. Both pickups will also have extra ammo, so if something happens to the Hummer, and you can't get ammo, get back to the staging area and resupply. We'll also have water and MREs in the trucks. I have no idea how long this will last. It could turn into a siege."

"Do we know where the staging area will be?" Clay asked.

"I don't know, but it will probably be at least a mile away. We don't know how far out they've expanded patrols since Danny and JC paid them a visit." Nick winked at Danny. "We'll do a quick comms check, and we'll roll out."

They had eight radios for the compound, the two Baofengs that Nick had stashed in the EMP shed, two they'd taken from Gorbold after they'd killed him, three more they'd salvaged from the men who'd attacked the farm, and the one Danny had lifted from the guard Antoine shot at the airport.

The radio in the Humvee had been destroyed by the hand grenade, but Nick had managed to wire one of the radios into the Hummer's antenna for extended range. Nick and Steven would share that radio. The other seven radios were distributed among all the members of the team, except for Catfish and Gwen.

Nick handed two of the three remaining hand grenades they'd taken from Gorbold to Danny. "I've got one of these, you take the other two. You never know when they'll come in handy."

Danny held them. "They're heavy. My pack is already packing a lot of weight. Besides my water, ammo, and medical kit, I've got the pistol grip shotgun for breaching doors in my pack."

"Then give one of the grenades to Alisa. Split the weight up."

Danny placed a grenade in his pack and gave the other to Alisa.

Nick watched. "I know it weighs a lot, but you should have bolt cutters and a pry bar."

Antoine held his hand up. "I've got those items in my pack." He turned around to reveal the handles of the bolt cutters protruding from the top of his pack.

"Good." Nick nodded his approval. "Chris, Jack, I know you guys have some night vision, but I wouldn't have it mounted on my weapon if I were you. We're pretty close to a full moon tonight, but besides that, everyone else is going to be using flashlights. We'll be in close quarters with the headlights from vehicles everywhere, and the enemy will be using the best lights they can get a hold of to try to spot us. If they shine a heavy duty flashlight in your scope, you'll be blind. You might want to take them along in your pack, but don't utilize them as your primary sight."

Nick walked by each person. "Everyone has a tactical light on their weapon, but try to operate using just the moonlight and the lights from the enemy. If you turn your light on in combat, it gives the enemy a target to hone in on."

Nana walked out to where they were preparing to leave. "I'm gonna speak a psalm over you before y'all head out. Now bow your heads."

Everyone complied and Nana opened her Bible. "The Lord is my light and my salvation; whom shall I fear? The Lord is the strength of my life; of whom shall I be afraid? When the wicked, even mine enemies and my foes, came upon me to eat up my flesh, they stumbled and fell. Though an host should encamp against me, my heart shall not fear: though war should rise against me, in this will I be confident. One thing have I desired of the Lord, that will I seek after; that I may dwell in the house of the Lord all the days of my life, to behold the beauty of the Lord, and to enquire in his temple. For in the time of trouble he shall hide me in his pavilion: in the secret of his tabernacle shall he hide me; he shall set me up upon a rock. And now shall mine head be lifted up above mine enemies round about me: therefore will I offer in his tabernacle sacrifices of joy; I will sing, yea, I will sing praises unto the Lord." Nana closed her bible. "Lord watch over these, your precious children and give them victory against the heathen. Be with them as you were with the children of Israel going out to fight the Canaanites. Amen."

After the prayer, Catfish took the driver's seat of his truck, with Danny riding shotgun. The girls all rode in the bed of Catfish's truck. Chris drove the F-150, with Clay in the passenger's seat. Jack and Antoine rode in the back of the F-150. Steven drove the Humvee, which would be at the head of the convoy, with Nick sitting next to him. The shattered glass had been knocked out of the Humvee's windshield as well as the F-150's. Nick had decided that being shattered, it acted as more of a hindrance than a help.

The cab of Catfish's truck was quiet on the way to Pickens. Danny was beginning to feel the tension of the battle they were heading towards. It seemed that even Catfish had run out of smart-alecky comments under the pressure of what was to come.

The convoy arrived at the flea market grounds. The man at the gate waved the Hummer on and directed him toward the gun tent. Catfish followed the Humvee, and the F-150 stayed close behind Catfish and Danny.

Ben walked out and greeted Nick, then instructed Chris and Catfish where to park. Everyone poured out of the vehicles and gathered around Ben.

The weathered old soldier pointed towards the mess tent. "They're clearing out the tables right now. We're going to brief everyone on the battle plan at four."

"You've already got a plan put together?" Nick asked.

"No. We've got a map and a general idea of the layout, but I wanted to hear what Danny has to say about what he saw when he was there. Why don't you two come with me over to the command center?"

Nick nodded. "Chris and Clay are both airmen. And pretty lethal, I might add. They fought their way home from Texas."

Ben nodded with a smile. "Then y'all come on with us."

Danny looked at Antoine. "Can you keep your eye on the girls?"

"Sure thing, Danny." He smiled.

"Let's go look at what the vendors are selling!" Dana led the pack.

"Thanks, Antoine." Danny waved as he walked away, knowing he'd just handed the big man a daunting task.

Ben led them back toward the trees where Nick had spotted what he thought was a comms repeater. Chris walked close to Ben. "We've got a .338 Lapua. Clay and I are both pretty good shooters and pretty good spotters. We switch off."

"That could come in handy. How are you set for ammo?" Ben turned to him.

"We might have eighty rounds left. It weighs in at about a pound for every ten rounds, and a large portion of our trip home was on foot, so we were limited on how much we could haul. But eighty rounds will yield at least sixty kills if you can set us up within five hundred yards of a target rich environment."

Ben nodded as he walked. "We might have just the place for you. I don't know if you'll be able to take out eighty men from where I have in mind, but if you can kill ten, that's ten less we'll have to deal with up close and personal. Once the chaos starts, though, we might need you to drop the rifle and move in with the rest of us."

"We can do that. We're versatile," Clay said.

"Good." Ben continued around the trees, to a rugged wooden structure. It was somewhere between a cabin and a storage shed. Danny guessed it had been some sort of office for the flea market.

Ben opened the door. "Welcome to the inner sanctum."

Danny and the others followed him in. There was an old desk. It was very large and looked like it might have been an antique. Danny figured it would be quite valuable if it had been better cared for. On the desk was a giant, hand-drawn map of the streets that ran around the TD convention center.

Ben pointed to the map. "As soon as you left yesterday, we managed to get a hold of a Greenville street map that one of the men had. Evan is our head cook. He also has a knack for drawing. He used that little bitty street map and drew this out. It seems to be pretty close to scale, as far as I can tell. We ain't doin' no surveying with it anyway. It will suit our purpose just fine.

"Here's the convention center. Danny, can you tell us what you saw when you were there?"

Danny walked over to the map. "We came in from the back. The convention center is right here, facing the airport."

"Can you sketch it in for us?" Ben handed Danny a pencil.

"It's not going to be as good of a drawing as Evan has done."

"That's not important. And here's something, if you need a straight edge." Ben handed Danny a ruler.

Danny drew in the front wall of the convention center. "You have three entrances along the front. All the security was at this center entrance when we hit it." Danny sketched out the main entrance with the walkway, as well as the two entrances on either side.

"We can bet that they'll have guards at all three entrances this time." Ben stroked his beard. "Isn't this a parking lot?"

"Yeah, have you been there?" Danny asked.

Ben nodded. "It's been a while. Just put a P with a circle around it. That tells us it's a parking lot."

Danny followed the directions. "They had a few Deuce and a half in this parking lot when we were there. You've got one more entrance with like a circular drive, right here on Eisenhower." Danny marked the entrance and what he remembered to be a roundabout. "Next to that, there's a service entrance with one or two loading docks, also on Eisenhower, but the main loading docks are along the back side. This area behind the loading docks is all wooded, the best I can remember."

Ben took the pencil from Danny and began scribbling in some trees. "Yep. You're right about the trees. That's probably going to be our main avenue of approach." Ben pointed to the other side of the map. "This is Bob Jones University. My pastor went to school there. There's a big parking garage right here at the university. It's about three quarters of a mile back. We'll be using the parking garage for our staging area. We'll also have a field hospital with a nurse practitioner set up there. Then, we've got a surgeon, a family physician, and three nurses who'll have a makeshift trauma unit set up here at the flea market. Several of the men's wives are volunteering to help out at one medical site or the other. We'll get casualties back to the field hospital, the nurse practitioner will get them stable, and then we'll transport them back here. Bob Jones University is about twenty-five miles from here."

Danny liked the sound of that. Cami had a few fancy bandages at the farm, but anyone with a serious injury was never going to get the type of care they needed.

Chris looked the map over. "Where were you

planning to put us?"

Ben looked over at Danny. "Seems to me that the air traffic control tower is about right here. Does that sound right to you?"

Danny looked at the map. "Yeah, we were right here, behind this lot. I think I remember seeing the tower back here."

Chris shook his head. "If the map is scale, or close to it, and it's three quarters of a mile to the parking garage, then the tower is only two hundred yards away from the closest entrance of the convention center. If I were Schlusser, I'd have guards in the tower myself."

Ben smiled. "Which would have to be taken out before we could get inside anyway. The Humane Society is right around here. I got my two dogs from there. It's a two-story building all the way at the other end of the runway. If there are men in that tower, you should be able to get a clear shot of them from the roof of the Humane Society."

"Let's say we kill one man in the tower. The others are going to duck and take cover. They'll probably put in a call while they're laying low."

"Good point," Ben said. "But if you've only got a hundred and fifty men at that location, how many can you dedicate to the tower? I'm guessing only two. You might shoot one, or you might get lucky and get a shot where they're both lined up. .338 at that range, it'll easily travel through two skulls."

Clay shook his head. "You're asking for the impossible."

Ben put his hand up. "Hear me out. We can have a breach team near the entrance to the tower, we can send them up to secure the tower as soon as you take the shot. They can take out the other guard.

"The way I count, Schlusser has half his force going out on raiding missions in the daytime, and the other half working security. So seventy-five guys for security, divided by three shifts, leaves twenty-five men standing guard when we hit them. I promise you he's not going to have an eight-man squad standing idle in that tower. If they put in a call, they'll be scrambling to secure the convention center, not sending reinforcement to the tower."

Chris asked, "If he's sending half of his men out on raiding missions, why don't we wait til they're gone? Hit them in the daylight, then we'd only have half as many to fight."

"Unless they get called back in and flank us from behind." Ben looked at Chris.

Chris nodded. "You're right."

Ben resumed laying out the basic plan. "We've got eighty men who'll be participating in the raid."

Nick cut him off. "Eighty? I thought you were going to be calling up more men?"

"We did. They'll be providing security here and at the staging area. That's another forty. If you count the medical personnel and volunteers, another eighty. All those folks are going to serve us better as support. Most of them have no experience or training. They'd get in the way on the battlefield. Besides all of that, we need them functioning in the capacity that I've assigned them for."

Ben pointed toward the back side of the convention center. "Our main force, consisting of sixty men will come in from the north and take up positions in the wooded area. I'll have a smaller force right along Eisenhower. We'll line up shots for the guards on the outside and time them to be taken out at the same time you take your shot from the Humane Society. As soon as you take out your man, head straight to the tower. Nick, you take your other fire team into the tower and clear it so it's ready when Chris and Clay get there. They can focus on getting set up and picking people off whenever they get a shot. By that time, there will be too much going on for anyone to figure out where the sniper fire is coming from.

"We'll kill anybody who sticks their head out the door, forcing them to hole up inside the convention center. Next, we'll breach the entrance on Eisenhower. If I remember correctly, it's a big glass entrance."

"I'd hate to be the guy driving through the entrance," Danny said.

"So would I," Ben replied. "That's why I think we'll just put a brick on the gas pedal of an old van. Might as well fill it up with some field expedient explosives since won't none of our boys be in it. A couple of the fellows in the Pickens militia used to participate in some historical reenactments from time to time. I'm sure I can scratch up some cannon fuse and maybe some gun powder as well. Either way, I can rig something up to detonate a little diesel fuel and fertilizer. It'll make a nice flash bang. As the smoke is clearing, we can rush in and hit them hard. We'll clear the entire convention center, one room at a time if we have to."

Nick raised his eyebrows as he looked at the

map. "I like it. I think it's a good plan. Chris, Clay, Danny, what do you guys think?"

Danny waited to see what Chris and Clay thought. Both nodded. Danny said, "It sounds good to me."

"Good, then let's go fill in the troops." Ben rolled up the map.

Nick, Chris, and Clay hurried out the door and back toward the vehicles. Danny took his time.

Ben caught up with Danny. "You don't see yourself as a leader."

"Why should I?"

Ben chuckled. "Humility is a rare quality, and a fine one, at that. But don't let it get in the way of you fulfilling your purpose."

Danny continued walking and looked over at Ben for the explanation to his riddle.

"I'll see you at the briefing." Ben turned off of the path and headed to another tent.

Danny watched as the man walked away. "That was rather cryptic." He scanned the vendors' booths for the girls. "I should be able to spot Antoine." He looked above the heads of the people. "There he is." Danny made his way over to where he'd spotted his friend.

Alisa met him there. "We found some clothes for Antoine! The guy only wants like three rounds of ammo for each thing."

Danny pursed his lips. "I'd hate to see Antoine not need those clothes tomorrow for want of three rounds of ammo tonight. How about we get through this and come back tomorrow and do some shopping."

Dana smirked. "Spoilsport."

Danny rolled his eyes and looked at Antoine. "If those clothes fit you, I doubt there's much risk of anyone else buying them before we come back."

Antoine smiled. "That's fine, Danny. I'm not in any hurry."

"That will be awesome if we can come back tomorrow. That'll give us a chance to look through our stuff and see if we have anything to trade." Gwen sounded pleased with the proposition.

"Look, real crutches!" Dana held up a pair of gently used crutches.

"For who?" Danny asked.

"Steven," she replied.

"He's getting around with a cane. He doesn't need those." Danny protested.

Dana raised her eyebrows. "This is Steven we're talking about. He gets shot in the leg like every other day."

Danny shook his head to show his disapproval of the jest made in extremely poor taste.

"What did you guys talk about?" Alisa asked.

"I can tell you what I know so far, but I would expect there to be some tweaks put on the plan by the time we have the briefing." Danny relayed to Antoine and the girls everything that Ben had told him about the mission, the field hospital and the trauma center as they made their way back to the vehicles.

When they arrived, Dana sat in the Humvee next to Steven. "We're coming back to go shopping tomorrow!"

Steven looked at Danny. "Did you approve this

extracurricular activity?"

"We'll need a little fun and distraction by tomorrow." Danny was doing his best to stay positive. He knew there was a good chance he'd be burying more of his friends, or they'd be burying him on the following day. He also knew it wouldn't help morale to issue such a caveat for the well-deserved shopping expedition.

A middle-aged man with a classic military haircut wearing US Army BDUs approached the vehicles. He approached Nick with his hand extended. "Are you Nick?"

"Yes." Nick shook the man's hand.

"Ben sent me over to introduce myself. I'm Lucas. I'm in command of the squad who will be covering your left flank. If you guys . . ." Lucas glanced at Alisa, Dana, and Gwen with a smile. ". . . or gals, get into a mess over there, you just give me a shout. We're ten, two fire teams of five each. We'll be coming in from the staging in a Deuce and a half. One of the old guys, Randy, is our driver. He'll be dropping us off then staying close by, in case we need an evac. Ben will assign location codes at the briefing so the enemy won't know what we're talking about if we have to call for an evac. If anyone on your team gets a scratch and needs to get out, you just call Randy and give him your location code. He'll come pick you up."

"Thanks. It's an honor to serve with you," Nick said.

"You, too. See y'all at the briefing."

At a quarter til four, Danny and the others

headed to the mess tent, where Ben and his two top militia leaders went over the plan. The map they had worked on in Ben's office was taped to a large chalk board. It had been gone over with a black Sharpie to make it easier to see for the crowd of more than one hundred to see. After the presentation, time was allotted for questions and answers, which helped bring clarity to the mission.

Afterwards, Ben dismissed Danny's team and the Pickens militia. "We'll get the table set back up in here and start serving dinner around seven. We roll out at nine. If you can sneak a nap in, do it. We're in for a long night."

The next few hours were filled with anticipation and speculation of what the night would bring. Nick went over the individual roles of everyone from the farm for the next two hours. Afterwards, Danny and Alisa lay down in the bed of Catfish's truck which was parked beneath a shade tree. Danny hoped to steal a quick cat nap, but it was no use. He wasn't going to sleep.

Dinner helped to pass the time. Afterwards, Nick went over the plan one more time and did a final gear inspection. Ben came around at eight-thirty and did a comms check to ensure everyone on Danny's team was tuned into the same frequency as the militia.

Then, at nine o'clock, they loaded up and headed to the staging area.

CHAPTER 10

I returned, and saw under the sun, that the race is not to the swift, nor the battle to the strong, neither yet bread to the wise, nor yet riches to men of understanding, nor yet favour to men of skill; but time and chance happeneth to them all. For man also knoweth not his time: as the fishes that are taken in an evil net, and as the birds that are caught in the snare; so are the sons of men snared in an evil time, when it falleth suddenly upon them.

Ecclesiastes 9:11-12

"Can you see okay, Catfish?" Danny noticed that

the old man was straining to see the Humvee in front of him. Ben had called over the radio for everyone to cut their lights when they entered the city limits of Greenville.

"I can see good enough." Catfish leaned forward over the steering wheel.

Danny had a different definition of *good enough* than Catfish, but they would soon be at the staging area, and he'd be sure that Catfish left his truck in the parking garage.

Once they arrived, everyone got out of the vehicles and tried to make as little noise as possible. Ben positioned the various squads next to the other squads they'd be working with. He passed by Danny's group, giving them one last inspection. "We're going in at 10:00. You'll have just seconds to get into position. We start firing on the enemy at 10:10."

Danny nodded and looked around at the rest of his fire team. Steven and Nick would be driving Chris and Clay to the Humane Society building, then bringing them to the air traffic control tower to rendezvous with Danny and the others.

Lucas came by. "You guys want a ride?"

"I'm driving. We're fine," Catfish answered abruptly.

Danny politely stepped forward. "We'd love a ride." He turned and whispered to Catfish, "You don't want your truck getting all shot up for no reason."

Catfish looked annoyed, but said, "You might have a point."

Jack and Antoine would be accompanying

Danny's team until Chris and Clay returned. They all loaded snuggly into the rear of the old military truck. Lucas stood on the back bumper and held onto the truck, patting the side of the vehicle to signal to the driver that they were ready to go.

The truck pulled out of the parking garage, passed the tennis courts and onto Pleasantburg Drive. They were at their drop-off point in less than two minutes. Danny jumped out, as did Antoine, Catfish, and Jack. Antoine assisted the girls in exiting the vehicle. They quietly made their way up Tower Drive, staying in the shadows of the trees and buildings, whenever possible.

Danny led the way, with Alisa directly behind him. They took cover in the shrubbery, right in front of the building with the air traffic control tower. Danny kneeled down so Alisa could retrieve the short-barreled shotgun with the pistol grip from Danny's pack. She passed it to him. He looked at his watch. It was 10:08, and they were in position. Danny prayed silently as the seconds passed, begging God to keep Alisa safe.

He glanced at his watch again. 10:10. He listened for the first shot.

POP, POW. Crack, crack, crack! He heard gunfire erupt from multiple directions. "Let's move in!"

Danny led the team to the glass door, which was locked. "Antoine!"

Antoine stepped forward with a pry bar and smashed out the glass. He reached in and turned the lock, pulling the door open for Danny and the others. Danny reached the door to the stairwell leading up to the tower. It was locked. He held the shotgun at a forty-five-degree angle from the lock and the door jamb, just as JC had taught him. He turned away and pulled the trigger. POW! The mangled fragments of the lock fell away and Danny kicked the door open. Dana and Gwen ran up the stairs behind Antoine and Jack as Danny handed the shotgun to Alisa to return to his pack.

"Catfish, you watch the stairwell. Call if you see trouble." Danny headed up the four flights of stairs.

Gunfire broke out from above, and Danny rushed to get to the air traffic control observation floor. When he arrived, the shooting had stopped. A large bullet hole in the glass revealed the origin of the round that had exploded the head of the dead guard on the south side of the tower. Jack and Antoine had exchanged fire with the second guard who was riddled with bullet holes. Danny scanned the tower then looked at Jack and Antoine. "Are you guys okay?"

Antoine looked himself over. "Yeah. I'm good."

"Me, too." Jack nodded.

"Good, let's clear the building downstairs. "Alisa, you and Dana keep a look out from the tower. Alisa, you watch the south side, and Dana, watch the north. Let us know if anyone is heading in this direction. Also, call me when you see the Humvee rolling up with Chris and Clay."

"Got it," Alisa replied.

Danny led the way back down the stairs where they cleared each room to be sure no one else was in the building. Alisa's voice came over the radio. "Dana saw six men coming from those buildings next door. They're coming this way."

Danny keyed the mic. "Roger. Take a shot if you get one." He motioned to the others. "We've got company coming. Let's try to keep 'em back from upstairs."

Jack looked at Danny. "Then we'll be trapped. I think we should hold them from down here."

Danny remembered the words Ben had said to him hours ago. "Jack, upstairs, right now! I'm the team leader, and you're part of my team until Chris gets back."

Jack hustled up the stairs without further objection, as did Gwen, Catfish, and Antoine. Danny pulled the door closed behind them and followed them up the stairs. Alisa and Dana were both laying down fire on the north side, through the glass.

Danny pointed to the stairwell. "Gwen, Catfish, and Jack, you watch this stairwell. When they come through the door downstairs, empty your mags. Antoine, see if you can knock that glass out so we can see what we're shooting at."

The glass was much thicker and harder than the door, but with the perforations from multiple rounds of steel-core 5.56, Antoine was able to clear out a gun port.

"Do you still see them?" Danny asked.

"They're behind that building!" Dana pointed to the building nearest to them.

Alisa shot three more rounds at the corner. "If they get across that short section of parking lot, we won't be able to hit them. They'll have cover from our building."

Danny quickly recognized the problem. "I need to take a team out on the roof, below the tower. Dana, Alisa, you keep them pinned down. Gwen, you'll watch the stairs. Catfish, watch the south side from the tower; make sure we're not getting flanked."

Dana and Alisa let out a volley of fire. Alisa yelled, "Six more just came through the far fence. We hit two, the other four are working their way to the first six. You better hurry!"

Danny darted down the stairs. "Antoine, Jack, follow me."

The three men descended to the third level and quickly found the roof access.

Danny tried the door knob. "Locked!"

"Want your shotgun?" Antoine was right behind him.

"Yep." Danny stood still, as there was no need to kneel for the tall man to access his pack.

Antoine passed the shotgun to Danny. Again, he quickly shot off the door handle and passed the shotgun back to Antoine to stow. They stayed low and made it to the northeast corner of the building. Danny and the others got into positions where they wouldn't be seen from the ground below. He called to Alisa. "Change magazines and give a couple of them a chance to run out."

"Roger." Alisa's gun ceased as did Dana's.

Five of the men, who had been standing behind the corner of the adjacent building, immediately dashed out from behind it, toward the tower building. Danny shot one, as did Antoine. Jack hit one in the leg.

"Wait! See if his buddy will come back." Danny put his hand on Jack's shoulder before he could finish the man off.

Sure enough, one of the men ran back. Danny shot him in the back. "Okay, finish him off."

Jack placed two more shots into the chest of the injured man.

"We've still got one who made it across. What do you want to do about him?" Antoine asked.

Danny called over the radio. "Gwen, one got through. Look sharp, he might be coming to the stairwell. I'm sending Antoine to watch the stairs from the third level. Don't shoot him!"

Antoine patted Danny on the back and headed back to the stairwell.

Rifle fire sprayed out from the corner of the building, and three more men ran across. Danny tried to stop them, but he had to duck to avoid the rounds that were hitting the roof line all around him. Danny pressed the mic. "We've got four downstairs now. Everybody stay alert." He looked at Jack. "There's no way we can let the other two get across. If one of them starts laying down cover fire, we're going to have to take our chances."

Seconds later, another wave of cover fire streamed from the corner. Danny looked at Jack. "Go!" Both popped up to see one more man running across. They each centered their fire on the man, and he fell in his tracks.

Danny tapped Jack on the shoulder. "There's nobody else to lay down cover for the last guy. You just keep him pinned. I'm going to go back up Antoine." Danny ran across the roof to the door and took a position at the edge of the stairwell.

Nick's voice came over the radio. "Danny, we're coming to you."

"We've got four hostiles trying to get into the building. Stay back."

"If I see them, I'll eliminate them for you."

"Thanks."

Danny heard the door open at the bottom of the stairs. "Here they come!" He took aim at a section of the stairs where he could see to the wall. Gunfire rang out from the direction of the convention center. Danny knew he had to clear this stairwell so Chris and Clay could eliminate the men who were most likely killing members of the militia. If their numbers became too depleted, the militia wouldn't be strong enough to breach the convention center, and the mission would fail.

He saw a leg and took a shot. Antoine was beside him with a slightly different target window. He placed several more shots.

"Did you get 'em?" Danny stayed focused.

"Nope."

"Me neither." A second man ran through, then a third. Danny fired ferociously, hitting the fourth.

Gunfire shot up through the stairwell, hitting very close to Danny and Antoine.

Danny kicked the door open behind him. "Back up, they have to come by here before they go upstairs. Only three left."

Antoine and Danny backed out onto the roof. Danny changed his magazine. "I've got a fresh mag. I'll cover the stairs. Change your mag. They've got at least another flight to climb."

Antoine quickly complied. "Ready!"

Danny waited. A man ran up shooting straight at the door. Danny and Antoine returned fire, killing the man, but letting the other two slip right by.

"Two hostiles coming your way, Gwen. Get everyone on that doorway!"

A hail of bullets rang out in the stairwell above. Danny wanted to run upstairs and eliminate the threat to his wife, but if he did, he risked being shot by one of his own team members. He could do nothing but wait for the shooting to cease.

Finally, the gunfire stopped. "What's happening?" Danny pleaded.

A brief period of silence preceded Gwen's voice. "All clear."

Danny rushed up the stairs calling on the radio as he ran. "Nick, we're down to one guy at the corner of the building next door."

"Which corner?"

"Southeast. Jack is covering the corner from our side. You could probably slip around from the back and take him out."

"Consider it done."

Danny stepped over the corpses of the fallen men to get into the air traffic control room. "Alisa! Are you okay?"

"Yeah!" She ran over and looked at Danny. "You?"

He gave a sigh of relief, hugged her and looked at the rest. "Anybody hurt?"

"My arthritis is been actin' up of a mornin'." Catfish had no sense of when to play around and when to be serious.

Danny remembered what Dana had once said about him being part raccoon. He thought she might be right about that. "Everybody, fresh mags in your rifles. Switch out your empties for full mags from your packs. Get a drink of water and get ready to do it again. As soon as Chris and Clay get up here, my team is moving out. Antoine, you and Jack will work security to make sure no one takes the tower. If you get more coming at you than you can handle, call, and we'll come running."

Danny heard several shots coming from the adjacent building. He keyed the mic. "Did you get him?"

"All clear." Nick replied over the radio.

"Antoine, do you want to go pull Jack in from the roof?" Danny made a circular motion with his hand, signaling for Catfish and the girls to rally around him so they could head downstairs as soon as Chris and Clay arrived.

"You got it." Antoine waved as he headed out the door. "You all be safe."

"You too, Antoine," Gwen said.

Chris and Clay made their way up the stairs shortly thereafter.

Danny pointed toward the large hole in the viewing glass. "Antoine took the liberty of setting you guys up with a gun port."

"Thanks." Clay smiled as he dropped the legs on the tripod of the sniper rifle.

"We helped with it, too." Dana said as she followed Danny out the door.

Danny led the way down the stairs. Steven and Nick were waiting outside with the Hummer. "Let's go. Lucas is pinned down on the southwest side of the building." Nick motioned for them to hurry. "When we get there, I'm going to start sweeping with the .50. You guys all find good solid cover, like a tree or something, and snipe anyone who sticks their head up. Hop in the back. I'll give you a lift up to Eisenhower. But jump out when we turn off of Tower Drive. The Humvee will be a big target, so keep your distance."

Danny helped the girls step up on the bumper and into the open back of the vehicle. Catfish took the passenger's seat, since Nick was standing in the turret. Steven sped off down the short stretch of road and stopped at the corner. Nick pointed to the parking lot across from the convention center. "Use those cars for cover. Remember, an engine block will stop a bullet, but a windshield won't. Think about what you're hiding behind when you take your position."

Danny jumped out and helped Alisa and the other two girls out of the back. Catfish rolled out of the passenger's side, and Steven drove toward the action. Danny waved for his team to follow him to the edge of the shrubs. "Let's keep a low profile."

They followed the tree line to the parking lot. "Catfish, Gwen, you guys take a position between these two cars. We'll go down a ways so we're spread out."

Gwen and Catfish got low and found a place where they had a decent field of fire. Danny hunched down to stay behind the cars and led Dana and Alisa to a spot between two other vehicles, about five cars down from Catfish and Gwen.

Danny lay down on his stomach and took aim. "We'll run this just like the fox hole on the farm. When I run out of ammo, one of you two take over while I change mags." Danny watched as Nick opened up the .50 caliber machine gun on the guards outside of the convention center. He watched as they began running for cover. He led his front sight in front of one guard, who he could see was making a run for cover behind a truck. Danny unleashed several rounds in the path of the man. At least one round found its target, and the man dropped. He watched as three others were cut down. Two by Nick's rapid fire from the Humvee and another from a shooter in the direction of Lucas's squad.

Suddenly, gunfire erupted and the glass in the windows of the car above Danny began to explode. "Put your head down! Cover your eyes!" Glass rained down on his back and head like hail.

Lucas's voice came over the radio. "I've got two men down. Randy, I need an evac at location eight."

"Roger," a voice responded to Lucas.

"Where is it coming from?" Alisa asked.

"I think they're on top of the building!" Dana kept her face to the ground.

Danny keyed the mic of his radio. "Chris, we've got shooters on the roof of the southwest corner. Can you see them?"

"Roger that." Chris's voice came back.

Danny crawled back behind the cars and traveled three cars further down the lot so he could see the roof line. Six men were firing down at Nick. Danny took aim and began spraying bullets in their direction, hitting one man.

Rifle fire was still coming from Lucas's direction, killing two more men on the roof. Danny saw Steven trying to maneuver the Humvee out of harm's way as it was the sole target of the men on the roof, at this point.

Another of Schlusser's goons fell forward off the roof. Danny supposed it was the force of the .338 from behind that had launched him over the side.

Steven's voice came over the radio. "Nick is hit."

Lucas's voice replied. "Is he responsive? If so, get him over to location eight. Evac is on the way here."

Steven came back. "No."

Danny pressed the talk button. "Where is he hit?"

Steven answered, "I can't tell. He's slouched over in the back. There's a lot of blood."

Danny knew that wasn't good. "Take him on over to location eight then."

"As soon as you drop him off, come pick me up." Clay said over the radio. "Somebody has to be on that .50."

"Roger," Steven replied.

Danny moved from car to car to keep the shooters on the roof guessing where he'd pop up next. He instructed Alisa and Dana to stay behind the cars, but they didn't listen. They began mimicking his whack-a-mole tactic, jumping from car to car, taking a few shots, and then relocating before the shooters from the roof could get a bead on them.

Soon Steven was ripping back up the street with Clay firing the .50 cal at the roof line.

Lucas's voice came back over the radio. "Mason's squad is taking heavy fire from inside the convention center. They've got the loading dock doors open and are hammering down on him and the squad next to him. They've got multiple casualties that they can't get to safety. They'd sure appreciate it if you could put that .50 on the loading docks long enough for them to clear the wounded.

"We're on it." Steven's voice was followed by a massive volley of fire from the machine gun mounted on top of the Humvee.

Danny stepped out to fire at the snipers on the roof who were pelting the Humvee with lead. Alisa and Dana did the same.

"Ouch!" Dana yelped. Something hot just hit my arm! I think it was a rock."

"Get down!" Danny pulled Dana to the ground.

Alisa looked at her arm. "You're hit."

Danny pulled his pack off and took out one of the compression bandages Cami had given him. "It's bleeding on both sides. It looks like it went straight through."

Dana's forearm was pierced halfway between her wrist and her elbow. "It was a bullet?"

"Yes, sweetie, it was a bullet, but it's not bad. Just stay calm." Alisa put her arm around Dana as Danny wrapped the wound.

Once he'd finished wrapping her wound, he keyed the mic. "Lucas, did that evac truck already leave?"

"Yeah, but he can come right back in five minutes. Where do you need him?"

"We'll get her to location eight." Danny looked

at Dana. "Let's get you to the truck."

Dana looked at the growing red stain on the bandage. "Okay."

"Who's hit?" Steven asked over the radio.

"Dana, but it's not bad at all."

"We'll come pick you up," Steven replied.

"Stay on mission, Steven. It's not bad," Danny replied.

"Danny, I'm coming to get Dana. I'll get right back in the fight."

Danny shook his head as he heard the roar of the Humvee's engine speeding in their direction. The vehicle pulled into the lot that was still taking heavy fire. Clay continued to direct the .50 caliber toward the roof line.

Steven got out of the Humvee and hobbled around to open the passenger's door.

"Get back in the truck, Steven!" Danny yelled as he helped Dana to the Humvee.

Clay made a horrible sound in between the gunfire.

Danny loathed the thought of looking up, but he had to. When he did, he saw that part of Clay's lower jaw was missing; he had his hands over his neck attempting to stop a torrent of blood.

Steven turned to look at what had happened, and a round hit him in the back, knocking him to the ground.

"Steven!" Dana yelled as she dropped to her knees.

"Help me get him in the vehicle!" Danny yelled to Alisa.

Alisa and Danny picked Steven up and laid him

in the back of the Humvee. Danny looked at Dana who was horrified over Steven. "Can you get the guns and put them in the truck?"

Dana seemed to be in shock. "What?" She slowly turned around to look at the guns on the ground. She picked them up and placed them in the Hummer.

Alisa held Dana's arm up as she stepped into the Humvee. "You have to keep your arm elevated."

Danny jumped in the driver's seat, threw the Hummer in gear and tore out of the lot toward the staging area. He raced around the block and headed north on Pleasantburg Drive. He pulled into the parking garage in just over a minute.

Dana threw the door open. "Medic, we need a medic!"

Two volunteers ran up to the Humvee with a stretcher. "Who's hurt?" one asked.

Danny pointed to Steven who was gasping for breath. "He was hit in the back."

The volunteer yelled. "Nurse! This one is hit in the lungs."

Dana stood by silently, staring at Steven, with her injured arm up and her other hand stroking his head.

The nurse practitioner was trying to stabilize multiple patients for transport back to the trauma center. She ran over and looked at Steven as Danny and the volunteers hoisted him out of the Humvee and onto the stretcher. "Is there an exit wound?"

Danny shook his head as he looked at Steven's heaving chest. "I don't think so."

Alisa pointed to Clay who was motionless on the

floor in the center of the Humvee. "Clay was hit, also. I don't know if he is still alive."

The nurse looked at Clay and let out a sorrowful sigh. "Oh no." She turned her attention back to Steven. "Let's get him to the table." The two volunteers carried the stretcher over to a folding table set up in the parking garage. The nurse took Steven's pulse and looked up at Danny. "He's been hit in the lungs. No exit wound. It was likely a hollow point, so there's probably a lot of damage." She instructed the volunteers to roll him over. She cut his shirt off and placed a chest seal on the entry wound. "I can't do much else for him here, except make him comfortable." She took out a syringe and stuck the needle in Steven's arm.

Danny watched as the drug took effect and Steven's breath grew shallow. "But he could pull through, right? I mean, there's always a chance."

"There's always hope." The nurse looked at Danny and gave a sympathetic smile. "But he doesn't look good."

Dana took Steven's hand. "Steven, if you can you hear me, I love you. Please stay with me."

"Danny, where are you guys?" Chris's voice came over the radio.

Danny keyed the mic. "At the staging area. Steven and Clay were both hit."

"Is it bad?"

"Yeah, that's why we wanted to get them over here right away."

"Okay, come pick me up. I'll pull Jack and put him on the sniper rifle, I'll run the .50."

Danny looked at Steven. "You hang in there,

buddy." Then he closed his eyes and looked up. "God, please watch over Steven, keep him alive and guide the doctors as they try to save him."

Danny swallowed the knot in his throat. "Alisa, you stay with Dana and Steven. They might need you."

"No way. I'm not injured. I'm going back with you!" Alisa kissed Dana on the forehead. "Stay with Steven, we'll be back." She got in the passenger's seat of the Hummer.

Danny started the engine. "Alisa, it's not safe."

"It's war Danny, of course it's not safe."

"I mean the Humvee, it's a death trap. Look how many people it has gotten killed."

She shook her head as she checked her weapon, replacing the magazine with a full one. "Just go!"

Danny drove out of the garage. "Okay, but I'm dropping you off with Catfish and Gwen. I have to get Chris."

Alisa bit her lower lip. "Why do you have to drive? Why can't Catfish or Antoine drive? You do everything. You infiltrate the camp, you're always putting yourself on the front line, and I get to sit and worry. Worry if I'm going to be like Pauline, or Tracey, or Melissa . . . or Cami . . . or like Dana . . ." Alisa's voice cracked.

Danny wanted to stop the car and hold her in his arms to comfort her and tell her everything was going to be okay, but he couldn't. She was right, the list of widows and girlfriends left behind was growing by the minute. "I'll be back, Alisa. I promise." Danny pulled to the curve behind the parking lot where Gwen and Catfish were.

"You better, Danny." Alisa grabbed her rifle as she exited the vehicle.

Danny raced toward the air traffic control tower. He keyed the mic. "Chris, your ride is here."

"Be right down."

Danny used the time to grab more ammo for his AK from the back of the Hummer. He also stuck several magazines for Alisa's AR into his pack.

Seconds later Chris bounded out the door and toward the vehicle. He jumped in the turret.

"Watch your step, it's wet." Danny couldn't bring himself to tell Chris that it was Clay's blood all over the floor beneath the turret.

Chris didn't ask for clarification. "Thanks. Give me a second to check the ammo box. If it needs to be changed, I'd rather do it here than under heavy fire."

Danny nodded and waited for Chris to tell him when to move out.

"Yep, this box is empty. Looks like we've only got one more box. Let's make it count." Chris changed the ammo box, opening the top of the weapon and starting the fresh belt.

"How long will that last us?" Danny looked over his shoulder.

"It's one hundred rounds, so not long. As soon as it's dry, let's get out of dodge and ditch the Hummer. No point being a lead magnet for nothing. Just wheel us to cover, and we can link back up with another fire team. Okay, I'm ready to rock. They need some help along the front entrance. Just take me to the corner. We don't have to drive down Exposition Drive, but keep moving."

Lucas came over the radio. "All squads, watch your six. We've got two Humvees coming in from the west. Probably a patrol that was out and got called back in when we launched the attack."

Danny's heart skipped a beat. "Alisa, they're coming right at Alisa! We've got to get over there."

Chris said, "Nope. We've got to get to the corner and dump this box of ammo. It won't take three minutes if you can get me in close. Let's do this, then we can get to Alisa. If the broader mission fails, she dies anyway."

Danny gritted his teeth. He stomped the gas pedal and sped down Tower Drive. He slowed down from the time he cleared the trees on the corner of Exposition until he reached Eisenhower. Chris unleashed a firestorm of ammo towards the goons who were holding a position at the main entrance. As Danny passed Eisenhower, he hooked a sharp U turn so Chris could get another pass. Once again, he directed heavy fire on the main entrance as Danny continued down Tower.

"Are you empty?" Danny yelled.

"I've got enough for one more pass. Take it a little slower, I want to run out the rest of this box."

Danny hooked another U turn and slowed as he reached Exposition. The .50 caliber rang out, filling the air with a persistent barrage of loud bangs. Finally, it ceased.

"Are you out?" Danny kept his eyes on the road.

"Yep, and I'm hit. See if you can get me to location eight." Chris crawled into the passenger's seat, holding his right shoulder.

Danny looked over. "Is it bad?"

"It hurts like heck, but it didn't hit an artery. Feels like it shattered my collar bone." Chris winced in pain.

Danny hurried toward location eight which was on the corner of Tower and Pleasantburg. He spotted the Humvees. "There's those two enemy patrols. I think they just spotted us."

"Let's leave the Hummer and get into the woods." Chris's voice showed his agony.

Danny turned around and stuck the Humvee in the lawn of the hotel on the corner. "Can you walk?"

"I can run, but that's about it."

Danny led the way across the street and into the woods. He found an obscured place and motioned for Chris to sit down. "I've got some Quickclot." Danny dropped his pack and fished out the blood clotting agent. He tore Chris's shirt open and placed the Quickclot in the wound. Next, he applied a battle dressing. "This is a rough place to dress. You'll still have to keep pressure on it with your hand."

Chris nodded. "Send them to pick me up when it's clear."

"Can you fire your pistol if you get in trouble?"

Chris struggled to pull his sidearm with his right hand while keeping pressure on the wound with his left. "Yeah. Probably can't reload, but I can empty one mag."

Danny drew his Glock and laid it on Chris's leg. "Make it two mags."

"Thanks. Now go get your wife." Chris forced a smile.

Danny grabbed his AK-47. "You've got your radio. Call if you get in trouble."

Danny dashed through the shallow wooded lot between him and the parking lot where Alisa was. He jumped the fence then stayed low until he could get to her, Gwen, and Catfish. He reached the row of cars where he expected them to be but saw no one. What was worse, the two enemy Humvees had just turned onto Eisenhower Drive and were heading his way. Danny fell back to the second row of cars and rolled under a truck to hide. He looked around beneath the other cars in the lot to see if he could get a visual on Alisa's feet. He took his radio and whispered loudly. "Alisa, where are you guys?" He adjusted the volume lower so not to give away his position.

"We're in a red Ford van, at the rear of the parking lot."

"Okay, I'm under a silver truck. I'll come to you."

"No!" Her voice was insistent. "One of the Humvees just turned into the lot."

Danny sighed and looked toward the entrance of the lot. He saw the wheels of the Humvee several cars away, but rolling in his direction. Then he heard gunfire erupt. It sounded like the militia was firing on the Humvee. He saw the boots of Schlusser's goons get out of the vehicle to take up defensive positions. He had a perfect shot at their legs and feet, but it meant his position would be revealed immediately. Danny hesitated as he lined up the shot, visualizing which set of feet he would move to for his second, third, and fourth shot. He keyed his mic and whispered loudly. "Alisa, I'm getting ready to do something stupid. I need you guys to back me up in about ten seconds."

CHAPTER 11

What doth it profit, my brethren, though a man say he hath faith, and have not works? can faith save him? If a brother or sister be naked, and destitute of daily food, And one of you say unto them, Depart in peace, be ye warmed and filled; notwithstanding ye give them not those things which are needful to the body; what doth it profit? Even so faith, if it hath not works, is dead, being alone. Yea, a man may say, Thou hast faith, and I have works: shew me thy faith without thy works, and I will shew thee my faith by my works. Thou believest that there is one God; thou doest well: the devils also believe, and tremble. But wilt thou know, O vain man, that faith without works is dead?

James 2:14-20

"God, this is crazy. I can't do it without you, but I feel like something inside is telling me to take this shot. Please help me get through this." Danny pulled the trigger, sending two shots into the first set of feet. He quickly did the same for the second and third set of feet. Those three men were lying on the ground, one of them staring straight into Danny's eyes, and the rest of the feet were scattering to locate him. Danny fired on the man looking at him. He quickly took aim at the other two downed men who were positioning their rifles towards him. Danny unleashed a volley of lead toward the men, who quickly fell limp. Danny looked around. There were feet coming in from every side. He took aim and pulled the trigger, but nothing happened. "I'm empty! Not good! Not good!" He had to fight to pull a magazine from his vest since he was laying on it.

He had just extracted his magazine when a voice belonging to one set of the feet yelled out, "You're dead!"

Danny saw the man kneeling to take a shot. Suddenly, shots rang out from all around, and the feet were joined by their bloody bodies. Danny rushed to get his magazine in and racked a round into the chamber. He rolled out from beneath the truck and looked up to see Alisa kneeling down beside him.

"Danny! You're okay!"

His eyes were wide with surprise. "Yeah, how are you?"

"Great, but get up. We've got to keep moving." She grabbed his hand and helped him sit up.

Gwen and Catfish were bent low as they scurried between the truck and the car where Danny and Alisa were.

"Thanks guys. How are you all set on ammo?"

Alisa tugged her vest. "I re-upped in the Humvee. I've got three more mags."

"Just spent my last bullet on that ornery critter who was fixing to put your lights out." Catfish patted the empty magazine pouches fastened to his overall straps.

Danny nodded, removing his backpack. "What about you, Gwen?"

She switched magazines. "This is my last full mag."

Danny handed five magazines to Catfish, two to Alisa, and four to Gwen. "Check these guys we just shot. See if we can find a few more mags. That's all I have besides the ones on my vest."

Gwen crawled on her hands and knees to the closest fallen goon. "He's got some fresh AR mags."

"Good!" Danny crab crawled around the vehicle to check the other fallen guards. "AK!" he looked at the curiously small AK magazines in the man's vest. "Never mind. These are for a 74, not a 47."

Danny continued to the next body. "More AR mags." He stripped them out of the man's chest rig.

"Here's some AK mags, Danny!" Alisa whispered loudly from behind the adjacent automobile.

"Good, give Catfish two more and stick the rest in my pack." Danny motioned for everyone to get close to him so they could work their way closer to the convention center.

Lucas's voice came over the radio, but Danny had the volume so low, he couldn't hear him. He quickly adjusted the volume. "Lucas, this is Danny, can you repeat that?"

"Yeah, Danny, I need you to bring your team to the southeast corner of the lot where you are."

"Roger." Danny motioned for Alisa and the others to follow him, while staying low behind the cover of the vehicles. They reached the corner of the lot in just over a minute. Danny quickly spotted Lucas who was kneeling beside six other men.

"Is this all you have left?" Lucas's face was grim.

"Jack and Antoine are still in the tower. But yeah, everyone else is dead or injured." Danny had been trying to avoid thinking about that reality. He put in a quick call for Randy to pick up Chris. "I need a man evaced. He's in the wooded area to the north of location eight. He's conscious and can walk, so he'll probably come out when he sees you pull up."

Lucas pursed his lips. "This is what's left of my squad. The whole militia was hit hard. We're down to about thirty total, including your team."

Lucas looked at the remaining handful of men with him then back at Danny. "The good news is, their numbers are lower, too. We've wiped out at least a hundred and forty. And the ones who are still alive are holed up inside the convention center."

"So you think about ten left?"

"No way. More like sixty."

"Sixty? I thought we were going on the assumption that there were only a hundred and fifty goons."

Lucas nodded. "A hundred and fifty goons, plus around fifty non-combatants."

"But we don't have to worry about them, right?"

Lucas glanced toward the convention center. "Funny thing about non-combatants, as soon as you try to invade their stronghold, they suddenly get combative."

"Yeah, I guess they do. What if we get inside and it's like women or girls who have been doing the cooking?"

Lucas continued to look toward the entrance on Eisenhower. "Easy, anyone who is doing anything except lying face down with their hands interlaced behind their head gets shot, regardless of race, color, sex, religion, age, or creed. I've got zip ties." Lucas pointed at Alisa and Gwen. "These two can be at the rear of the entry team. They can go through and restrain anyone with the good sense to surrender as we penetrate past the prisoners. Can you call your other two guys in? They did a great job sniping, but we don't need them up there as bad as we need them when we go in."

Danny keyed the mic. "Antoine, Jack, rendezvous with us in the southeast corner of the lot closest to location eight. We're waiting on you for phase two."

"Roger, be there in less than five," Antoine said.

Danny took the time to get a drink of water, offer some to the rest of his team, and ask Lucas if any of his men needed ammo. Minutes later, Antoine and Jack arrived.

Danny watched as the old white van, which had been loaded with explosives, pulled up to the Eisenhower Drive entrance. The van stopped outside then began charging toward the door. Danny could see that the driver, who had gotten out and was now running in the other direction, was Ben.

"That's our cue!" Lucas motioned for his men to be ready to move out.

Danny ducked his head as the van crashed through the glass and busted into an inferno of blazing fire. As soon as the explosion had detonated, he motioned for his team to follow him. They sprinted behind Lucas's team. When they reached the entrance, the fire was still burning too hot for them to enter. Ben ran up from behind, leading another squad. He pointed through the fire. "My team, on my lead, we're running right through that opening in the flames. If you catch fire, stop, drop and roll, but not until you've cleared the debris field. You don't want to be rolling around in shrapnel and broken glass."

Danny watched as the old man dashed like an action hero into the fire, leading eight other dedicated soldiers. "Wow!"

Lucas held his hand out. "You guys want to go next?"

Danny looked at his team. They all nodded that they were ready, so he motioned for them to follow and they all darted through the blazes.

Lucas's team followed next. Once they'd all reached the other side of the flames, Ben pointed to three doors. "We'll take the first room, Lucas, that one's yours, and Danny, your team take the last one.

Danny nodded, leading his team toward the third door. It was unlocked, Danny hoped the unsecured entrance implied that no one was inside. But to be safe, he cleared the room using the method JC had taught him. Indeed, the room turned out to be unoccupied.

When he came out of the room, Ben's team was moving toward the main exhibition hall. Ben called out, "We'll clear this area together. Stack up and get ready."

Ben gave the signal. His lead man breached the doorway and Ben's team poured into the exhibition hall. Gunfire rang out from inside the room. Danny's legs froze, but Lucas gave him a less than gentle nudge. "Go, Danny!"

Danny reached down inside and went against everything his body was telling him. He rushed through the door, into a room with bullets flying in every direction. He saw men with guns at the far side of the exhibition hall behind a make-shift barricade, constructed of bleachers and tables. Obviously, they had planned for this eventuality. In so doing, they'd left nothing to be used as cover for the invading force. Danny ducked low to reduce the height of his profile and ran toward the bathrooms. Antoine, Jack, Catfish, Gwen and Alisa did likewise. Lucas's team made a mad dash to the concession stands to meet up with Ben's team.

Danny's team didn't have a clear shot from the

entrance to the bathrooms, but they had good cover.

Danny retrieved a grenade from his pack. He looked at Antoine. "How is your football throwing arm?"

"It's been a while," Antoine replied.

Danny looked him in the eye. "But it's safe to say, you probably have a better shot of getting it in the bleachers than I do."

Antoine nodded. "I'd say that's accurate."

Danny handed him the grenade. "It's set for five and a half seconds. Pull the pen then count it off for two seconds, one Mississippi, two Mississippi, then throw it."

"Are you sure, Danny?"

"Positive. JC had me count off the first one we ever used. It's exactly five and a half seconds. If you throw it too soon, they could have just enough time to pick it up and throw it right back to us. And trust me, I've seen one of these things go off, it will ruin everybody's day."

Antoine blew out a deep breath as if he were steeling himself for the toss.

Danny keyed his mic. "We're sending in a surprise. Everybody keep your heads down for a minute." Danny knelt close to the floor and motioned for Jack to come next to him. "We're going to lay down some heavy cover fire. Don't worry about hitting anything, but we need to keep their heads down so Antoine can wind up for a good toss."

Jack nodded.

"Okay, pull the pin. We'll start shooting. Release the lever and count it down. On three. One, two, three!" Danny and Jack took prone positions near the corner of the entrance to the bathroom and began firing.

Antoine stepped out into the open. "One Mississippi, two . . ."

Danny saw the grenade make a perfect arch through the air, hit the wall behind the barricade, and drop straight down. Men began scattering from behind the barricade, but it was too late. Their fates were sealed. The bright flash of the grenade and the piercing boom filled the exhibition hall with sound and light. Danny and Jack began shooting at the men who were still moving. Lucas and Ben's teams were catching them in a cross fire, cutting down the survivors.

Lucas led his team to extinguish the remaining stragglers. Anyone not killed by the grenade was in bad condition. As Danny had already seen, the militia's medical team was way past capacity. He hated to see injured hostiles being gunned down like that. But he figured, under the circumstances, it was the most humane thing that could be done for them.

One man from Ben's team had been shot in the stomach, and another from Lucas's team caught a bullet in the head. Ben sent two men to carry the one who'd been gut shot. They took the injured man to the front door, where he would be picked up by Randy. The dead man would be carried out after the entire structure had been cleared.

"Rally around me, and let's move out. We've still got the rear expo hall and the offices to clear." Ben changed his magazine. "Danny, can your team handle the office?"

"Yes, sir." Danny followed Ben's direction to the office.

"Stack up behind me." Danny checked the knob. It was locked. "Antoine, hand me the shotgun."

Danny took the shotgun from the man behind him, held the barrel at an angle, and shot the lock. He flung the door open and Antoine rushed in, followed by Jack, Catfish, Alisa, and Gwen.

"Face down!" Jack screamed.

"On the ground, face down, do it now!" Alisa's voice rang out.

Danny stepped through the door just in time to see one of the women in the room leveling a revolver. He took aim and fired, but not before she'd taken three shots. The woman fell dead. The other women were screaming with their hands on their heads, complying with the demands to lie face down.

Immediately, he looked at Alisa. "Are you okay?"

"Yeah," Alisa answered keeping her AR-15 leveled at the women.

Gwen looked shaken, but she was in good enough shape to keep her rifle trained on the detainees.

Antoine called to Danny. "Jack is hit."

Danny's stomach sank. Jack was on the floor and blood was spurting out of his thigh. "It's his artery!" Danny dropped his rifle, removed his pack and retrieved a tourniquet. He quickly tied it around Jack's leg, and the blood stopped pumping out like a fountain. "Antoine, can you carry him over your shoulder? The Humvee is parked in the grass across from location eight. We need to get him back to the trauma unit in Pickens as soon as possible."

"You got it." Antoine took the keys from Danny.

Danny looked at Jack. "How are you feeling?"

"Weak and cold."

"You just try to stay alert until Antoine can get you back. Keep that tourniquet tight. If your leg starts bleeding again, turn the little bar one more time and lock it in the white clip. And don't loosen it, even if it feels like your leg is going to sleep or getting numb. Understand?"

Jack nodded.

"Good. Catfish, go with Antoine for security, just in case he runs into more trouble on the way. You guys get going. We'll catch up," Danny said.

Antoine gently picked Jack up and draped him over his shoulder, the way a child might carry a pet cat. Jack wasn't a large person, by anyone's definition, but hanging over Antoine's shoulder like a fox stole, he looked quite small.

Danny watched over the women as Gwen and Alisa began restraining them. He counted seven women besides the dead one. All the prisoners had managed to get to the opposite side of the room from the woman who had fired the pistol. It was a smart move on their part, because Danny had missed almost as many times as he had hit the dead woman. Anyone on either side of her would have likely caught at least one stray bullet. Once they were all restrained, Danny said, "Stay here with them, I'll go see how Ben is doing and let him know we have prisoners."

Alisa held her rifle at a low ready position.

"Okay, hurry back."

Danny found Ben and informed him of the detainees.

"Good work. We've got the rest of the building cleared." He put his hand on Danny's shoulder. "We did it. We shut Schlusser down. It cost us dearly. A lot of men paid with their lives; ours and yours. But better to cut this thing off at the root than let it grow." Ben looked around. "It seems like a high price to pay for a crummy old convention center, but the building isn't what we took here today. We took back our freedom. We couldn't have done it without you and your team."

Danny looked the old soldier in his eyes. "I hate to cut out on you, but do you have anyone who can watch the detainees? We've got a couple wounded that didn't look good at all. My team, we're all family . . ."

Ben cut him off. "Of course, Danny. You get out of here. We'll take care of the prisoners." Ben motioned for one of his men to follow Danny back to the office. "Carter, can you keep an eye on some detainees for me until we get a transport over here to pick them up?"

Carter nodded. "Yes, sir."

Danny led Carter to the office and called to Alisa and Gwen. "Girls, let's go."

The three of them proceeded out the nearest exit door.

"Are we going to walk back to the staging area?" Gwen asked.

Alisa paused and looked toward the parking lot where they had spent so much time fighting. "What about that Hummer in the lot?"

"Let's check it out." Danny turned toward the parking lot, still watching for possible hostiles. "Stay alert. We're not safe until we're home."

They walked the length of the convention center and finally reached the southwest lot.

Alisa looked the tan-colored vehicle over, which was still idling right where they'd left it. "It's in better condition than ours."

Gwen opened the passenger's side and got in. "Wow! Their seats aren't all ripped up and blood stained, and it still has the radio."

Alisa shared a seat with Gwen. "And best of all, it still has a windshield."

Danny sat in the driver's seat. "But no .50 caliber. I still like our green one better."

"That machine gun doesn't help much without ammo," Alisa said. "I like this one better. Besides, I'm tired of machine guns."

Danny put the vehicle in gear and began driving back toward the staging area. He was tired of machine guns too. That cursed .50 caliber had cost Nick and Clay their lives. Of course it had also sent many of Schlusser's goons to meet their Maker as well.

When they reached the staging area, Danny looked around the lot. "Catfish's truck is still here. So is the F-150."

"Did they leave the keys?" Alisa asked. "We can both drive a truck back."

Danny drove over to the F-150. "I don't know if Chris did, but I can guarantee that Catfish didn't. He started sleeping with them in his pocket after JC *commandeered* his truck." Danny jumped out to check the ignition, visor, and floor mat of the F-150. "No dice. I guess we'll get them later."

Danny climbed back in the Hummer and headed back to Pickens. He wasn't in a hurry to get there. The last time he'd seen Steven, his friend was still breathing. For the short drive back to the flea market grounds, the man who had told him about Jesus, walked with him to the altar when he'd accepted Christ as his Savior, and stood by him at his wedding was still alive. The friend who'd encouraged him in his Christian walk, believed his crazy dream, prepared with him before the lights went out, and fought beside him on the journey to the farm, still had a heartbeat when Danny left him to be taken back to the trauma center in Pickens. And he could sense it in his stomach, in his very soul, the next time he saw Steven, it would only be a lifeless corpse; the shell of his long-time companion who had crossed over and gone before him.

Danny glanced over at Alisa. A single tear was solemnly making its journey from her eye to her chin. His heart ached for Steven, and for Nick, yet he found such magnificent gratitude to his heavenly Father welling up from the center of his being; utter thankfulness that God had protected Alisa, and not left him on this miserable planet without her.

Danny prayed silently that God would preserve Jack and keep him alive. Although their injuries were not life threatening, he prayed for Chris and Dana. And beyond their physical wounds, he prayed that God would somehow heal Dana's heart as it was most certainly shattered over the loss of Steven, and Chris's heart that must be crippled over the death of Clay, a man who had been like a brother to him. Danny prayed that God would comfort his sister, Cami, and give him strength as he told her of the brave sacrifice Nick had made for the good of them all.

Finally, Danny prayed for JC. He didn't know if JC was still alive, but if he was, there would be no rescue attempts anytime soon. Danny's group had been decimated, Chris and Jack would be on the mend for weeks, and the Pickens militia had been utterly massacred, leaving only a fraction of their original numbers.

He pulled into the parking lot of the flea market grounds and got out. Alisa and Gwen ran ahead to the trauma area. Danny trailed behind, each step feeling heavier than the last. The first tent was the waiting area for less serious injuries. He caught up with Alisa and Gwen who had located the rest of the group. Catfish and Antoine were sitting in foldable metal chairs, comforting Dana, who had her arm in a sling and was sobbing like a baby. Catfish and Antoine instinctively stood up to give the chairs to Alisa and Gwen who both sat down and covered Dana with their arms.

Danny didn't have to ask, but he did anyway. He needed to hear someone say it out loud. As painful as it was, it was the first step in dealing with the reality, mourning the loss of his friend, and the subsequent healing process. But for now, it would bring only pain. He looked at Catfish who was staring at his shoes, obviously avoiding Danny's gaze. "Is Steven gone?"

Catfish's lip quivered as he gave the subtlest nod.

Tears streamed down Danny's face as he quietly grieved.

Danny wiped his eyes and turned to Antoine. "Any word on Jack or Chris?"

"Jack is in surgery. They sedated Chris until they can get him on the operating table, which might not be until tomorrow. They're completely overwhelmed with injured people. Jack's injury had to be addressed right away, so they took him straight in.

"Chris was in a lot of pain, plus his bereavement over Clay. The doctor said sedation was the best thing for him. At least he can get some rest. He'll have plenty of time to cry over his buddy once they get his shoulder fixed up."

Danny took a deep breath and let it out. "Can you try to find out where they have Chris's things? He has the keys to the F-150. We need to get those and get back. I'm going to locate the morgue. We have to get Steven, Clay, and Nick's bodies back. I still have to tell my sister that her husband is dead."

"Sure thing, Danny." Antoine pulled Danny to his chest and gave him a tremendous bear hug.

Danny looked up and forced a smile. "Thanks." Then he set out on the gruesome task of locating the corpses of his best friend and brother-in-law.

Danny asked one of the returning militia men who directed him to the morgue. It was behind the operating tent. He found an attendant who directed him to the bodies of Nick, Clay, and Steven. Like the other bodies, all three had been washed up and wrapped in clean sheets. The attendant unwrapped them enough for Danny to make identification. Steven looked serene and peaceful. Nick did not. Part of his scalp was missing. He was recognizable, but the bullet which had killed him had severely traumatized his face. Danny hoped Cami wouldn't look, but he knew she would. A large portion of Clay's lower jaw was missing. He looked even worse. Danny retrieved the tan Humvee and the attendant helped him to load the corpses. He then drove back around to the waiting area.

He walked in and put his hand on Dana's shoulder. "Are you cleared to leave or are you still waiting for medical attention?"

Dana dried her eyes and looked up. "They cleaned the wound, but said I need stitches. The lady said it might be tomorrow evening by the time someone can stitch me up."

"Cami can stitch you up. Why don't you come on home? I've got Steven, Clay, and Nick in the vehicle. We still have to go back to the staging area to pick up the trucks. Antoine, can you drive the green Hummer back?"

"Sure."

Danny looked at Gwen. "Can you drive the F-150? Catfish will drive his truck, I'm sure."

She agreed and they all made their way out to the vehicles. Danny led the way back to the staging area. Catfish and Gwen got out to retrieve the trucks.

Ben was in the staging area unloading boxes of supplies they'd taken from the convention center. He saw Danny drive up and walked over to him.

"How are you set for gas?"

Danny looked at the gauge. "Enough to get home."

"We found his diesel stash. He had it stored in water totes, inside the loading dock. I guess he didn't trust keeping it outside after what you pulled in Charlotte. Drive on back down to the convention center and fill up before you leave. We're going to give all the food and supplies we took to the widows of the fallen. Do you know Nick's wife?"

"It's my sister."

"Sorry for your loss." Ben waved to one of the men. "Bring two cases of MREs and put them in that white F-150."

Ben turned back to Danny. "You tell your sister that she married a hero and give her those boxes."

"Thanks."

"We'll get some more for her as soon as we figure out what's what. When will I see you again?"

Danny shrugged. "Tomorrow I guess. I've got one in recovery and another waiting for surgery back in Pickens."

Ben looked toward Catfish's truck. "Do they have enough gas to get home and back?"

Danny nodded.

"Good. Then bring the trucks to Pickens tomorrow. I'll make sure they both get fill-ups as well."

Danny waved as he put the Hummer in gear. "Thanks for everything, Ben."

"Thank you, Danny." Ben saluted Danny as he drove away.

The next afternoon, Danny pulled the F-150 into the drive, after returning from getting Jack and Chris in Pickens. Melissa and Annie Castell raced out to greet the two wounded warriors. Chris had ridden back in the truck with Catfish and was able to get out on his own. Jack, however, was still heavily medicated for his pain and had ridden home in the bed of the F-150. Danny and Alisa got out and lowered the tailgate to help Jack out. Gwen also walked over to lend a hand.

"Come on, big guy. Let's see if you can get to your trailer on your crutches." Danny took Jack's hand to help him sit up.

Gwen held the crutches that Ben had given him. "Good foot on the ground and take the crutches, one at a time."

Jack kept his injured leg elevated, took the crutches, and lurched forward on his good leg. He almost stood up, but lost his balance and began falling. Gwen quickly wrapped her arms around him to break the fall. She was unable to keep him up, but took him to the ground slowly, breaking his fall with her body.

Jack embraced Gwen as he lay on the ground next to her. "You are so pretty!"

Gwen blushed. "Thanks, but I think that's the morphine talking."

Jack's speech was slurred. "Nope. It's the morphine making me not care what my dad will say about us dating, but I've thought you were the most beautiful girl in the world since the first time I saw you."

She giggled. "Jack, I'm four years older than

you. And like you said, I doubt your dad would approve."

"I'll catch up. I'll be eighteen next year. And if you help bring my dad home, what can he say?"

Nana walked out on the porch. "Chris, you get on in here. I've got you a ham biscuit. Ain't nothing like ham meat to cure what ails you. Catfish, get over here and help Glenda get this boy up off the ground and bring him in the house so he can lay down for a spell."

Danny put his arm around Alisa and watched as Jack continued to embarrass himself. It was amusing, a welcome distraction to the misery all around. The day was only half over and Danny was already exhausted. He, Antoine, and Catfish had spent all morning digging the graves. Then, he'd cleaned up and driven out to Pickens to get the Castell boys. And before the day was over, he still had to come up with a message for the memorial service that evening.

With JC gone, and Steven and Nick dead, he was the one everyone was looking to for leadership. He was the tactical commander, the compound administrator, and he would also have to step up to the plate to take on the role of pastor.

His mind drifted as he considered what scripture he would use for the memorial. He muttered a verse from Job, "the LORD gave, and the LORD hath taken away; blessed be the name of the LORD."

As he looked around the compound and noticed the growing number of widows, he wondered how many other American wives, like Cami, Tracey, and Pauline had lost husbands in the grand contest for liberty. He contemplated how many sleepless nights had been spent by women like Melissa, who had no closure, wives of prisoners of war, not knowing if their husbands were dead or alive.

Danny considered the great sacrifices which had been made throughout time by American soldiers to grant the United States her freedoms. In stark contrast, he pondered what little pains had been taken by the American people, the elected leaders, and the American church at large, to keep the once-great nation on a straight path and a sure moral heading so that the country might retain the blessing, protection, and covering of her Creator, the Lord God Almighty.

DON'T PANIC!

Inevitably, books like this will wake folks up to the need to be prepared, or cause those of us who are already prepared to take inventory of our preparations. New preppers can find the task of getting prepared for an economic collapse, EMP, or societal breakdown to be a source of great anxiety. It shouldn't be. By following an organized plan and setting a goal of getting a little more prepared each day, you can do it.

I always try to include a few prepper tips in my novels, but they're fiction and not a comprehensive plan to get prepared. Now that you're motivated to start prepping, the last thing I want to do is leave you frustrated, not knowing what to do next. So I'd like to offer you a free PDF copy of *The Seven Step Survival Plan.*

For the new prepper, *The Seven Step Survival Plan* provides a blueprint that prioritizes the different aspects of preparedness and breaks them down into achievable goals. For seasoned preppers who often get overweight in one particular area of preparedness, *The Seven Step Survival Plan* provides basic guidelines to help keep their plan in balance, and ensures they're not missing any critical segments of a well-adjusted survival strategy.

To get your **FREE** copy of ***The Seven Step Survival Plan***, go to **PrepperRecon.com** and click the FREE PDF banner, just below the menu bar, at the top of the home page.

Thank you for reading
A Haunt for Jackals
Seven Cows, Ugly and Gaunt: Book Three

Reviews are the best way to help get the book noticed. If you liked the book, please take a moment to leave a five-star review on Amazon and Goodreads.

I love hearing from readers! So, whether it's to say you enjoyed the book or to point out a typo that we missed, drop me a line.
prepperrecon@gmail.com

Stay tuned to PrepperRecon.com for the latest news about my upcoming books, and great interviews on the
Prepper Recon Podcast.

Keep watch for
Vengeance
Seven Cows, Ugly and Gaunt: Book Four

If you liked *A Haunt for Jackals*, you'll love
The Days of Noah

In *The Days of Noah, Book One: Conspiracy*, The founding precepts of America have been destroyed by a conspiracy that dates back hundreds of years. The signs can no longer be ignored and Noah Parker is forced to prepare for the cataclysmic period of financial and political upheaval ahead. Watch through the eyes of Noah as a global empire takes shape, ancient writings are fulfilled, and the last days fall upon the once great, United States of America. Start reading today.

And check out the follow-up series to *The Days of Noah*,
The Days of Elijah

This series picks up where *The Days of Noah* left off. It chronicles the struggles of ex-CIA analyst and new believer, Everett Carroll, as he tries to survive the total onslaught of ruin brought on by the tribulation, a coming period of wrath promised by the Bible to be unparalleled in destruction and suffering.

Made in the USA
Columbia, SC
28 March 2021